# CLOISTER OF WHISPERS

## AN ELA OF SALISBURY MEDIEVAL MYSTERY

### J. G. LEWIS

*For my friend Julie Fell, fellow horse-lover and companion in adventures of both sides of the Atlantic.*

## ACKNOWLEDGMENTS

Once more I am very grateful to Rebecca Hazell, Betsy van der Hoek, Anne MacFarlane and Judith Tilden for their careful readings and excellent suggestions. Many thanks also to the formidable Lynn Messina. All remaining errors are mine.

# CHAPTER 1

*S*alisbury, August 1227

ELA STOOD on the castle mound, where the cloister quadrangle once stood between the former bishop's palace and the stone shadow of the once-grand cathedral it served. She'd watched both be demolished at the behest of Bishop Richard Poore, who'd since erected the great new cathedral and a far grander palace down in the water meadows. The bright summer sun glinted off the helmets of the two young men riding to opposite ends of the old cathedral grounds.

"Don't kill your brother," she murmured to Stephen, the younger but more warlike of her two sons, mounted on his father's magnificent black destrier.

"Don't worry, Mama, Richard can hold his own."

Beyond the far end of the quadrangle, Richard, also in full armor, sat atop a broad chestnut, his lance in his hand.

Ela knew it would show a lack of faith in her sons to cross herself at this moment, so she murmured a silent prayer under her breath as they spurred their horses into motion. It was surely a sacrilege to use such formerly sacred ground to practice the arts of war, but she'd been forced to admit the practicality of a training ground inside the castle walls.

Her sons, if they survived this morning's exercise, would grow up to fight in battles where not only their lives but the security of the kingdom or the fate of all Christendom might be at stake. It was her lot as a mother to dig her nails into her palms while they trained for their roles as defenders of the king and the faith.

Hooves thudded across the close-grazed grass as two small pieces of her heart charged toward each other, lances raised.

"My lady!" A voice behind her tugged at her attention, but she didn't dare take her eyes off her two bold sons, only eleven and thirteen, riding such powerful horses at speed.

"My lady, there's been a murder!"

Ela turned to see a young messenger running toward her. In the distance, Albert the porter shuffled after him.

A great clash jerked her gaze back to the mock battle, and she gasped as a thrust knocked young Richard from his saddle. His horse kept cantering as he slid—in slow motion— around its neck until he was hanging under it, legs dangling in front of its powerful chest.

Ela heard her own scream pierce the air as Richard crumpled to the ground amid the thundering hooves of his mount. She flew toward him as his horse spun and reared up, eyes wide.

"I'm fine, Mama." Richard's voice came from somewhere inside his helmet. Bill Talbot hurried toward him, more slowly than she did, and offered him a hand to rise from the ground.

Ela watched as Richard climbed gingerly to his feet and

removed his helmet. A nearby guard had seized the chestnut horse, who now pawed and stamped at the ground nearby.

"There was no need to scream, Mama," hissed Richard, a look of fury in his eyes.

"I'm sorry." She was, truly. Poor Richard had been bested by his younger brother, and she'd compounded the humiliation with her excess of motherly concern. "You both rode well."

"I fell like an oaf."

"You did," said Sir William Talbot. His face showed the relief Ela felt, but he'd been more dignified about showing it. "Once you can't get back in the saddle, you're supposed to push yourself away from the horse in order to land far from its feet."

"I know," said Richard sulkily. "Good ride, brother."

Stephen, helmet under his arm but still astride his great black mount, grinned like a court jester.

"Don't congratulate yourself too hard, young man," said Bill. "Your form was far from perfect. You carried your lance too high and almost missed him."

Now Ela did cross herself. And turned her attention back to the messenger. She wished he hadn't heard her cry out. "You have news of a murder?"

"Yes, my lady. At the Abbey of St. Benedict near the Chute Forest. A priest lies dead."

"Has the coroner been alerted?"

"A guard went to look for him."

"Call for a jury to attend. I'll head there myself at once."

ELA'S HORSE, Freya, proved lame from a stone bruise, so by the time she'd mounted another horse and made her way—

with her entourage of guards—to the monastery, the bells for Nones had sounded.

At least seven horses stood tied outside the monastery gate, suggesting that Haughton and the jurors had beat her here. She prayed that no one had yet disturbed the body or the scene.

A white-faced lay brother with an uneven, wheat-colored tonsure led her through the gates and into a large cloister. Rows of intricately carved columns lined the wide stone halls of the cloister, rising to an impressive vaulted stone ceiling. The cloister quadrangle bristled with herbs and close-pruned fruit trees in neat beds edged in fragrant lavender. A hum of voices drew her gaze to the far end of the long row of columns where a group of men huddled around what must be the body.

Ela hurried toward them over the smooth stones. Like the floor, the carved stone columns of the cloister were crisp and clean, reminding her that this monastery was only a few years old.

"My lady." Giles Haughton stepped from the crowd. "The murdered man is Father Edmund de Grey. I'm afraid the scene is rather gruesome."

Ela doubted it could be more disconcerting than the sight of her beloved sons charging at each other across the grounds of her ruined cathedral.

The gathered men—she recognized several jurors among them—parted so she could approach the body. She stifled a gasp at the sight of the dead man spread-eagled on the stones, eyes staring, mouth gaping, and a ghastly halo of blood already drying on the stones around his head and torso.

Ela crossed herself and murmured a Hail Mary under her breath.

"He appears to have died from a mortal wound to the

heart or from loss of blood from the same," said Haughton. "Though I'll know more once I get him into the mortuary. His clothing is torn in multiple places from what look to be stab wounds made with a knife or similar blade."

Ela nodded. The dead priest's garments were new and fine, trimmed around the cuffs and hem with embroidered ribbon. Priests wore more layers of clothing than the average person and she didn't know the names for most of them. The richly trimmed brocade chasuble covered them all. Whoever stabbed Father de Grey had taken on more than they bargained for, which perhaps accounted for all the stab wounds required to pierce his flesh effectively.

She glanced up at the other monastics and found them all in brown homespun, which seemed a marked contrast. "Is he the highest authority in this monastery?"

"Nay, my lady," replied a redheaded monk. "Th-there's Prior Hode and Father Billow."

"Where are they?"

"On-on a pilgrimage to visit the r-relics of James the Apostle, my lady."

"They're traveling to Santiago de Compostela?"

"Yes, my lady. They've been gone nigh on three weeks."

"And Father de Grey is in charge of the monastery in their absence."

He nodded.

"Who is to be in charge here now that he's dead?"

The red-headed monk looked around. Several other brothers looked at each other. "Br-brother Alban is the most senior. He's the oldest. But he-he-he..." The redheaded monk's stutter made Ela's nerves jangle. She chastised herself for the unkind thought. He could hardly help the affliction.

"He's not sound of mind, my lady," cut in another monk with a close-cropped gray tonsure. "Or body, due to his great age. He rarely leaves his cell."

Most of the monks—and she could see at least fifteen of them from where she stood—were quite young, between twenty and forty. It appears that in the absence of the prior and the second priest, now away on a long pilgrimage, the monastery had been left a headless body.

But that was a problem for another day. "When was the body found?" Ela asked the question of Giles Haughton.

"It was found this morning after Prime."

"So long ago? Why the delay before the hue and cry was raised?"

Haughton looked at the monks, who looked at one another. "W-we prayed over the body seeking grace for his immortal soul," said the redhead.

"For several hours?"

"Prayer is our calling, my lady," said the wheaten-haired man who'd ushered her in. "And the fate of the soul our highest concern."

Ela could hardly argue with that. Still... "Who found his body?"

"We all did, my lady." The gray-haired man spoke up. "We emerged from the chapel after Prime service and found him here."

"Did he not read the psalms and devotions himself?"

"He did, my lady, but he commanded us to pray ten decades of the rosary before returning to our duties. Which we did. On leaving the chapel we found him bleeding in the cloister."

"Were any of you missing from the Prime service?"

"Oh, no, my lady," said the gray-haired monk. "Our lives revolve around the Hours, and of course the Mass."

Ela looked at Haughton, then back at the monk. "What servants do you have here who perform tasks while you're all in the chapel?"

"The lay brothers, my lady," stammered the red-haired

"When did this theft happen?"

"Last year, my lady."

"Was the theft reported to the sheriff?"

"It was indeed."

"And?" This must have happened during Simon de Hal's brief tenure as sheriff, before she'd proved his unfitness for the role and had him banished from her castle.

"The sheriff sent some men over here but they didn't find anything." The gray-haired man shifted uneasily from one foot to another.

She could tell there was more that he was unwilling to reveal. "And they pursued this outlaw?"

"I can't say, my lady." He frowned. "I never heard of anyone being brought to trial for it."

"No offense to the o-office of the sheriff, m-my lady," interjected the red-haired monk. "But they seemed more interested in the remaining valuables and whether the monastery was paying enough in tithes."

"That's enough, Wilfred," said the gray-haired monk in a curt tone.

So, de Hal's main interest had been in how he might line his purse with the wealth of the monastery. Hardly a surprise. "Have no fear, we shall concern ourselves with solving the crime, not attempting to profit from it," she said. Nothing she could learn about de Hal would surprise her. For all she knew he'd hired someone to pose as an outlaw to steal the goods for his own coffers. She was glad he'd been banished far from Salisbury, though no doubt he was making mischief somewhere else. "We shall inquire into the matter of the stolen property as well as the whereabouts of the outlaw."

She looked at the jurors, who'd stood silent until now. "My guards shall seek him and bring him to the castle for questioning. Do you have any further questions for the brothers?"

The jurors cast their eyes down to the dead man's body, then they seemed reluctant to raise them. Perhaps they were intimidated by the monastic environment and the presence of the holy brothers who spent their days and nights in prayer.

"Was anything stolen today?" asked Peter Howard, the baker, an older man with long experience on the jury.

"Not that we're aware of," said the silver-haired monk. "But with all the to-do over the murder we may have missed something. We'll be sure to take a full accounting of the monastery's goods and stores."

"Report to me once you've made your assessment. Rest assured, we will hunt Father de Grey's killer until he's brought to justice. The killing of a man of God is a grave mortal sin as well as a crime. I know God will guide us in seeking redress for this cruel murder."

THEY SPOKE to the guard stationed at the gate, who said that he had seen no one unusual entering or leaving the abbey that morning. Giles Haughton supervised the removal of the body onto a cart headed for the mortuary at Salisbury castle. Ela left the monks to mourn their dead priest and to send word to their two fellow clerics now on their pilgrimage on the Continent.

As soon as she arrived back at the castle she headed to the mortuary, keen to get Haughton's private opinions of the details of the murder.

Inside the cool, dark room, the dead priest was now laid out on his back on the table, his layers of garments removed but his modesty preserved by a linen cloth spread from neck to knees, stained in places by the blood congealed around his wounds.

Giles Haughton washed his hands in a bowl of water, and dried them on a clean cloth after she entered.

"A very sad business, Sir Giles," she said. She crossed herself before approaching the body. "A man of God murdered in his own cloister."

Haughton put down the cloth and walked toward the table. "Would you like me to show you the wounds?"

Ela drew in a shaky breath. "Yes." This was her least favorite part of her job, and one she could easily leave to Haughton, but she didn't want him to think she didn't have a strong enough stomach to review all the evidence properly.

Haughton whisked back the cloth, but it stuck to one of the wounds. Dried blood had glued it in place and he had to tug it twice to rip it away. Ela managed to keep her breathing inaudible as the dead priest's bare chest was exposed.

"I cleaned up most of the blood." He gestured to a bowl of water and a small pile of soiled rags. "So I could see the wounds. As you can see these cuts appear to have been made with a short weapon like a knife or small dagger, thrust in quite deep, possibly up to its hilt. The cuts run right to left." The incisions, while not regular, left the slit-like wounds running sideways on his torso.

"You can see here where his blade hit the ribs and didn't plunge fully in." He pointed to one shorter cut, higher up on the torso. "The others, five of them, lay in the belly area, where they puckered the priest's sallow, almost hairless skin.

"An act of revenge," said Ela. "What else could motivate such savagery?"

"It's an odd business, my lady. He was stabbed almost twenty times. Some of the marks were made after he'd already fallen to the ground, mortally wounded."

"How can you tell?"

"The stab marks on his back were the fatal wounds. One just below his rib cage pierced his heart and he would have died almost immediately from that. It appears that he fell backward, and the rest of the stab wounds are on his chest and arms. They're not as deep but more like punctures made in a fit of rage."

"So perhaps someone with a personal grudge against him?"

"Or who wanted to be very sure he was dead. The monks were not very forthcoming about who it might be. If they were all in Prime with him just moments before his death I'd suspect that at least one of them knows more than he's saying."

"They mentioned the outlaw."

"Outlaws make a good scapegoat. They're already on the run for a crime they've committed and they're hard to find and bring to justice."

"So you think that story about the Fox was an invention?"

"Not entirely, but I can't imagine his motive in striding into the monastery cloister in broad daylight and running his blade into Father de Grey. Certainly not more than once."

"If Father de Grey is the reason he became an outlaw in the first place, he might have cause to nurse enough of a grudge to kill him."

Haughton inhaled deeply. "I don't think the crime that drove him to outlawry was committed in Wiltshire. If it was I've never heard of it. I suppose the man they call the Fox might have a history with Father de Grey elsewhere."

"I shall return to the monastery once the initial shock of his murder has passed and seek more details about Father de Grey's history," said Ela. "I got a sense that all the monks were watching each other and none of them was willing to risk saying the wrong thing in front of his brothers."

"I had the same impression. Did you notice how the

oldest one scowled at the young redhead when he mentioned that de Hal had wanted to increase their tithes?" Haughton frowned. "I wonder at robbery as a motive, though. As a priest in his own cloister, it's unlikely he was carrying an item valuable enough to incite theft, unless he held the silver chalice from the altar in his hands. Hopefully the monks will account for any missing items. I did find two keys on his person." He glanced at them where they lay on a small table that held bottles filled with embalming fluids and the like.

Ela moved to the table and picked up the two iron keys. One large, like a door key, and the other smaller, like the key to a chest. "May I take these?"

"Of course."

She averted her eyes as Haughton turned the body face down on the table. It was a shame that murdered men and women had to suffer the indignities of their investigation. Once the priest's buttocks were safely covered with linen, she looked at his bony back. "I see the thrust that claimed his life." One single knife plunge, wide enough to suggest the knife went deep into his body, just to one side of his spine.

"It would have stopped his heart and felled him instantly," said Haughton.

"Yet the killer took the time to stab him repeatedly once he already lay dead. A crime of passion. Who would do such a thing to a priest? One can hardly blame a cuckolded spouse or a jilted lover."

"Or could one?" Haughton didn't look up at her.

Ela stared at him for a moment. "I suppose we must make inquiries about how closely he obeyed his vow of celibacy."

"I've found that discreet inquiries produce much more useful information than asking questions in front of a crowd," said Haughton. "A return visit to the monastery where the monks are questioned individually might produce useful information."

"I quite agree. None of them likely wishes to betray a trust or even reveal enmity in front of his fellows. It will be interesting to see what each of the brothers has to say when questioned by himself."

Haughton had now turned the priest onto his back again and covered him. He did pull out a hand, though, and showed it to her. "No torn nails or other signs of struggle. His hands are well kept. No calluses and his nails are buffed quite smooth. Clearly he did not partake in manual labor at the monastery."

"I'd imagine that's left to the lay brothers so he can spend his time in prayer and devotions."

"Quite."

"Keep the body here until I return to the monastery tomorrow to ask more questions. I want to make sure we get all the information we need before it's returned for burial."

"I must caution you that with the summer heat he must be embalmed and quickly or the body will start to decompose."

"You think we should return him to the monastery today?"

"Tomorrow at the latest, or the embalming process should be undertaken here."

Ela didn't really want to take on the trouble and expense when she was sure the brothers at the monastery would rather do it themselves. "I shall move forward in this investigation with all haste. Thank you, as always, for your prompt and thorough examination of the body."

She drew in a breath and turned for the door. Then she stopped and looked at him. "Before I go, do you have any insights into this case that might have escaped my notice? I value your years of experience as coroner."

"I wish I did, my lady. You've already observed that the killer acted with an excess of violence, which implies previous knowledge of—and even hatred for—the dead man."

"We must find out if this outlaw, the Fox, had reason to hate him enough to stab him repeatedly."

"The Fox hasn't been accused of a murder while I've been coroner, at least not in Wiltshire. I've heard talk of him at the Bull and Bear, though."

"What do they say about him?"

"That he's from up north originally. Comes out of the forest to commit acts of petty theft, then disappears back into it."

"So he's been a wanted man for years and no one can find him?"

"That's how they tell it."

"Well, now I want him and I shan't rest until he's standing before a jury in my hall."

# CHAPTER 2

*T*he next morning, Ela sat at a table in her great hall, helping her youngest daughter, Ellie, embroider a flower into the corner of a handkerchief. "Don't pull too tight or the fabric will pucker."

"Have I ruined it?" Little Ellie's worried eyes looked up at her.

"No. You can flatten it before you make the next stitch." She smoothed out the wrinkles in the handkerchief. A flurry of activity at the hall door made her look up. John Dacus, her co-sheriff, strode in with several men behind him.

The Fox! They must have found him. Her men had been hunting him all afternoon yesterday and since the wee hours of this morning.

Ela rose, scanning the group. "Where's the prisoner?" she asked as Dacus approached.

"We didn't see hide nor hair of him. No hint of a camp. No sign he's there in the forest at all."

"Did you speak to the forest wardens?" she asked.

"Yes, and they insist he can't be there. They've searched every corner of the forest for him."

"The monks said he stole from the monastery recently."

Dacus nodded. "The abbey at Pamber was robbed last month and a witness swears it was him.."

"Pamber is in Hampshire, outside our jurisdiction. I'll speak to the Sheriff of Hampshire and we can join forces to hunt him." Ela spoke with conviction she didn't entirely feel.

She hoped the Sheriff of Hampshire would cooperate. They weren't exactly on the best of terms but, as the two most powerful people in Salisbury, they maintained an uneasy peace. The sheriff of Hampshire lived in Salisbury—in Wiltshire—because he'd just built himself a fine new palace there. He was a man with his finger in many pies, always feeling around for a rich plum to pluck out and feast on.

The sheriff of Hampshire was Bishop Richard Poore.

ELA RODE for New Salisbury with her closest ally, Bill Talbot, at her side. Sir William had brought her back from exile in France as a young girl, and remained a faithful knight in her family's household ever since. He played a vital role in raising her sons to be trained knights as well as men of character, especially now that their father was gone. "Is it not odd for a man of the cloth to be a sheriff?" she said softly, once they were out of earshot of the guards.

"Not if he wants to enjoy confiscating properties and lining his purse by exacting fines," said Bill easily.

Ela was glad he voiced her thoughts aloud. "I suspect Hubert de Burgh chose him for the role. They've been hand in glove during King Henry's minority. I suppose I should be glad he didn't make Poore Sheriff of Wiltshire." She'd had an almighty battle securing the role for herself. "Do you suppose

Poore concerns himself much with matters of justice in Hampshire?"

"I don't imagine the good men and women of Portsmouth and Southampton are traipsing to his palace in Salisbury with their concerns. His co-sheriff, Gilbert de Staplebrigg, likely shoulders the load himself."

"We could approach Sir Gilbert directly, but why not hold Poore's feet to the fire?" She shot a smile at Bill. "I would hate for him to sit bored in the luxury of his fine new palace." She spurred her horse into a trot.

~

"HIS GRACE IS IN PRAYER," murmured the short, stout monk who greeted them at the door of the bishop's palace.

"We can wait," said Ela brightly. "May we come in? It looks like rain."

The monk's mouth set into an awkward slant. He looked up at the white sky, where rain undoubtedly hovered some-where, if not right there. "Most certainly, my lady."

Ela and Bill entered and took a seat in the now familiar sitting room where Poore greeted his guests. Bright tapestries, the ornately carved fireplace, and fine oak furni-ture reminded guests that he was Poore in name only.

"Shall I fetch you a cup of wine?" asked the monk, with a withering look.

"Don't trouble yourself on my account," said Ela. She shot a glance at Bill, who echoed her refusal. She and Bill sat in companionable silence for barely enough time for Bishop Poore to utter a decade on his rosary before he swept into the room, looking mildly peeved.

"My lady Ela!" he exclaimed. "Sir William. What a pleasant surprise." His flat tone rather undercut his jovial manner. "Have you come to seek a burial plot for a murdered

18

outcast? Or perhaps an infidel has been thrown in your moat again?"

Ela managed a cold smile. "I'm afraid I'm here today to inquire of you in your capacity as Sheriff of Hampshire."

An expression of perplexity crossed his wide, pale brow, as if he'd forgotten for a moment that he was indeed Sheriff of Hampshire. He gestured for her and Bill to rest themselves in one of the grand oak chairs. Once she was seated he settled himself heavily into another, arranging his embroidered robes and settling his pale hands across his plump stomach. "My co-sheriff handles most of the day-to-day matters." He twisted his big ruby ring. "As I am inconveniently located here in the heart of Salisbury, where I have many duties related to the cathedral and our new school."

"Quite. However, it has come to my attention that an outlaw known as the Fox has lived at large in the forest of Chute for some time—years even. Have you heard of this man?"

"Indeed I have. He seems to target religious houses for his crimes."

"Which ones?" She wondered if he'd heard of the recent robbery at the Abbey of St. Benedict.

"Some silver plate was taken this spring from Whirwell Abbey, and a silver and gold cup was stolen over the winter from the Pamber Priory. If I remember correctly there was a small silver cross studded with emeralds taken from Andwell Priory some months ago."

"Did anyone see him commit these crimes?"

"I don't think so. That's why they call him the Fox. He's in and out like a shadow."

"Then how do they know it was the same man?" Ela began to wonder if the mysterious Fox even existed. "And not several different thieves?"

"Not many men would dare to rob a house of God. Most

have at least a respectable fear of the fires of hell if not the laws of man."

Ela wasn't so sure of this. "Has anyone seen him, ever?"

"Oh yes, he's been seen in the forest. Led the forest wardens on a merry chase on more than one occasion. In fact I suspect he baits them on purpose to show them what fools they are."

Ela blinked. "You find the forest wardens ineffective?"

"Of course. One hardly selects the finest mind in the kingdom to patrol a few thousand acres of acorns."

She was surprised at his dismissive air. She'd always thought that England's kings, including the current young monarch, took the security of their forests and all the quarry in them very seriously. Stealing a stag or boar from the king's forest could even lead to hanging. Still, she could see how the work was rather dull and thankless.

"We need to find this Fox. If you and I join forces, sending men into the forest from both counties, he can't escape. His brazen acts of thievery were bad enough, but if he's now murdered a priest he must face justice."

Poore looked surprised. "A priest?"

"Yesterday, Father Edmund de Grey was found stabbed to death in the cloister of the Abbey of St. Benedict. The killing was savage, with multiple stab wounds, suggesting a degree of enmity for the victim."

Poore's pale eyes widened. He crossed himself with a plump hand. "May God rest his soul."

"Indeed, but I shall not rest until his killer is brought to justice."

"My men are at your service and I'll do anything I can to help." He looked truly shaken.

"My men sought him yesterday and this morning but found no sign of him. We must join forces with the forest wardens and make the forest so uncomfortable for this outlaw that he has no choice but to leave it. Once we flush him out he shall be arrested and brought to justice for all his crimes."

"Quite, quite." Poore called for a monk, then sent him to fetch wine. "You've shaken my nerves with this tale of murder."

"Did you know Father de Grey?"

"I can't say I did. Not that I recall, anyway. Of course, there are quite a few monastic houses in the vicinity and I concern myself with those under my direct control."

"Do you know anything about him?"

Poore looked blank. The monk came back with a carafe of wine and three silver cups. He then poured wine and handed them each a cupful. Ela and Bill took theirs without comment. Perhaps Poore needed the wine to steady his nerves but didn't want to be seen drinking alone at this early hour.

Poore took a steadying sip of his wine. "I do know that he's one of two priests at the abbey, under the management of an experienced prior. I'm sure they all shoulder the burden together."

"Unfortunately the other two are far away on a holy pilgrimage."

Poore perked up. "Oh dear. We can't have the holy brothers left leaderless in Father de Grey's absence. I shall see to it myself that they have good guidance."

Ela wondered what Poore would get out of this. He wasn't one to exert himself unless there was power or profit to be had. Likely he anticipated both.

"I'm planning to visit the abbey myself today to inquire further about de Grey himself," said Ela. "I'd like to know if he was popular with the brothers or if he had enemies either in the clergy or among the common people."

"I'm sure you'll find he was well respected by all. He's a man of God, after all."

"No disrespect to Father de Grey intended but not all men of God are godly. You'll recall the ugly matter I attended to in London last year."

"Indeed I do. Most unfortunate. And so clever of you to expose the evils of the wicked hiding behind the robes of Mother Church." He pushed an oily smile to his lips. "Surely you're not suggesting that Father de Grey was involved in... anything untoward. I've never heard ill mention of the man. Oh, his poor flock, left bereft of their shepherd and with his cohorts too far away to offer succor. I shall prepare some words to give them good cheer in their time of need."

"I'm sure your kindness will be much appreciated, Bishop Poore." Ela was surprised by this show of apparent generosity. "And if you learn anything about Father Edmund de Grey, or any useful information about his fellow priests or the brothers, I would appreciate hearing it."

"Of course, my dear lady. I won't shrink from bending your ear with any information that might be in the tiniest bit useful." He'd finished his cup and held it out for the monk standing near the doorway.

"If your men find the outlaw first, please have them bring him to Salisbury. I want him tried in the shire where the murder was committed."

He watched while the monk refilled his cup. "Quite understandable. Such a man must be brought to justice or chaos will soon rule the land." He lifted his cup. "To flushing evil out of the forest and restoring peace to the naves and cloisters in Wiltshire and Hampshire."

Ela nodded politely. "You'll send your men out today?"

"They shall be mounted within the hour."

WHILE NUMBERS of men set out from Salisbury on horseback for the Chute Forest with John Dacus leading them, Ela returned to the Abbey of St. Benedict with Bill Talbot to ask more questions. She arrived shortly before the bells for Nones.

The same red-haired monk with the slight stammer greeted her warily at the door into the abbey courtyard. "God be with you, m-m-my lady."

"And with you, brother…" She waited for him to say his name. He didn't. "What do they call you?"

His eyes widened and his face reddened. "Well, flame head, jitter jaws—"

"Your name, brother!" Did he think she intended to mortify him? "The one you were christened with."

"Oh." His face turned the color of boiled beetroot. "W-wilfred Bedulf."

"I need you to show me Father de Grey's room."

"Yes, m-my lady." He led her through the shady cloister. Monks or lay brothers hovered here and there, looking up from their weeding or sweeping as she passed. When they reached the end of the cloister the bells chimed, their sound filling the courtyard. The brothers hurried to put away their tools and file into the church for prayer.

Brother Wilfred hesitated, looking toward the door of the church and shuffling as if he were arguing with his feet about whether they should run toward it.

"The Lord will forgive you for missing Nones this one time in the service of finding Father de Grey's killer," she murmured.

"I'm s-sure you're right, m-my lady," he said, looking doubtful.

"On the morning of his death, Father de Grey ordered you all to pray ten decades of the rosary before leaving the chapel?"

"Y-yes, my lady."

This suggested to her that he intended to meet privately with someone while the others were all occupied. "Was such a thing unusual?"

"I c-can't say he did it often, my lady."

Since they were alone, Ela decided to ask the awkward question about Father Edmund's fidelity to his vows. "I wonder if Father Edmund had any relationships, of a secret or covert kind, I mean. With a woman, perhaps?"

Brother Wilfred stopped in his tracks and stared at her like she was mad. "F-f-father Edmund?"

"It's not entirely uncommon."

"I-I-I-certainly haven't heard of s-such a thing."

They still stood at the end of the cloister, now alone, with Brother Bedulf still gazing back longingly at the abbey. It seemed to pain him to be outside it, missing the solace of the sacred ritual. "Please proceed." She wanted time to examine the room before the monks flooded out again.

The red-haired monk shook himself out of his torpor and led her on through a carved arch and toward a long, low building with a row of small windows.

He opened a wooden door and cautioned her not to trip on the threshold. Ela stepped into a dark and gloomy passageway, lined with doors. "The monks' cells?" she asked.

"Yes, my l-lady. Father de Grey's r-r-room is upstairs." They walked the length of the passage, which had a flagged stone floor and smelled of damp, then turned to go up a tight wooden stair. No daylight penetrated the stairway and she wouldn't have been able to see her hand in front of her face if she'd lifted it. At the top of the stairs, Brother Bedulf opened another door and they stood in a wider passage with a polished wood floor and four carved oak doors.

"It does seem a good deal more salubrious up here. Which room is Father de Grey's?"

"This one." The monk gestured to the door on the far right.

"Do you have the key?"

"No. F-father de Grey was a private man and p-preferred to keep his own key. I suppose we could f-force the door. He won't mind now that he's d-d-dead, will he?"

Ela reached into her purse. "The coroner found two keys on his person." She pulled out the larger one, and pushed it into the lock. It turned almost silently and the door swung open to reveal a good-sized room with a bright window.

The room had a narrow bed pushed up against one wall. A prie-dieu stood in one corner, and there was also a writing desk with a rather flimsy looking wood chair. These were all things she'd expect to find in a priest's modest chamber.

It was the other items in the room that made her catch her breath and turn to Bill Talbot.

# CHAPTER 3

"This tapestry looks like one that my mother bought in Normandy." Ela peered at the colorful weaving. "It's made with mulberry silk thread, from China."

"Is it a biblical scene?" asked Bill. "I can't place it."

Ela scanned the array of figures and lush foliage. "It looks more like a hunting scene. What an odd thing to find in his room. And the curtains are rich damask." They reminded her of the ones on her own bed that had been recently repaired and rehung. "These are surprising luxuries for a priest's room."

"Father de Grey liked nice things," said Brother Bedulf.

"I wonder if that's why the Fox made him a target," said Ela. "But then why are these items here and not stolen?"

"A tapestry is not an easy item to make away with and hide in the forest," observed Bill. "Perhaps he stole more moveable items."

The inkwell on Father de Grey's desk looked like brass inlaid with lapis lazuli and garnet. "This is probably imported from the Holy Land." An oak chest sat in one corner of the room. "I suspect I have the key for this as well."

Unsurprisingly the smaller key opened the chest. Ela expected to find a spare set of clean robes and a linen shift or two, but raised the lid to find an odd assortment of items. There were knives and belts and brass candlesticks. A prayerbook. A new pair of shoes and a hair comb made of tortoiseshell.

Several small bags lay stacked across one end, and she picked up one and opened it. Inside she found an assortment of coins, but also two rings, a slim gold band with the name Mary crudely engraved on it, and a silver braided band. "These are women's rings. They're too small for a man to wear."

Another bag held more coins, all silver, and a chain, of the kind that might be used to hold a cape together in front of the wearer's chest. The chain wasn't gold—brass perhaps—but its fine craftsmanship meant it was valuable enough. Another bag held yet more coins and a small polished mirror.

Ela stopped looking and stared at Brother Bedulf. He looked as surprised as she felt. "Why would he have all this money? And all these items? These women's rings can't be his own possessions."

"I don't have any idea, my l-lady."

"You didn't know that he had a treasure hoard in his room?"

"No. He didn't let anyone in, even to clean. The lay brothers are supposed to sweep and dust for the monks but he said he preferred to do it himself. Said he wanted to keep humble to guard his soul from pride."

"I suspect avarice was more of a problem for him than pride," murmured Ela, fingering another chain, this one likely meant to adorn a lady's waist. "But how did he acquire these? This hoard looks more like something I'd expect to find in the Fox's lair than in a priest's cell."

"Perhaps the items have sentimental value?" suggested Bill. "And he brought them here with him when he left home. Some of these men come from wealthy backgrounds and may find it hard to part entirely with worldly luxuries."

"True." Ela's own family members had traditionally joined the monastery at Bradenstoke—founded by her great grand-father—once they reached a great age. Though so far her mother had resisted taking the veil, and her father had died young, so she didn't personally know any of the ones who had.

"This is a Benedictine house," said Brother Bedulf. "While the men who enter do not directly swear a vow of poverty they do promise to strictly observe the monastic way of life, and poverty is implied."

"Apparently Father de Grey had his own ideas about monastic life," said Bill. "There must be fifty pounds in coins here, if not more."

"It's certainly a great sum." Ela frowned. "Perhaps he was collecting it for a particular purpose? A dedicated chapel, or a pilgrimage?"

"Perhaps." Brother Bedulf peered into the chest, looking rather stunned.

"I wonder if the other clerics knew about this chest," said Ela.

"Unfortunately we'll have to wait several months until they return from their journey," said Bill.

"The trial certainly can't wait until then," said Ela. "Pre-suming we can catch his killer, which I certainly intend to." She closed the chest.

"What w—will happen to all this money?" Brother Bedulf opened his mouth in protest. "S-surely his wealth belongs to the abbey."

"That will be determined by the ecclesiastical authorities." Otherwise known as Bishop Richard Poore. As she locked the door behind them, she pondered that Poore was entirely capable of just taking it all and keeping it.

Ela wondered if the brothers would find themselves overwhelmed by temptation if they'd knew this treasure was stored over their sleeping heads. Then again, what would a group of cloistered monks do with all the coins in the world?

And more importantly, what did Father de Grey intend to do with them?

~

AT SUPPER THAT NIGHT, Ela's oldest unmarried daughter Petronella picked at her fish. "Why haven't you caught the killer yet? He killed a priest! A man who dedicated his life to serving God. His wickedness is inconceivable."

"Men from two counties are combing the forest even now." They'd sent guards to patrol the entire forest perimeter so the outlaw couldn't escape.

"I prayed all night last night that you'd find the killer. I couldn't sleep for thinking about the cruelty of—"

"Darling, don't scare the little ones." Ellie and Nicky were within earshot. She didn't want them tossing and turning and picturing a murderer prowling in the woods. She tried to keep her duties and her family life separate, though it was almost impossible when the business of the county took place in her own hall. "Do keep praying, though. The outlaw we seek has evaded the law for some time."

"The soldiers say he hates priests and nuns. That he steals only from men and women of God. Why would anyone hate those who devote their lives to praying for our salvation?" Petronella intended to be a nun.

"I don't know. He must be both godless and fearless to risk the wrath of the Almighty as well as of the county courts." Ela grew increasingly curious about the elusive Fox.

Tales of his wicked deeds, and even that he used witchcraft to hide himself from human eyes, buzzed around the castle like flies. "But he can't evade justice forever. By tomorrow night he'll be in the castle dungeon, and the men and women in the religious houses of Wiltshire and Hampshire will sleep quietly again."

"Can I ride with you tomorrow, Mama?" asked Stephen. "Bill Talbot's taught me to hunt, and I suspect hunting a man is not much different than hunting a hind."

"You're too young," said Ela. Her roasted parsnips and trout cooked in butter didn't hold much appeal. The butter was hardening on her trencher. "And it's too far to ride."

"I could ride there, Mother," said Richard. "I'm old enough."

Should she let him? Richard was nearly fourteen. "I suppose you can. I do intend to ride there myself tomorrow. Bill Talbot can come with us." Then at least she could concentrate on her own duties.

"Sounds like an adventure to me, lad," said Bill, who sat nearby. "Meet me at the stables bright and early and we can supervise the grooms."

Richard's serious expression didn't change, but Ela detected a tiny glow of pride behind his eyes. More serious and bookish than his brothers, Richard wasn't the first to leap into action—unlike his younger brother Stephen—so Ela was proud of him for volunteering.

Stephen pouted. "It's not fair. I'm already riding Father's destrier, and Richard can barely ride a quiet palfrey!"

"Your brother is an excellent rider, and envy is a sin," scolded Ela. In truth, young Stephen had a rare gift with horses and had formed a bond with his father's temperamental black horse, who some of the grooms were afraid to even handle. Stephen was also tall for his age, almost as tall as his older brother. Sometimes she forgot the two years' difference in age between them. But Stephen could be impetuous and over-bold and lacked the maturity needed for this manhunt. "You'll go on other adventures, but not this one."

"You and I can pray for their safety," said Petronella. "We'll say the whole rosary together."

"I can't wait," said Stephen glumly.

"Is there a special punishment for a man who kills a priest?" Petronella asked. "I mean, it is worse than killing an ordinary man, isn't it?"

"The punishment for murder is death," said Ela. "Here on earth we don't have a worse punishment than death."

"I'm not afraid of death," said Petronella. "I'll be at God's right hand and sing with the angels in the choir."

Stephen rolled his eyes. "I'm not afraid of death either, because I'm brave like Papa. I'll travel to Jerusalem and fight the Saracens when I'm older."

"Hopefully there won't be a need for that because Jerusalem will be safe in Christian hands," said Ela. She hated the idea of her sons disappearing on a long and dangerous crusade, as her husband had done.

"I shall take Papa's sword with me," continued Stephen. "And swing it over my head and—"

"Stephen! Don't speak of bloodshed during supper," said Petronella sharply. "Besides, you can barely lift Papa's longsword."

"I can too! Ask Bill."

"Attend to your supper," scolded Ela. "There are children going to bed hungry in England tonight."

"Here in Wiltshire?" asked Ellie.

"I do hope not," said Ela. *But, yes, probably.* She provided alms to local families here in the castle walls and down in Salisbury and the surrounding hamlets, but the county was large and there were whole villages she'd never set foot in.

She tried to set a good example by eating a few mouthfuls of her fish and parsnips, but her stomach remained unsettled and she soon stopped trying.

Father de Grey's chest full of coins filled her with deep unease. Was the priest a holy man of God whose murder should fill all good Christian men with horror and raise a cry for vengeance of his death? Or had he been up to something immoral at best or criminal at worst?

ELA'S HUSBAND had hunted in the Chute Forest at the late King John's invitation on more than one occasion. Ela herself had never ventured more than a mile or so into its leafy groves, on well-traveled tracks, despite its proximity to her castle mound. It was unsettling to realize that a forest so broad and dense that a man could hide there for an entire day, let alone months on end, lay right at her doorstep. She was curious to see the outlaw's hideaway.

Bill Talbot and Richard, mounted on a sensible bay, rode with her along with four other guards. The forest rose from a sheep-grazed meadow, and Ela was glad to see guards stationed along the road, and also riding the perimeter of the forest where it met the adjacent fields.

She and her party took the road into the forest, where the trees closed around it, narrowing it into a thin track. As they rode on, dense canopies of great oak and beech trees shaded out the sun and thick undergrowth snatched at their clothes.

The Chute Forest proved to be largely trackless and unmanaged. Branches, vines and undergrowth soon tripped and slowed their every step. This seemed a remote and forlorn corner of Wiltshire compared to the bright wild-flower-specked meadows and pollarded copses near her home. "What a waste of potential farmland," she muttered, as they picked their way over yet another fallen tree and through another tangle of vines. "The king could harvest this timber and put the land to good use."

"I can't speak for the current king, but his forbears saw hunting as a good use," said Bill cheerfully.

Richard murmured agreement. "And don't forget about the wild creatures, Mama. The badgers and stoats and hares."

"Not to mention wolves and wild boar the size of ponies," said Bill. "The forest wardens keep the forest this large and wild to entertain quarry fit for a king should he wish to chase it."

"I can't imagine it would be any easier to hunt four-legged quarry in here than two-legged."

"I suspect there were chases cut through the brush in areas where King John and his father liked to hunt. They've been neglected in recent years, with our current king being so young. But if he sends a few men out here with scythes and strong backs there'll soon be room to gallop from end to end, won't there, Richard?"

Her son nodded enthusiastically.

"I'm not sure King Henry has an appetite for blood sports," said Ela. "He's a pious and thoughtful young man."

"All men have an appetite for blood sports, my lady." Bill surveyed the wild tangle that stretched in all directions. "It sharpens our wits for war."

Ela inhaled deeply. She hadn't quite recovered from seeing her young sons charging at each other yesterday. Of course learning such skills prepared them to defend their lives on the battlefield one day. And Bill managed their training carefully so as to keep them as safe as possible.

"I think I hear someone." Ela reined in Freya and listened. Which was hard with all of their horses breathing and shifting and shuffling in a group.

"I do, too," said Bill quietly. "A man on horseback." He

stood in his saddle and peered into the dense tangle of woodland. "Two men on horseback."

Ela's gaze followed his, and she soon saw the bright blue cloak of a young man. His companion wore red trimmed in silver. "I hardly think that either of them is the outlaw, but in those getups they're not guards from Salisbury or garrison soldiers either. Please summon them to us."

Bill called out and, after a pause, one of the men responded. The two groups rode cautiously toward each other, pushing aside branches and vines, until Ela stood face-to-face with two young men on tall horses. After casting a surprised glance in her direction, both men fixed their attention on Bill. "Good morrow, sir."

Bill tipped his head slightly.

"What is your business in these woods?" asked Ela.

Again they looked at her in surprise, as if a horse had started to talk.

"This is my lady Ela, Countess of Salisbury," growled Bill. "Pray answer her question."

She could feel Bill getting ready to put his hand on the hilt of his sword.

"I'm Robert de Halpin," said one, a callow-looking youth with blond curls. "And this is my brother Philip. We're here at the behest of Bishop Poore to capture the outlaw known as the Fox and bring him back dead or alive."

"He must be captured alive. He's only accused of this crime, not convicted," said Ela firmly. These men were likely young nobles from Hampshire, though she didn't recognize the name. They didn't seem to be professional soldiers, which alarmed her. She didn't want every young huntsman to see this as an opportunity to chase human quarry as an exciting change from deer. "If you find him please restrain him and summon my men. They're spread throughout the forest." Or at least she hoped they were, though she hadn't actually seen any since entering it. A forest that spread over a hundred square miles was not easy to search, even with a large force of men. "Have you seen any sign of him?"

"Not a hair," said Robert de Halpin. "Though you'd be hard pressed to find anything smaller than a horse in here, it's so dark and dense."

"Do all of Bishop Poore's men have orders to bring the Fox in dead or alive?" Ela wondered who these forces were that Poore had raised and how he'd instructed them.

"That's what we were told. There's a bounty of ten pounds if this Fox is captured."

Ela managed not to exclaim in shock. On the one hand she had to admire Poore's ingenuity in galvanizing the local gentry. On the other she resented this perversion of the natural course of justice. "I see. I shall honor the bounty if he's brought to Salisbury, but only if he's captured alive. A dead man can't tell the truth."

"A live one can spout lies," said Robert de Halpin.

"Watch your tongue, lad," said Bill, gruffly. "We seek the truth rather than hasty retribution. We have many questions for this Fox, if we can find him."

"If he can be found at all," said dark-browed Philip de Halpin, who had a rather more serious face and tone than his brother. "The villagers say no one can see him unless he appears to them on purpose. We've combed these woods for hours and haven't found any sign of him."

"He's a mortal man and shall be found and caught. Good luck to you in your search but remember, the outlaw must be alive for you to claim the bounty, no matter what Bishop Poore has suggested."

She intended to have sharp words with Poore when she returned to Salisbury. She couldn't have him telling the men of the shire to dispense justice with their own swords, or chaos would soon reign.

They rode off in different directions. Once the men were out of earshot, Ela turned to Bill. "I wonder why Bishop Poore would give such strange instructions. He wants the man badly enough to offer ten pounds for his capture but doesn't care if he's not alive to stand trial?"

"Very odd," said Bill. "There's much information to be gleaned from the outlaw. According to all accounts, this murder is not his first crime—if he even committed it. I'm sure the abbeys and monastic houses that have been robbed would be glad to get their stolen items back, and he can't tell us where they are if he's dead."

Ela reflected that those items were likely sold and converted into coin long ago, but didn't have the heart to say it aloud.

"We shall find him ourselves, Mama," said Richard. "Before Bishop Poore's men do."

"While that would be most satisfying, we must remember that he's dangerous and could ambush us," replied Bill.

Ela found herself glancing over her shoulder at every sound. The outlaw knew the forest as his home. Its hollow oaks and dense thickets were the keep of his castle. The forest was anything but silent. Birds chirped and rustled in the canopy overhead, small creatures stirred the leaf litter and dead branches snapped underfoot. Every step their horses took set off an echo of rustling and crunching that seemed deafening as her ears strained for a single footfall by an unseen outlaw.

"What's that?" Richard stared off to his left. They reined their horses to a halt. Had he imagined something? One of the guards' horses stamped his foot impatiently. Then Ela heard it. A rumbling sound. Not like the thundering hooves of a horse, but something smaller, lighter, charging toward them...like a man running.

"What is it?" Richard whispered to Bill.

Bill's muscles strained and his head was cocked, searching the sound for clues. "Boar. It's a wild boar."

Ela felt her breath catch.

"They're dangerous, aren't they?" Richard spoke under his breath.

"The most feared quarry in the woods," murmured Bill.

"So we should kill it, to be safe, shouldn't we?" Richard's hand was already on the hint of his sword.

Ela found herself muttering a prayer under her breath.

"That boar belongs to the king," said Bill. "Who might take a dim view of us slaying it."

"The king is my cousin," said Richard. "I don't think he'd mind."

Bill glanced at Ela, who in turn looked at Richard. The boy's face was alive with excitement and not a small amount of terror. "Can we chase it, Mama?"

Ela nodded her assent. She didn't relish the prospect of a wild boar nipping at their heels. The great beasts with their sharp teeth and deadly tusks had finished many a bold knight. She'd rather have Bill and Richard chase it on their terms than find them stalked as its prey.

"I'll stay here with two guards while you give chase. And you shall write the letter to the king and his forest wardens in the event that you take it."

"I will, Mama." Richard looked ready to explode with excitement as he and Bill gathered their reins and, with the other two guards, turned to pursue the still-hidden quarry.

As Bill and Richard disappeared from view into the thickness of the forest. Ela found herself uttering another fervent prayer under her breath—for their safety and the preservation of her son's confidence as well as his life.

"We shall stay right here until they come back." She hoped they wouldn't lose track of her in their excitement. Bill was an experienced huntsman, but she didn't want to make life more difficult for him by wandering around the forest.

Ela peered into the depths of the forest, wondering where the rest of her men were. She'd like to pass on the message that the Fox must be captured *alive* to every armed man in the forest. A robin caught her eye on the branch of a tree, then flapped up into the canopy. Pale sunlight barely filtered through the branches, here in the forest depths, and she found herself staring up toward it.

She was mentally composing her clipped but angry speech to Bishop Poore, scolding him for encouraging his men and others of the shire to break the Lord's commandments, when it happened.

## CHAPTER 4

$\mathscr{H}$e fell on her fast and with so much force that he knocked the breath right out of her lungs. Ela tumbled from her horse and landed on her back on the ground, with a hooded man standing over her. She tried to cry out but couldn't gather enough breath to make even a squeak.

"Ela, Countess of Salisbury," said the man's voice.

She couldn't see his face. His hood cast it into shadow.

Where were her men? Why did they not intervene? She could hear scuffling but couldn't see it from where she lay on the ground. Her horse had spooked, and she could hear it crashing away through the undergrowth.

"Help." The voice finally emerged from her throat, so strangled and tiny that she could barely hear it herself.

"I've heard good things about you, my lady." He spoke English with a rustic accent.

"The Fox?" she managed. Her chest felt deflated and she struggled to take a breath.

"They call me that who don't know my real name."

"What is your name?"

He laughed. Then his laugh stopped abruptly. "That doesn't matter. What matters is that I didn't kill Father Edmund de Grey."

Her first instinct was to assume that he was lying. "Who did?"

"That's not my business to tell you."

"Did you know the priest?" Her breath was back and her brain now functioning enough to form thoughts. While part of her wanted to panic and scream—where were the guards? —the rest of her ached for information about the dead priest with his odd stash of coins.

"I know of him. A wicked man, greedy and cruel, extorting money from the townspeople who could scarcely buy bread. I won't say he deserved what he got, but I won't shed a tear for him."

Ela frowned. This was not the kind of speech she'd expect from an outlaw. She became conscious that she was still lying on her back on the forest floor, with this man looming over her, his worn shoes only inches from her cheeks. She tried to struggle onto her elbows.

To her surprise he held out a hand and lifted her to her feet. She glanced around and saw her guards trussed and gagged and bound to nearby trees.

*He's not alone.* She scanned the woods but didn't see anyone else.

*If he wanted to kill me he could do it right now.*

But he didn't, or he'd have done it already.

The outlaw was barely taller than her and not a broad man. He'd overpowered her with surprise and speed rather than brute force. Not young, either. From this new angle she could see a glimpse of weathered cheek among the shadows cast by his deep hood.

"The brothers at the Abbey of St. Benedict say you stole from them."

40

A harsh laugh jolted her nerves.

"I stole from them? They steal from the people with their tithes and fines and rents. Wringing pennies from the weak and the sick and the old using threats and extortion. Taking food from the mouths of mothers and babes. Piling their wealth up in their coffers while the people outside their high abbey walls are left to starve."

Ela could feel herself frowning. "I can see you resent the tithes demanded by the abbey, but the brothers pray day and night for the souls of all men and women in the district and in our world. Surely the hope of eternal life is worth a few bags of corn or flour."

"Let them pray to repent for their own sins and leave the people in peace. I took nothing from them that they didn't steal from someone else."

"Tithes due to the church are no different from taxes due to the king. Just because you don't want to pay them doesn't mean you can break the laws of the land." She peered into the shadowed visage, and could just make out the gleam of dark eyes.

"I'm an outlaw. The laws of the land mean nothing to me."

"How did you become an outlaw?"

"That doesn't matter."

"Where did you become an outlaw? There's no record of you in Wiltshire until recently." She felt oddly calm, alone in this trackless forest with a known criminal. Curiosity overwhelmed her fear. None of the legal records she'd called up from the clerks found his birth or any other proof of his residence in the shire, and his accent placed him further north.

"That doesn't matter either. These woods suit me because they cross between two shires so I can find myself neither here nor there." She thought she saw a glimmer of amusement in his eyes.

"Bishop Poore is the sheriff of Hampshire and has put a

bounty on your head. His men have been told to bring you back dead or alive."

"Bishop Poore is a bloated old fool."

Ela stiffened. She wasn't a keen admirer of the bishop but she'd never stoop to blistering insults aimed at a representative of God's holy church. "You should mind your tongue. I could clap you in the dungeons for insulting God's bishop."

"Apparently you could lock me in your dungeons for any number of things—if you could only catch me."

Ela racked her brain for how she could overpower him and take him prisoner. She had a knife in the belt at her waist but nothing to truss him with—even if he wasn't honed to hard muscle by the demands of living by his wits in the woods.

She drew in a steadying breath. "You despise the church and its representatives. Why do you feel this gives you the right to steal from them?"

"To take back what was taken from others and return the goods to their rightful owners."

"That suggests you're stealing back sides of beef or sacks of carrots, when instead I've heard that you stole valuable candlesticks and cups and other treasures."

"It all amounts to the same. Candlesticks are more portable than fleeces or bags of grain."

This man's arrogance astonished her. "So you hand the candlesticks over to a starving peasant woman so she can repair her thatch?"

"Not quite."

She spied a chink in his armor of confidence. "It seems I can retire as sheriff because you see yourself as dispenser of justice, attacking the thieves and returning the stolen goods to their—in your mind—rightful owner."

"Now you understand." He took the bait, and she saw the

hint of a smile twist his mouth. She could make out slightly more of his face now. Not a familiar face to her.

"Indeed I do not. Tithes and taxes are essential to the running of the parish and the country. It's my job as sheriff to ensure that they are collected and that our clergy and our king receive their due."

"And the sheriffs stick their fingers in the jar and line their purses with the proceeds of their labors."

"I most certainly do not," Ela spat. She took pains to keep all her activities above board and avoid any appearance of impropriety or avarice. She tried to calm her temper. She could scarcely believe this man had the arrogance to speak to her thus. If Bill Talbot were here—

Where was Bill? He'd gone to hunt the boar, with her beloved son, but now she realized the sounds of a boar were likely a ruse so the Fox could get her alone and pounce on her and her men. The guards couldn't even wriggle in the tight bonds that held them to their trees, and their mouths were gagged so they couldn't talk. She still didn't see any sign of other men in the outlaw's band.

As she looked at one of her guards, he arched his neck and let out a stifled cry.

*Bill! Listen and come rescue me.* She'd be glad of the sight of Bishop Poore's men right now, swords bared to kill the Fox.

"The townspeople will tell you I didn't kill the priest."

"Stand trial and prove it."

Again that harsh cackle of a laugh. "I wouldn't stand a chance in a trial. The upstanding men of the jury take a dim view of any man who lives beyond the reach of society and its petty rules." He leaned in until she could almost smell his breath. "And I'd sooner be dead than in your dungeon."

*That can be arranged*, thought Ela, before realizing that she'd started to think like Bishop Poore.

The Fox executed a small neat bow, then seemed to

clamber up into the tree like a squirrel. He then jumped to another tree and disappeared into the forest canopy leaving her standing there staring after him.

She came to her senses and whipped around to look behind her in case his men were there. Not seeing anyone, she hurried to the guards and cut through their bonds. They pulled the gags from their mouths and rushed to the horses, who—mercifully—still stood nearby.

"Stay here," she commanded, her voice rising. "You must guard me. He's already escaped."

"I'm so sorry my lady. They overpowered me that quick I didn't know what happened," muttered one guard, a big, barrel-chested man a little older than her. "Never seen anything like it."

"They? Were there other men with him?" Ela hadn't seen any.

"There must have been." The men looked around in confusion.

The younger guard was red-faced with fury or embarrassment or pique at being bested by a band of brigands, or—far worse—one very nimble outlaw. "I'm sorry, my lady," he half hissed.

They probably wondered if they'd be dismissed or punished or worse. A not irrational fear. Their one duty here was to guard her, and they'd failed miserably.

"I'm unharmed, thanks be to God. But I am concerned for the others. I fear they've left us and fallen into a trap."

"I can call for them, if you wish, my lady," said the older man.

Ela nodded her assent.

The guard pulled out a small horn from the bag on his belt and blew into it. It emitted a squeal sharp enough to startle the birds from the trees. He blew into it twice more.

Ela heard an answering squeal.

"That's Sir William Talbot," said the guard. "We arranged the signal if we should need it."

Soon Ela heard the distant thud of hooves moving slowly but steadily through the thick undergrowth, twigs snapping and vines swishing around them. Bill and Richard and the others appeared, looking flushed, their horses sweated up and blowing.

"The Fox waylaid us," said Ela. "Dropped out of a tree and knocked me off my horse, and two of his men must have tied up the guards."

"More than two," muttered the older man gruffly. "A crowd of them, it felt like." Ela wasn't so sure of that. In fact she wasn't sure he hadn't ambushed them entirely alone, but she didn't see any point in contradicting him.

Bill looked appalled. "Where is he?"

"He gave me a lecture on how the church takes money from the poor of the parish, then he disappeared up into the trees again. More like an owl than a fox," said Ela. Her heart had stopped pounding and her encounter seemed more strange than terrifying. "He insisted that he didn't murder Edmund de Grey, though he had nothing good to say about the priest. He told me to speak to the local people about who murdered him."

Bill frowned deeply, probably mortally offended for her— and for himself—that a lawless ruffian had lectured his countess while he was off crashing around in the woods.

"We didn't find the boar, Mother," said Richard. "It got away."

"I'm not sure there ever was a boar," said Ela. "I suspect the outlaw feigned the sounds of a boar to draw you away and split up our party."

"Which we should never have done," said Bill, his voice a full octave deeper than usual. "Thank God you're unharmed or I'd never forgive myself. We must catch him at once."

"He said he'd rather be dead than stand trial," said Ela. "He said he'd never get a fair trial, and he's probably not wrong."

"He can't just get away!" protested Bill. "Not after insulting you."

"Perhaps he won't," she replied. "Maybe Richard Poore's men will bring him in, tied to a spit like a dead hind." Suddenly that prospect didn't bother her so much. "But my main concern is finding Father de Grey's murderer, and I find myself inclined to believe the outlaw when he said he didn't kill the priest."

Something in her heart told her that the Fox was honest. He'd put himself in her way deliberately. He'd also freely admitted to stealing from the church, following his own misguided beliefs that the thefts were justified.

"It's not safe for you to be here, my lady," said Bill quietly.

"I can't argue with you about that," said Ela. "The Fox outwitted us. He could have killed me and got away. That he didn't intrigues me."

"He doesn't want to bring every man in Wiltshire and Hampshire down upon his head," growled Bill. "Which would unquestionably happen if even one hair of your head were harmed."

"Every man in Wiltshire and Hampshire is already chasing him, and he's apparently laughing at them from the treetops," said Ela. She inhaled. "But I'm ready to leave. I want to follow his advice and interview the people of the nearby village."

"How do you know he's not setting another trap?" asked Bill.

"I don't."

~

ELA FOLLOWED Bill's advice and they headed back to the castle, deposited Richard safely at home, and return the next day to visit the people who lived nearby. Even their horses were tense and jumpy as they rode away from the forest. Not only had they failed to catch the Fox, but he'd snared them all in his own trap and made Ela doubt everything she'd believed when they set out that morning.

Back in the great hall, Stephen hovered around her like a bumblebee. "Mama, Bill said you found the killer. Why isn't he in the dungeon?" They'd finished their evening meal and sat around the table, half listening to a young musician who'd been hired to play tunes on his lute.

"He found me, rather than the other way around," she said wryly. "I wish he was in my dungeon, but instead it appears his name is well chosen." She felt like a chicken who'd survived a coop raid. "The men are out hunting him still."

"Can I come hunt him tomorrow?"

"Absolutely not. The woods are a tangled thicket and quite unsuitable for riding. If I'd known that I'd never have gone myself."

"Is that how he crept up on you?"

"Indeed it is. The forest wardens should maintain it better." Of course, if they did, the Fox would likely make himself scarce. She intended to address the wardens on that matter and recommend that they rectify it.

"Are there wolves in the Chute Forest?" asked little Nicky.

"We didn't see any. No one's seen a wolf in this part of the country for some time."

"That doesn't mean they're not here, though," chimed in Bill. "A brave knight in training should be prepared to meet a wolf any time he rides out."

"I'm not afraid of wolves," said Nicky. "Or outlaws. I'd have run him through with my sword."

Richard, who'd been flushed with excitement over his day

of hunting and the close encounter with the outlaw, had grown quiet as each person asked him why his quarry had got away. Ela suspected he now felt personally responsible for her being left poorly guarded and humiliated by the outlaw.

"Running people through with your sword is not acceptable behavior except during battle," she said curtly. "We have juries and justices who decide who must be punished by death. We can't have men—even knights of the realm—taking justice into their own hands."

"But the outlaw killed a priest," protested Stephen. "Which is about the worst thing you could ever do."

"We know the priest was killed, but we don't know for sure who killed him. The monks at his abbey said that the outlaw was a possibility. The outlaw himself insists on his innocence."

"Well, he would, wouldn't he?" said her daughter Petronella, glancing up from her embroidery. She was stitching a row of rather stiff looking lilies around the hem of a handkerchief with a skein of brown thread. "He's lying so he won't be hanged."

"That is possible. He told me to talk to the townspeople and ask them about the priest."

"You're not going to follow his advice, are you?" asked Petronella, sounding scandalized.

"I am going to speak to the villagers who live near the forest. Not because the outlaw told me to but because—as sheriff—I must investigate the circumstances of the priest's death."

"The servants were talking," admitted Petronella. "The man who transported the body here from the abbey said there was blood everywhere."

"Ewww," cried out Nicky. "Did they clean it up?"

"I don't know. Maybe you'll slip in a pool of it if you go walk near the mortuary. We could go look. It's not dark yet."

"Don't taunt your brother," chastised Ela. Petronella sometimes grew impatient with her younger siblings. Ela knew she yearned for the peace of the cloister, but Ela herself wasn't yet ready to part with her daughter. She'd already lost her three oldest to marriage, and each departure felt like her heart was being plucked from her body and put back inside her chest with a piece missing. "I viewed the body myself, and it was a violent death. Your prayers for Father de Grey's soul are surely welcome."

Ela certainly didn't intend to tell her children that the priest had been accused of extorting money from the villagers. She wasn't fool enough to believe that every man of the cloth was a saint or an angel sent to walk the earth among us, but she was shocked that a man trusted with caring for the poor and needy of the parish should seek to exploit them so cruelly.

The Fox's words had unsettled her. Did the wealth paid to the church place an undue strain on the people? Everyone complained about taxes—she certainly did—but she never begrudged money due to those whose prayer paved the paths of all men and women on earth toward Heaven.

She resolved to set out the next morning and ask the townspeople what they knew about Father Edmund de Grey and also about the outlaw known as the Fox.

CHAPTER 5

*E*la felt restless as she performed her morning rounds of the castle and grounds. All seemed in order—the boys fed the pigs, the gardeners pulled summer weeds around the vegetables and herbs in the gardens, different lads had swept the hearth and sprinkled the ash on the paths...but the outlaw remained at large. No one had reported his capture overnight—and his insult to her person rankled more rather than less with the passage of time.

*He could have slit your throat, but he didn't.* Reminding herself of this fact didn't calm her. Worse yet, she found herself believing his protests of innocence. She hated the way he'd crept under her skin and into her thoughts.

Outlaws went against everything she stood for as sheriff. They defied the strict laws of social order, having no place in the village or castle—as serf or freeman—and paying no taxes or allegiance to any lord. Their very presence prickled like a burr under the saddle, a threat to the maintenance of law and order.

If a charismatic and commanding outlaw was known to be at large he could amass a gang of thieves and scoundrels who might waylay travelers and terrorize the roads of the shire. It was her duty as sheriff to make sure that didn't happen.

~

ELA AND BILL set out again with carefully hand-picked guards—all armed to the teeth and told to be on high alert at all times. The Fox, it seemed, had taken pleasure in tricking her party, confounding her guards, and catching Ela by surprise, and she didn't intend to give him another opportunity.

"We don't need to go into the forest at all," she said briskly, as they rode out through the castle gate onto the road beyond. "No one lives within its boundaries, or at least not legally. But there's a village near the abbey and our focus is on the people there who would have interacted with Father Edmund de Grey in their daily life."

She'd learned that de Grey, along with his fellow priest, conducted Mass every day of the week, so he would have had plenty of opportunity to interact with the local people, beyond placing the blessed sacrament on their tongues.

Ela had learned what she could about the people who lived near the Abbey of St. Benedict. "There's only one village near the abbey, called Biddesden. It's on land owned by Sir Geoffrey de Wakefield, who funded and built the abbey on a part of his manor that was partitioned off and dedicated to the purpose."

"I don't know Sir Geoffrey myself," said Bill. "Though I've heard his name."

"He has several manors in Oxfordshire," said Ela. "He spends little time in Wiltshire. His estate is managed by a steward, so he'd have little reason to conduct any business with the abbey."

"Except for paying tithes to it," said Bill.

"True, though I'd imagine the steward handles all that in his absence. And since he built the abbey himself he'd hardly resent the tithes. He has two grown sons, but they also live in Oxfordshire from what I hear. I suppose we should speak to the steward. He likely attends Mass at the abbey."

"If he's a good Christian, he would," said Bill. "He could at least give an opinion of Father de Grey."

"Indeed." Ela liked the idea of beginning with the steward. He would likely be a man with at least some education. It could be very tiring to attempt a conversation with peasants, who spent more time with animals than people and who'd never seen a book, let alone read one. "We shall visit the manor and call on him."

THE MANOR HOUSE stood on a small rise on the approach to the forest, easy to see from the road. It had likely been forti- fied at some point in the distant past, but now it was a long, rather squat house with a thatched roof and weathered timbers. Too old-fashioned for a knight of any pretensions to inhabit as his residence but too solid and picturesque to tear down or abandon.

The thatch was in good repair, suggesting that someone lived there, either the steward or a tenant. They rode up toward the house through daisy-strewn meadows. A decrepit wooden paling separated the house from the surrounding fields. Once inside the gate, they dismounted and approached the door along a somewhat weedy path. A few chickens scattered as they approached, and before Bill could knock, the door opened.

A young man with curly light brown hair peered outside, scowling and squinting in the sunlight. Beardless and smooth-skinned, he looked to be barely in his majority, certainly no more than twenty-five.

"We seek the steward for Sir Geoffrey de Wakefield," said Bill.

The occupant peered at them with odd pale green eyes. "You've found both the steward and Sir Geoffrey de Wakefield."

There was an awkward pause. "This is Ela, Countess of Salisbury and High Sheriff of Wiltshire," said Bill gruffly. He obviously found the young man's enigmatic answer rude in its obtuseness. "Who might you be?"

"I'm Geoffrey de Wakefield."

Another pause. "I've met Sir Geoffrey and he's a man almost my own age," continued Bill, growing unsettled. "Are you his steward?"

"I am, and I'm also his son, of the same name." The young man seemed to be enjoying the confusion he'd sown.

Ela wondered why the namesake son of a wealthy landowner would be living far from his main estates in this rustic dwelling. Still, that didn't matter right now. "Are you aware that a priest was murdered in the Abbey of St. Benedict earlier this week?"

The young man's eyes hardened slightly. "I did hear tell of it."

"What do you know of Father Edmund de Grey?" asked Ela. "Have you met him?"

"Of course. I attend Mass on Sundays like anyone else." He tilted his chin as if defying her to prove otherwise. Ela suspected he hadn't set foot over a church threshold in some time. "Though I hadn't had time to get to know him personally."

"Did he collect tithes from your manor?"

"I couldn't say. I haven't been here long enough to pay the tithes. I arrived from Oxfordshire less than two months ago."

"The steward paid them?"

"I suppose he did."

Ela found herself growing irritated with his half answers. "Where is the steward?"

"In front of you. There was no need for the old steward now that I'm here. I sent him on his way."

Ela felt her heart sinking. They'd lost a source of valuable information, unless the former steward could be found. "What was his name?"

"John Goodson. I believe he went to Wales, where he had connections of some kind."

Of course, an area as large as it was wild and remote. It might take months to locate him, if the effort was even worthwhile.

"Did you ever live here before two months ago?" she pressed.

"Never."

"But you attended church, so you spoke with Father Edmund de Grey."

"Yes, I've met him at the abbey. But now fate has sadly deprived me of the chance to get to know him." Something like humor shone in his pale green eyes.

Ela wished she could slap the arrogant smirk off his face. "Until his killer is found, every man in the shire is a potential suspect."

She wasn't sure what she expected him to do, but he bowed low, like a palace courtier. "I am at my lady's service to find the killer and bring him to justice."

*He's mocking me.* Ela felt fury rising in her chest. "That won't be necessary. But do contact me if you hear of any pertinent information." She glanced at Bill, then turned and walked back to her horse.

"His arrogance was—" Ela found herself at a loss for words as they rode away.

"Infuriating," muttered Bill. "I'd like to take the little twit and—"

"Never mind about him. We'll head into the village and talk to the people who've lived here more than two months."

THE VILLAGE of Biddesden proved to be small and mean: two narrow, dusty lanes at a crossroads pecked by scrawny chickens. There seemed to be a persistent drainage problem that had washed away a part of the road into the village. They had to ride around the edge of a field to approach the hamlet in order to avoid negotiating a steep gully that cut through the middle of it.

The residents—fewer than forty souls, including their children—were all serfs in hereditary bondage to the ancient family of de Wakefield. They seemed flustered to the point of speechlessness by the arrival of Ela and her party, and Bill and the guards had hard work even getting them to come to their doors.

"Outlaw?" The red-faced peasant in a greasy brown tunic blinked in surprise once he'd been pried from the dark innards of his cottage. "In these parts?"

"He lives in the forest," explained Bill. "He's taken to stealing from the religious houses, and we're told he gives the money to the poor of the parish."

The man blinked again. "I don't know nothing about that."

"We did hear about Father de Grey's death," muttered one middle-aged woman in a faded green kerchief. "God rest his soul."

"You all attended Sunday Mass at the Abbey of St. Benedict?" asked Ela.

"It's the only church left that you can hear the bells from

here. Used to be a little chapel out in the fields that we went to of a Sunday, but it was torn down some years hence when they built the abbey."

Ela nodded. The loss of their little chapel probably pained them as much as the loss of the old Salisbury cathedral she'd loved as a child. "And you went there every week?"

"Yes, my lady," the woman said quietly, but with enough hesitation to make Ela wonder if she was lying.

"So you were familiar with Father de Grey and Father Billow as the shepherds of your flock?"

"Yes, my lady."

"Do you know of anyone who might have reason to want him dead?"

The woman shook her head quickly. "It's a terrible sin to kill a priest."

"At the abbey they suggested that the outlaw known as the Fox killed him," said Ela, hoping to prompt at least a trickle of information about either the outlaw or the murdered man.

But the woman's lips only seemed to clamp tighter shut.

ELA WALKED FARTHER along the lane, disturbed by the state of the cottages, with their rotten thatch and rain-washed plaster. The residents seemed to cower in their dismal dwellings until Bill knocked loudly on the doors. Even the children were quiet creatures with lean faces. The strips of garden in the fields behind the houses should have been flush with growth at this time of year, but instead they were sparse and weedy, possibly due to a lack of the water that had destroyed their road at some point.

"You're all serfs in the service of Sir Geoffrey de Wakefield?" asked Ela, of the dismal body of people finally assembled outside their cottages.

"Aye, my lady," said one older man, leaning heavily on a knobby cane. "But he lives far distant and doesn't pay attention here beyond collecting dues from us. Bleeds us dry, he does."

Ela could easily believe that. "Are you aware that Sir Geoffrey's son is in residence here now?

"Aye." The grizzled serf hesitated. "But he's no different than his father. If we all starved he'd grind our bones to make his bread."

"Pa! Come now. It's not as bad as all that." A thin woman in a ragged dress hurried forward, wiping her hands on her apron. She tried to usher her father back into the doorway of her cottage. The interior was so dark—with soot from the chimneyless fireplace—that it looked like a black hole. "Don't mind my father. He doesn't mean what he says."

"That I do! It's a shame for a lord to treat his people thus," stammered the man, as his daughter dragged him away into the dark interior.

Ela couldn't help but agree with him. Though surely some of the blame went to the steward who'd been left to run the manor in his master's absence. She intended to have stern words with the new occupant of the manor as to his duties as manorial lord.

They had heard of the outlaw, though. "Oh, aye," said a mother with two young children clutching at her skirts. "The monks told us to be very careful and keep a look out for the outlaw. Might cut our throats in our sleep, they said."

"Has he stolen from you here in the village?" asked Ela.

"Stolen what?" asked a young man with a scar on his cheek. "We've nothing to steal except the food on our tables and the clothes on our backs."

"Have you ever seen him?"

There was an odd hush before they all muttered a quiet chorus of noes.

~

ELA AND BILL rode away from Biddesden no wiser than when they'd entered it. Ela felt her belly grumble. Part of her wanted to return to the castle and take some wine to fortify her flagging spirits.

But a sense of unease propelled her forward. "Someone's not telling the truth."

"I got the same feeling," said Bill. "They're like frightened sheep."

"But who's frightened them? If it was de Grey, he's dead, so can't come back to harm them. And why would they be frightened of a parish priest?"

Bill shook his head. He probably also wanted to put his feet up in the great hall. Still…. "Since we're in the vicinity, I intend to go back to de Wakefield's manor and have words with him about the condition of his village."

~

THE YOUNG SQUIRE emerged from his house before they could approach it. "Back so soon?"

Ela didn't dismount from her horse. "We've just spoken with the residents of Biddesden. The village is in a miserable state of repair and its residents scraping by in the most unprosperous fashion."

"It's not my fault if they're not industrious."

"It's hard to be industrious on an empty belly," said Ela. "Or when your roof is letting in rain. There are no materials to repair thatch or make limewash in the village, so they'd have to buy them and they clearly can't afford it."

"Blame the abbey for that," he muttered. "I went to collect rents and they all pleaded poverty on account of giving their worldly goods to the priests."

"What? Why didn't you mention this earlier?"

"You didn't ask." Perhaps her look alone scolded him, but he straightened up and continued. "And I didn't think of it. But they said Father Edmund had squeezed every penny and chattel out of them."

"How? Why?"

"Payment for their sins or something. That's what one old crone kept muttering over and over. She wasn't in her right mind, though."

Ela looked at Bill. No one had mentioned that Father de Grey had wrung their few pennies out of them. Why hadn't they told her?

She gave young Geoffrey a clipped speech about his responsibilities as lord of the manor and how his tenants would be happier, healthier and also more profitable if he saw to their material needs. When he returned a blank look she gave an extended metaphor about his horse and how it would fail him in battle if it wasn't nourished and raised and trained to help him instead of fail him.

At last he agreed to see to repairs and improvements in the village, and Ela told him she'd be back to make sure his deeds matched his words.

"Young Sir Geoffrey's news about the priest taking money from the villagers explains the hoard of coins in his room," said Ela as they rode away from the remote manor.

"And if he kept them in his room, it's likely he was squeezing a private income from them rather than collecting funds for the abbey."

"It's a motive for murder," mused Ela. "Which I suppose is why the villagers were afraid to say anything. A penny can be the difference between life and death for a poor man, if he doesn't have it when he desperately needs it. We must go back and press them for details."

~

THEY RODE BACK TO BIDDESDEN. Ela could hear the bells for Vespers, but the summer day would be long enough to accommodate more questions.

She trotted right into the main part of the village where the cottages clustered together. This time she dismounted. She didn't want them to think they could dust her with pleasantries and she'd ride away. She handed her horse to the guard and, with Bill at her side, she approached the nearest door, which she remembered belonged to the woman who'd said—truthfully—that it was a terrible sin to kill a priest.

The woman opened the door, face pale aside from a smudge of soot on her forehead. "My lady."

"I've learned that Father de Grey was in the habit of collecting money from parishioners. Did he press you for coins?"

"I haven't got any coins," said the woman in a shaky voice. Her eyes darted behind Ela, and she lowered her voice almost to a whisper. "But he did take my three chickens that I couldn't afford to lose."

"He insisted that you give them to him?"

She nodded. "He said it was a penance."

Ela frowned. "A penance after confession?"

The woman's eyes dropped to the floor and her scrawny chest rose inside her faded gown. "Yes."

*For what?* What did this poor woman have to confess that could be worth the chickens that sustained her family?

Ela knew the secrets of the confessional were sacred, so she shouldn't ask. Still, how did he have such a hold over these people? "Did he threaten to reveal your confession if you didn't pay?"

The woman raised her eyes almost to Ela's, then they dropped back to the floor again. "He did."

Ela looked behind the woman into the cottage. Smoke from a cooking fire further obscured the dark interior, but she could make out the movement of at least one other person in there. "Come with me." She drew the woman out of the door way, motioned to Bill to stay put, and walked with her until they were just out of earshot. "I shall never reveal to anyone, ever, what you've confessed, if you'll just tell it to me now. I want to know what kind of confession he found worthy of extortion."

# CHAPTER 6

*T*he woman hesitated, lips pressed tight together. Ela braced herself. Would she confess to the murder of Father de Grey and Ela would have to keep a murderer's secret or break her word?

"I confessed that I had unkind thoughts about my husband. That he's lazy and makes me work hard enough for both of us." The woman's voice was barely audible. "He'd beat me if he heard me say that."

"I don't doubt it," said Ela softly. "But why did you confess that to the priest?"

"Because it's a sin to have such selfish thoughts about my own husband. I don't want to burn in hell for all eternity." The woman's whisper grew impassioned as the fires of hell licked around her thoughts.

"Of course. I quite understand. And I don't judge you at all. I suspect every married woman has unkind thoughts about her husband from time to time and it's only natural to seek relief from the burden of them in confession."

Ela would never in a thousand years confess any of her marital dissatisfactions to Bishop Poore, or even the castle chaplain. She bore the burden of those sins on her own soul. This woman's simple faith and trust was a credit to her—but had built a snare for her in the hands of an unscrupulous priest.

"Are you aware of other villagers who were forced to pay him to keep secret?"

The woman glanced up and down the lane. No other people were outside, which was odd. Likely they stood huddled behind their doors and walls, waiting for Ela and her intimidating men-at-arms to leave them in peace.

She leaned into Ela and whispered. "I couldn't say why he did it, but I do know that John Thistle gave the priest his best bull three months ago. He used to charge for the breeding of it, and that's how he kept himself. He's been hard off ever since."

"Which house does he live in?"

The woman pointed down the road to a reasonably sturdy wattle-and-daub dwelling with a paling fence behind it.

"What is your name, mistress?" asked Ela.

Again she hesitated, "You're not going to say anything to my husband, are you?"

"I promise you on God's holy word that I will not." Ela spoke sincerely. Though it was entirely possible that the woman's words might be raised before the jury, not attached to her name but as part of a body of evidence, there was no reason to believe that they'd ever get back to the lazy husband.

"My name is Agnes Crumb, my lady."

"I thank you for your assistance."

Agnes screwed up her face slightly. Her skin, though pale, was weathered by sun and wind. "But why do you need to know? The priest is dead, isn't he? He'll never be punished for his wrongdoing."

"True. God will be his judge. But it's my job as sheriff to find his killer."

Panic flashed in her eyes. "I didn't kill him, I swear. I'd never kill anyone."

"I don't think for a single moment that you did. But if he extorted money from other people, perhaps one of them grew angry enough to kill him."

The murder—with multiple stab wounds—was a crime of passion. It seemed likely that one of the villagers had grown angry enough to end the priest's extortion.

"Perhaps it was the outlaw that killed him," said Agnes, her voice rising. "Outlaws are criminals, aren't they? That's how they become outlaws."

"That is certainly a possibility, and there are armed men currently swarming the forest in an attempt to arrest him." Ela found it interesting that Agnes had tried to push her suspicion from the villagers to the outlaw, who they'd apparently never heard of until Ela mentioned him earlier that day. Perhaps she felt guilty that she'd now introduced John Thistle as a potential murder suspect.

"All possibilities will be thoroughly investigated." Ela wanted to reassure her. "And the suspect or suspects will be tried at the assizes by the traveling justice. There won't be any hasty hangings, I promise you."

Agnes Crumb looked very slightly reassured. "I'd better get back inside."

"Of course. But if you learn anything more about who killed the priest or about any other people he teased money from, I'd appreciate it if you bring that news to me at the castle. I'll make it worth your while."

Ela knew that Agnes Crumb would more likely walk all the way to Scotland than come through the castle gates, if she even had any means of transportation other than her own feet, which was unlikely. There wasn't a single horse, or even a donkey, in the entire village. No cows or sheep either. However did these people live?

Agnes Crumb had now disappeared back inside her cottage. From where she stood, Ela could hear raised voices as her husband likely demanded to know what she'd been gabbing about with the noblewoman who wanted to get them all into trouble.

A tiny stab of guilt pierced her chest. The information she'd shared would cost Agnes one way or another.

Ela beckoned to Bill and the guards to follow her down the road, and she walked the hundred yards or so to John Thistle's dwelling, which was set somewhat apart from the other hovels. Bill approached and rapped on the door.

The scarred wood door opened slowly to reveal a big, burly man with a face reddened by the wind. Bill stepped back to where the guards stood. She'd told him to keep a discreet distance in case she needed to pry secrets out of this man.

"God be with you, Farmer Thistle," said Ela.

"How do you know my name?" he said quickly.

"I learned it from your neighbor Agnes. She told me that a priest at the abbey insisted that you bring your prize bull to him as payment."

He glanced toward Agnes's cottage with a look of shock and anger. "I don't see how that's any of her business."

"She told me that she'd been forced to pay with her chickens. It seems that the priest was extorting goods and money from the villagers."

"All that money they have to put up fancy buildings with stained glass windows and scrolled ironwork and they have to bleed us dry to pay for their luxuries when we can't hardly keep a roof over our heads. It makes me sick." His anger rolled off him so hot Ela could almost feel it in the air.

*Is he a suspect?* Caution prickled inside her. "You attended church at the abbey?"

"Not every Sunday, I admit it, but I went when I could. Until that greedy priest stole my means of living out from under me."

"What was his pretext for wanting the bull?"

"Why does anyone want a bull? To breed good cows, of course." He looked at her like she was simple.

"I mean, how did he manage to force you into it?"

He hesitated and frowned. "Said it was a penance for my sins. But whoever heard of a penance that beggars a man?"

"Did you protest it?"

"Of course I did. I begged and pleaded with him and all. But he kept at me until I gave up and he won."

Ela spoke softly. "He threatened to reveal a secret you'd told him during confession?"

"What's spoken in confession is between a priest and his parishioner. He's not supposed to ever tell a soul."

"But did he? Threaten to tell someone?"

John Thistle peered at her with his beady brown eyes. Ela could feel him sizing her up. "Aye."

"Who did he intend to tell?"

He shifted his weight awkwardly, lumbering from one foot to another. A black cat emerged from the darkness so suddenly that it made Ela jump before it slunk away around the cottage. She hadn't realized how tense she was.

"I already gave him my bull so what's the good of my telling you? It won't get my bull back. I heard he sold it in the market at Marlborough and fetched a high price for it."

Ela could hardly remind him that she was hunting for the priest's murderer. John Thistle had more motive than anyone she'd come across. "It appears that the priest was extorting money from his parishioners. I'm trying to put together an account of his wrongdoings so the church can put a stop to such behavior."

He peered at her suspiciously. *He doesn't believe me.*

"I have no interest in your sins. I'm just trying to find out what was going on."

"Ask Alfie Fletcher, then. Maybe he'll be angry enough or fool enough to tell you what the priest took from him. My confession is between me and my God and if I had it to do over again—"

He seemed to catch himself midsentence.

"You'd what?" Ela tried to keep her voice calm. John Thistle was a big man with a broad back. He'd have no trouble overpowering a priest who spent his days hunched over prayer books and goblets of consecrated wine.

"I'd tell him to do his worst and leave me my bull. I don't know how I'm going to keep body and soul together come the winter. I used to get a penny per breeding for that bull in all the villages around these parts—I'd walk him hither and yon on a rope, he was that tame—and that money would keep me all year long. Produced the best milkers for miles around."

"He does sound like a very valuable animal." Ela felt sorry for John Thistle over the loss of his prized beast. "How did you hear of Father de Grey's death?"

"I don't rightly know. Folks were talking about it, I suppose. I haven't been near the abbey since I had to take my bull there. Don't want to ever set foot there again, truth be told."

"Don't let the actions of one dishonest man keep you from seeking comfort in the solace of the church and finding the blessings of the Lord." It infuriated Ela that Edmund de Grey had taken advantage of these people's simple faith. John Thistle must have confessed something quite compromising for de Grey to be able to pry his precious bull away from him. "Men of God can fall prey to temptation as we are all fallible humans."

"I'll keep my sins to myself from now on," he muttered. "If God's priests aren't to be trusted not to thieve and lie like common criminals."

*Speaking of which...* "What do you know of the outlaw they speak of? The one who lives in the Chute Forest?"

"He's a finer man than Father Edmund de Grey." He said the priest's name in a mocking tone. "I'll tell you that much."

Ela's curiosity flared up. "What makes you say that?"

"He cares about poor people. He thinks it's wrong that the riches of our countryside are stored up in the tithe barns of abbeys and castles. The people that toil to fill them are going hungry and cold in the winter while fat priests and lords feast on our chickens and burn our wood and drink the milk from our cows."

Ela thought of her own dining table, often groaning with such fare. And the fire blazing in the dead of winter, as they sat around it laughing and drinking spiced wine. Still, it was the way things were: some men were rich, some poor; some strong, others weak.

"Your lord provides protection and land for you to live on here on his manor, and your priests provide a spiritual home for your soul during your time on earth, to help you find your place in Heaven."

He stared at her, face reddening. "What *protection* does my lord provide?

"Protection from enemies. From someone bigger and stronger coming to throw you off this land and take it as his."

He seemed to ponder that for a moment. "It's not mine anyway, is it? I'm just a serf. Couldn't leave it if I wanted to. Maybe I'd prefer it if some oaf came along and threw me off it."

If Bill were next to her he'd tell this man to mind his

tongue! Ela was tempted to do the same. It might be hazardous to the peace of the shire if serfs were able to wander the countryside spouting such discontent.

*You talk like a man who has nothing to lose. A man who might be tempted to risk everything for one final rebellious act.*

Should she arrest John Thistle on suspicion of murdering Edmund de Grey?

Something stopped her. This man had taken the risk of confessing a sin terrible enough for Edmund de Grey to take his bull as payment for silence. Confession, in addition to being an act of contrition, was a statement of faith. Like Agnes Crumb, he'd put his faith in a man of God, and thus, in God himself.

If he killed the priest he'd damn his immortal soul to the fires of hell for all eternity. A man of true faith would never do that.

She burned with curiosity to know the nature of his expensive sin. But perhaps she could learn of it from another villager. "Alfie Fletcher was the man you said I should visit?"

"Aye. Lives in the middle of the village. You won't have trouble finding him."

Ela thanked him for his time and summoned Bill and the guards to walk back to the sad cluster of dwellings that made up the village. A pinched woman swept her yard, and Ela could hear a baby crying inside.

"Where may I find Alfie Fletcher?"

"Between a rock and a hard place, my lady," said the woman, her flinty eyes peering out of a suspicious face.

"He's dead?"

The woman laughed, an eerie, unsettling sound. "Nay, though he sometimes seems like he is. Lost his wife last year and his daughter this one."

"May God rest their souls." Ela crossed herself.

"Two doors down. Daub falling right off the walls and won't lift his finger to fix it."

Ela recalled the cottage, wondering if its occupant had died. The brittle old daub had crumbled right away in some places, exposing the woven wattle structure of the walls. She thanked the woman and walked to his door, where she knocked briskly.

A stirring sound from within told her the occupant was home. "Who is it?" called a sleepy voice.

"Countess Ela of Salisbury, Sheriff of Wiltshire."

A sharp clang spoke of something falling to the floor, and she heard more shuffling. Then stillness. "Come on in and arrest me. I don't care if I die here or in the dungeon at Salisbury castle."

"Let me enter first," said Bill quietly. Ela stepped aside and watched him push the door open with his fingertips, the other hand on the hilt of his sword. The door opened to reveal a pitch-dark interior. There were no windows, so the only light followed them through the door in a long shaft. She heard a mouse—or rat—scurry somewhere off to the side.

But, stepping into the room, she could smell a man. "Where are you?"

"Here on the bed."

"Rise up at once," commanded Bill. "Your countess is present."

There was a short pause, then a pile of rags seemed to shift in one corner. Slowly a man sat up. She could see the gleam of his eyes in the darkness though his face was smudged with soot or dirt so she couldn't make out his features.

"Stand at once!" She could feel Bill growing agitated beside her. Why did this man behave so oddly? More like a ghost than a living human.

The man staggered to his feet and swayed a little, like a drunk. But she didn't smell any liquor.

"State your name," barked Bill.

"Alfred Fletcher," he said listlessly. "You can arrest me now. It was just one loaf of bread for my starving child and she's dead now and I'd sooner be dead myself than living here alone."

A cold sensation formed in Ela's gut. "My deepest condolences on your terrible loss. May God guide and comfort you."

The man didn't reply.

"We're not here to arrest you. John Thistle said that you, like him, were forced into giving up goods by a priest of St. Benedict's Abbey."

"Took my last sack of grain," he said, growing suddenly animated. "Or said he'd tell the sheriff I stole bread and I'd be locked up in the dungeon and my daughter would be left alone. She were only three years old and..." His voice trailed off. "I should have let them arrest me as then one of the neighbors would have taken little Maisie in and my bag of grain would have kept her alive while I rotted in the dungeon." He paused. His eyes glittered in the dark with what looked like tears. "Now they're both gone so it was all for nothing. And I'll burn in hell anyway for what I'm feeling over it all." His voice fell to a hushed whisper.

*Did he kill the priest?*

If he lost his daughter as a result of the priest taking food from her mouth, any man with a heart would understand his anger.

"Do you own a knife?" She asked in a light tone.

"Of course I own a knife. What man doesn't own a knife?"

Bill stiffened. "Fetch it at once, man."

The man's eyes glittered in the dark. "What if I don't?" His voice was barely a whisper.

71

"Then you'll feel the sharp edge of my sword," growled Bill. Ela could tell he found this man's lassitude unsettling. She did, too. Such depths of despair smelled almost of the sulfur of hell—as if he were living in a hell here on earth.

"Where is the knife?" she asked gently. "My men can find it."

"It's under my bed I suppose."

The man sat back on his bed, leaned forward and groped around underneath the bed, which—from what she could make out in the dark—was a rickety affair made from repurposed wood, just high enough off the earthen floor to keep the damp from his ragged bedding. He pulled out a good-sized knife and brandished it fast enough to make Ela gasp.

"Sorry my lady. I didn't mean to startle you." She wasn't sure if he intended to mock her or not.

"Bill, please take the knife outside and examine it."

Bill snatched the knife from him and headed outside, murmuring something unintelligible to the guards as he passed them. They moved in closer to her, hands hovering over the hilts of their swords.

"Do you know why John Thistle felt compelled to give up his good bull to keep the priest quiet?"

The man's eyes shut for a moment, making him almost disappear in the darkness. Then they opened and peered right at her. "You should ask him."

"I did. Naturally he worries that I'll seek retribution for whatever it was. I have no intention of doing that. I merely seek information about how the dead priest was extorting money."

"What does it matter? The priest is dead."

*But the person who killed him is alive.*

The villagers must know she was gathering details about them to determine which of them had stabbed the priest to death.

"Justice matters," she said quietly.

"There's no justice for the poor," muttered the man. "We're born, we suffer, and we die and no one remembers us afterward."

A chill settled in Ela's chest. She searched her mind for homilies to cheer and encourage him but couldn't come up with any that didn't seem like a cruel platitude under his desperate circumstances.

She decided to try another direction. "What do you know of the outlaw that they call the Fox?"

His gaze dropped to the floor. "Nothing."

"They say he helps the needy."

"They say a lot of things." His voice had taken on a defensive edge that told Ela he knew more than he was letting on.

"Have you ever met him?"

"Not knowingly. They say he's a master of disguise, and you won't know if you've met him or not half the time."

"So you do know something of him." She didn't manage to disguise the note of triumph in her voice. "Do you think he could have killed Father Edmund de Grey?"

His suspicious gaze faltered for a moment and he closed his eyes. When he opened them she saw the tiniest hint of fire in the gleam of his eyes. "Perhaps he did. He's the only one around here who seems to have any fire in him. The rest of us are all just lambs to the slaughter who let the lords and the priests bleed us dry. If I died today they wouldn't even notice. He's a man who makes them sit up and take notice."

"How?"

"By taking back their ill-gotten gains and returning them to those that were wronged."

Ela hesitated for a moment. She grew tired of hearing all these stories of the Fox's beneficence with stolen goods. So far she'd seen no evidence of it. "Did he give you back your bag of grain?"

The man drew in a ragged breath. "Nay. I'm nothing to him or to anyone else. My daughter, Maisie, was the light of my life and it's gone out now she's gone. I'm not worth a single grain without her. If I had any fire left inside me maybe I'd have murdered Father de Grey myself to stop him destroying other people's lives, but I don't."

"If you'd committed murder you'd have an eternity in hellfire to look forward to," said Ela, in a clipped voice. "Cruel as it sometimes is, our suffering on earth at least has numbered days."

The man's eyes widened, glittered in the darkness, and he let out a strange cackle of laughter. "What do you know of suffering? What do you know of hunger and cold and privations? What do you know of watching your only child slowly weaken until she couldn't even lift her head to greet me?"

*I've suffered*, she wanted to protest. *My husband was cruelly taken from me and every day is a battle I must fight by myself.* But she couldn't compare her suffering to his.

"I shall send alms. Your daughter wouldn't want you to give up and throw the rest of your precious life away. You have a purpose here on earth."

"To work my fingers to the bone for some lord who doesn't care if I live or die?"

Bill had come back into the room and stood there silently, still holding the knife.

"Any findings?" she asked him.

"It's rusty. No signs of blood or even recent use."

Ela wasn't surprised. This man didn't seem to have the energy to lift a finger to save his own life, let alone take anyone else's. She bid him goodbye and wished him the strength and courage to live on to honor the memory of his daughter. Then she promised to return to visit him.

He sat silently, no doubt hoping and praying that she'd disappear and never come back.

74

*E*la had vaguely noticed voices outside the hovel, and now her ears focused on the high-pitched shriek of an angry woman. "It's your fault anyway. Never mind a penny, you don't have a kind word or deed to bestow on man or beast!"

Ela emerged into the dusty lane to see a woman screaming at a man in a greasy linen cap.

The man hunched forward almost like a predator ready to spring at prey. "For richer or for poorer, you said." His beady dark eyes narrowed. "In sickness and in health."

"Sickness of the body, not of the mind," cried the woman. She was youngish—less than thirty—with a rosy, handsome face and tendrils of dark hair escaping her kerchief. "I thought I knew you when I married you. I thought you were solid and steady and would soften with tender care. Instead you hardened like leather left out in the rain."

A snarl twisted the man's face. "Too much rain makes a flood."

"Well, your flood might be someone else's spring!" spat the woman.

"Silence!" Bill Talbot's commanding voice boomed out over the fracas. All the villagers had emerged from their squalid dwellings and stood either in their doorways or clustered around the unhappy couple. "Your countess doesn't need to hear your petty squabbles that should be kept behind closed doors."

Ela wished she could scold Bill for interpreting her thoughts, which ran in a completely different direction.

She stepped forward. "Why are you chastising your wife?" she asked the man. She already found herself favoring the errant woman over this pinched ferret of a man.

He hesitated, staring at her, as if he suddenly realized he'd stepped into a river and was now over his head. "Brought me no end of trouble with her whoring ways. It's a sin as well as a crime and cost me my plough."

Ela had a hunch about what had happened and why he picked this moment to accuse his wife. "How did she cost you your plough?"

"The priest took it or said he'd tell everyone in the village that my wife was—" His gaze fell to the ground. Then jerked back to meet Ela's. "All because this strumpet was fool enough to confess her disgusting deeds."

Ela looked up and down the lane. She also had a suspicion about who the other man was in this depressing little love triangle. John Thistle was nowhere to be seen.

"I'd like to speak to you alone," Ela said to the woman.

"About what?" About Ela's height, the woman looked ready to argue with anyone. "Are you going to have me arrested for adultery?"

"I wish to speak with you about another matter."

The woman frowned. She clearly didn't trust Ela and expected to be clapped in irons if she backed down an inch.

"Obey your countess," snapped Bill. He'd clearly had

enough of this rag-tag group of villagers. He mostly dealt with people who'd come to the castle on business, fully prepared to bow and scrape and show all due respect to their countess. "Or you'll be clapped in irons for your insolence."

Ela didn't remember seeing Bill this cantankerous before. "That won't be necessary. I'm sure you won't mind just stepping over here by this tree." She pointed to a great spreading oak—by far the most imposing and beautiful feature in this dismal village—that stood about a hundred feet from the last house.

The woman swallowed and adjusted her kerchief. "I suppose I must, mustn't I?"

Ela silenced Bill with a look. Once again he had his hand on the hilt of his sword. Did he anticipate having to hold it to the throat of one of these sorry serfs? She beckoned for the woman to come with her and for Bill and the guards to stay behind.

Once they'd reached the shade of the tree, Ela introduced herself quietly and established that the woman's name was Minnie Frost. Ela explained that she knew the priest had sowed a bitter harvest in the village by extorting money from anyone who'd made a compromising confession.

"I wouldn't have confessed if I'd known he'd hold it over my head. I'd never go near the abbey again," said the woman with some vehemence.

"So you stopped going to confession. Did others do the same?"

"Of course! Who'd confess to someone who'd squeeze the lifeblood out of them later for it?"

Ela wondered if the priest had grown used to his income stream of ill-gotten riches and when he found it drying up, he'd taken a risk that got him killed.

"Who else fell into the priest's trap?"

"You mean who else did he demand money from? Agnes Crumb and Mildred Rucker both gave him their laying hens. And I'm pretty sure he got the milk cow from the Weathers family. He didn't even want the animals but sold them in the market." That explained why his chest was filled with coins and not chicken feathers.

Ela wondered at the number of sinners in this valley, each with a sin great enough to be worth a bribe. She struggled to think of a single act she'd committed where the revealing of it would make her give away her worldly goods to stop it becoming public.

"It sounds like you all have reason to be angry with him."

"We do. He gained our trust by taking confession for months before he started demanding money. I suppose that's why they do confession, isn't it? So they'll have something to hold over our heads."

Ela blinked. "No, I'm sure that's not the reason for it. It's to release us from the burden of our sins and—" She realized she was engaging in a theological discussion with a serf who'd probably never seen a Bible let alone read one. "Edmund de Grey's behavior was a shocking aberration."

She didn't suspect this woman of murdering the priest. Her husband was another matter. From his complaints it was clear that he'd been cuckolded by his wife and forced into giving up his plough to cover it up or bear the shame of everyone knowing. Then—in his anger—he'd revealed the truth anyway. "Does your husband have a temper?"

Minnie Frost looked at her. "You mean, did he kill the priest? Much as I'd like to be rid of the hard-hearted old sod I am quite sure he didn't murder anyone. Doesn't have enough passion to squash a fly if it bit him."

Ela couldn't help asking, "What about John Thistle?"

The woman looked startled. She hadn't admitted that Thistle was the man she'd sinned with, and Ela didn't like to press her for details or she was little better than the priest. She straightened her kerchief. "He was very upset about losing his bull." She looked back toward the village. The villagers all stood about staring at them as if they were watching a group of mummers from a distance. "But I don't think so. He's a God-fearing man."

"Not so God-fearing that he didn't break the commandment about adultery," observed Ela.

The woman stared at her for a second. "Does God really judge adultery in the same breath that he judges bloody murder? I don't think so."

Ela blinked, not sure whether she was dumbfounded or impressed by the woman's lack of deference. She found herself growing exhausted by the expanding list of suspects and the dearth of any actionable information. "If you had to guess who killed the priest, who would you suspect?"

She frowned. "It's none of my business to suspect. I'm not the sheriff."

Ela now felt like she'd been slapped in the face. She was glad Bill didn't hear this piece of insolence. Not that it was entirely undeserved. She thanked Minnie Frost for her time and decided to retreat to the castle to mull over all this new information.

ELA SHARED the evening meal with her children, then sat watching while they played a game of blindman's bluff in the hall. The younger ones loved the game and her older children—with the exception of oh-so-serious Petronella—indulged them by playing with them. Right now little Ellie was blindfolded and striding toward Stephen, who held his finger to his mouth to keep the others from revealing his location.

Ela sipped her wine, which had relaxed her considerably, and beckoned Bill Talbot over. "You seemed on edge today."

"I don't like that village."

"Why?" Ela wanted to laugh at his grim expression. "It must be one of the sorriest places in Wiltshire now that the priest has picked its poor residents clean of all their worldly goods."

"Exactly. Those people have been fleeced of their chattels and their pride. They've nothing left at all. Makes them dangerous, if you ask me."

"I think it makes them pathetic. I feel sorry for them, not angry with them."

"Such weakness of character is despicable."

"They're serfs, Bill! Their entire lot in life is predicated on knowing their place and obeying their betters."

"I'd rather be dead than live like that." He spoke low so that no one but her could hear him.

Ela was shocked. "They've really unsettled you, haven't they? They were honest enough to tell their sins to the priest, and he turned on them. What I see as simple faith and trust, you see as weakness."

"They should have stood up to him."

"How?" Ela put down her wine cup. "They have no means to stand up to him."

"They could have come to the castle and reported his misdeeds."

"For that they'd have to air the information about their sins in this hall. They preferred to keep them quiet, as most good Christians would. They had no idea he was going to be murdered and all their dirty business would explode like blood spatter in their faces."

"They'd have done better to not sin in the first place."

"There do seem to be a lot of sinners in one small village. If I was a superstitious type I might ask a priest to exorcise the Godforsaken place. As it is I shall pray for them and for a speedy resolution of this whole ugly matter."

Bill took a sip of his wine. "Who do you think killed the priest?"

"Well…" Ela watched Ellie spin around, listening for where her siblings might be creeping about. One of Ellie's hands twitched as if she ached to lift her blindfold and take a peek. "At first I was inclined to suspect the outlaw since the monks at the abbey mentioned him as their first suspect. Having met him I think that's less likely."

"'Met him' is one way of describing him overpowering your guards and assaulting you in the forest." Bill's jaw grew tight. "Perhaps he's the reason I'm so furious at the villagers. They seem to almost revere him when they should be turning him in to the sheriff. I'll never forgive myself for letting you be attacked."

"I'm unharmed, if a little unnerved by the incident."

"It was all my fault. What was I thinking, taking chase of a boar and leaving you unattended in a forest with an outlaw at large?"

"You left me in the care of trained men-at-arms."

"Who should be horsewhipped for their carelessness."

"Or is it the outlaw who should be praised for his cunning plan of attack? I half wish I had him on my castle staff."

Bill stared at her like she'd entirely lost her mind.

"I'm joking, of course. But I am rather intrigued by his efforts to take the people's wealth back from those that seized it from them, in the belief that they need and deserve it more."

"It's no different than if you sent me to wrest the taxes you paid last year back from the king!" Bill spoke low. Even jesting about such a thing was probably high treason.

"Don't tempt me." Ela sipped her wine. "But you have to admit there's some genius to it. I'm so used to being in the position of collecting rents and taxes and tithes myself, that I've never really stopped to ponder the fate of those who have to offer them up but never collect them. I gnash my teeth and complain about parting with the profits of my many manors, but no amount of taxation and tithing takes food from my children's mouths. For these people the loss of a single animal can mean the difference between life and death."

"That's why the Lord suffers us to be charitable."

"But their lord is far from charitable. Both the old one and the new. If anything he's utterly oblivious to their plight."

"He sets my teeth on edge as well. Why would his wealthy and powerful father send him to such a desolate backwater?"

Ela peered at him and pretended to look affronted. "Wiltshire is the crown jewel of England."

"Not that lonely corner of it. The soil is thin and you can see the valley is alternately subject to torrents and droughts."

Ellie, who had been flailing around and had failed to catch anyone, stopped and stamped her foot. "I give up!"

"Hellooo," called out Richard, who'd been creeping about just a few feet from her. "I'm right under your nose."

Ellie lunged forward and Richard—who could easily have got away—made a big show of being captured, then lifted his triumphant little sister up onto his shoulders and carried her around the great hall like a queen surveying her newly conquered lands.

"Your sons are a credit to you," said Bill, with a satisfied smile.

"They're a credit to *you*," replied Ela. "Since you've played the largest part in their training. Their dear father was away for so much of their childhood I don't know what we'd have done without you."

"That said, I should not have given in to Richard's boyish

urge to chase a boar when we had more important and dangerous quarry."

"I won't argue that point with you." She sipped her wine with a wry smile. "Though perhaps it was for the best. I did meet the outlaw and get to hear his side of the story. I admit it changed my view of things."

"He's still an outlaw and a criminal, even if he isn't the murderer—which he absolutely might be."

Richard had now tied the blindfold around his head and, in typical thirteen-year-old boy fashion, was charging blindly around the room, bumping tables and knocking chairs, grabbing wildly for his siblings, who scurried around giggling and taunting him.

"Should we really let the children raise such a ruckus in the great hall of Salisbury Castle?" whispered Ela to Bill. "Sometimes I worry that the decorum of our hall should be more closely observed. I'm always quick to complain when the garrison soldiers get drunk and rowdy."

"It's hardly the same as an outlaw running amok in the king's forest and stealing treasures from the churches and abbeys."

Ela mused for a moment. "I do wish he'd go pursue his business far from Wiltshire."

"You see no problem with what he's doing?" Bill looked astonished.

"I see a great many problems with what he's doing. And with the way some lords milk the poor for their labor and give them nothing in return." She fingered her wine cup. "And, though I'd never begrudge the church the income they need to sing praises to the Lord and to provide spiritual succor to the people, I do now wonder if some of that money might be better spent on alms distributed directly to the people rather than rich treasures."

"I'm surprised to hear you say that. You are following in a

family tradition of bestowing great sums to endow new abbeys for the glory of God."

"And for the passage of my immortal soul and that of my husband. There is a selfish element to the beneficence," she admitted. She was glad of the noisy game of blind-man's bluff to hide this rather personal conversation. "But the religious orders are supposed to celebrate poverty and the liberation from worldly cares. Have you ever read the Rule of St. Benedict?"

"I have not," Bill admitted.

"It's the list of precepts written down hundreds of years ago by St. Benedict of Nursia to govern monastic life, but I'm afraid the execution often runs far from the principle in these troubled times. I find myself wondering how other affairs were conducted at the Abbey of St. Benedict."

"And how they are unfolding now in the absence of the prior and the priests—one dead and the others on the Continent."

"Indeed," said Ela. "Bishop Poore said he would take over the running of the abbey, which in itself is cause for concern. And he's the current Sheriff of Hampshire!"

"It does beggar belief." Bill's shook his head. "How is a man supposed to punish sins with one hand and forgive them with the other?"

Ela moved in closer. She didn't want anyone to overhear her thoughts. "I agree that it makes no sense. Bishop Poore is an ambitious man who has consolidated his power to an almost dangerous degree."

"He is a right-hand-man of both the king and the king's justiciar. As such he's gathering riches to augment his status and fortune."

"Quite contrary to the Rule of St. Benedict." Ela inhaled deeply. "I think tomorrow we should visit the abbey again with a view to examining their tithe barns and inquiring as to the wealth they've acquired in their short period of existence."

Bill looked confused. "To find out who might have motive to murder Father de Grey?"

"That as well."

# CHAPTER 8

*E*la and Bill rode up to the Abbey of St. Benedict as the bells rang for Terce. They left their horses with the guards and entered through the large wrought-iron gates manned by a single lay brother acting as guard, then walked along the carved stone cloisters and into the church itself, just as the monks burst into the familiar plea.

*O God, come to our aid.*

*O Lord, make haste to help us.*

Ela closed her eyes and silently joined in their entreaty. Their voices rose in song, filling the nave and echoing off all the carved and polished surfaces, gathering momentum and strength to carry their wishes to the Lord.

During the service she looked around for the red-haired monk, Brother Wilfred, who'd been so helpful thus far, and located him standing near the front. As the service ended she waited for him to file out so she could ask him to show her the tithe barns and examine their stores.

She was surprised when he hurried past her without so much as raising his eyes to greet her.

Taken aback, Ela looked around for another potential

helper and settled on the gray-haired man who'd been quite talkative and appeared to be a figure of some authority on her first visit, the day of the murder.

Luckily he didn't avoid her gaze, though he didn't exactly look happy to see her, either. "My lady." He bowed his head slightly.

"I must trouble you for some of your time as we continue to investigate the murder of Father Edmund. Could you please show us the contents of your tithe barns?"

A look of surprise passed over his face, then one of… knowing. Ela remembered with a sudden flare of embarrassment that the red-haired monk had mentioned that sheriffs were usually only interested in the goods and chattels of the monastery. She resisted the temptation to exclaim the purity of her purpose, but followed him there in silence as the other monks filed out into the cloister and scattered to perform their various duties.

Ela noted the fine carvings ornamenting the stone archways of the cloister, and the smooth and expert stonework of the walkways. No expense had been spared in the construction of this monument to the glory of God. She resolved to insist on similar attention to detail and quality of construction of the soon-to-be-built monasteries dedicated to the memory of her husband and herself at Hinton and Lacock.

The monk, whose name was established to be Brother Ethelstan, led them past the monks' quarters and along a paved path to a great stone-built barn with a slate roof.

"What a fine barn. It's built as sturdy as my castle," she exclaimed.

"No sense having a good store of grain get moldy from leaking thatch," muttered Brother Ethelstan. He pulled the key from the folds of his rough-spun robe and opened the door.

"How many of you have the key?" She was rather surprised that he didn't need to fetch it from somewhere.

"Normally just the prior and priests have the key, but since they're not to be found, I have one, Brother Wilfred has one, and I believe that Bishop Richard Poore now has a third."

Ah. "Bishop Poore has been here to oversee the running of the monastery."

Ethelstan looked at her for a moment as if trying to read her expression. "He was here long enough to inspect the stores and take hold of the keys."

The door creaked open, to reveal a roomy interior with no natural light other than what fell through the doorway. Sacks of grain were stacked higher than two men along one wall. She also saw a great pile of fleeces and various barrels and kegs.

"Will the monastery use all these goods for yourselves or will they be sold?"

"Whatever is unlikely to be used in time is sold. Or as fresher goods come in they sell off the older."

"It seems you are very well supplied. Are all these goods gathered from the village nearest to the abbey?"

"Yes, my lady."

"Do the people protest at giving up their stores of grain and their fleeces?"

"Oh, yes. And these barrels contain quantities of salted meat and fish. But it's all for the glory of God. How will the people go to Heaven without us to pray for their sinful and corrupt souls?"

"Thanks be to God in his mercy," she muttered, thinking that perhaps the people could pray better for their own souls if they had food in their bellies.

She'd have to speak to Bishop Poore about possibly redistributing some of these stores back to the people who'd given them. Much as she appreciated and supported the work of the brothers, this Abbey had benefactors and was not in need of wringing every last handful of grain from its parishioners.

"I'd like to visit Father Edmund's chambers again." She wanted to take another look at the chest with his goods in them—if it was still there.

Brother Ethelstan looked perturbed. "I don't have the key to his room."

"I do. In the meantime, I'd be curious to know what the rumors are about who killed Father Edmund. I'm sure the monks talk among themselves about the matter. What have you heard?"

She saw his Adam's apple move as he swallowed. "We're none the wiser, I'm afraid, my lady." He turned to walk toward the priests' chambers.

*He's keeping something from me.*

"Do the brothers still suspect the outlaw?" No one knew of her encounter with the notorious character. Richard and Bill were sworn to secrecy, and the guards would be far too embarrassed at their own failure to protect their countess to mention it.

"I suppose so, my lady. He's known to steal from the religious houses. I suppose he would hate a priest."

This line of reasoning made no sense to her. If—as he'd told her—he had a clear purpose in giving the people back their own goods, he'd only be endangering his mission by murdering the priest.

"Are you aware of any encounters between Father Edmund and the outlaw while Father Edmund was still alive?"

"I haven't heard of such, but I believe Father Edmund visited the sheriff asking for his arrest in the weeks before his death."

"He visited Bishop Poore?"

"Not Bishop Poore. His co-sheriff. I didn't even know Bishop Poore was the sheriff."

Interesting. Ela didn't know much about his co-sheriff, Gilbert de Staplebrigg, but she was fairly sure Bishop Poore had little interest in the day-to-day running of the county beyond opportunities to enrich himself and augment his power.

Ela and Bill followed Brother Ethelstan up the stairs into the corridor with the priests' rooms. "Have the two men on a pilgrimage been notified of the murder?"

"A letter has been sent, my lady. Whether it has yet been delivered, I'm afraid I don't know."

The letter had likely crossed the sea by now. "I'd imagine it's hard to deliver a letter when they could be in any number of places along the pilgrimage route."

"Indeed, my lady. It's a shame they'll have to abandon their pilgrimage to the holy shrine and return at once, but I'm sure they will."

"They are good men?"

He looked surprised at her question. "Yes, of course."

And odd curiosity tweaked her. "Would you describe Father Edmund as a good man, too?"

He blinked, obviously shocked. "Of course. He's one of God's holy fathers." His answer came a little too fast and loud to be entirely convincing.

She decided to press him further. "We heard from some of the villagers that he exacted...fines from them after hearing their confession." She downplayed it as she didn't know the full story and didn't want chaos to erupt inside the monastery. "Have you heard of such a thing?" They reached the closed door of Father de Grey's room. Ela pulled the two keys from her purse and inserted the larger one into the lock, where it turned easily.

Ela stepped into the room. Which had been stripped bare

of its treasures. The tapestry was gone, and a silver and wood crucifix that hung on the wall above his bed, and the chest. "Where has the chest been removed to?"

"I don't know, my lady."

"Did Bishop Poore oversee this?"

"I don't know, my lady."

She didn't entirely believe him. But what reason would he have to lie to her?

"I shall have to pay a visit to Bishop Poore."

ELA RODE to Bishop Poore's house that afternoon. She'd had a servant ride ahead earlier to confirm that he was at home to save her a wasted journey. This time only her guards attended her, since she'd left Bill to continue his important work of teaching her boys to be both knights and men of honor.

An odd sense of apprehension crept over her as she dismounted and approached the finely carved door of the bishop's palace. She'd recently visited the king in his nearby palace at Clarendon, and Bishop Poore's new residence was arguably finer.

A cowled brother opened the door and bowed, and ushered her in as if Poore was expecting her. She entered, heart still beating faster than usual, and stood in his glorious receiving room with its grand fireplace, gorgeous French tapestry on one wall, and finely carved furniture.

Ela thought of the villagers at Biddesden, in their mean hovels, all one misfortune from starvation, yet having to give a great portion of their meager goods to both their absentee (until recently) lord and the Abbey of St. Benedict.

"Ela, my dear." Bishop Poore swept in through the wide,

arched doorway, face wreathed in a smile too warm for the occasion.

"Your grace." She greeted him with a polite nod of the head. He took her hands in both of his and squeezed them. For a tiny moment she felt as if her heart was also being pressed between his meaty palms. "I hear you've taken charge of the Abbey of St. Benedict."

"Yes, I made haste to visit them and give them succor and solace." He shook his head. "What a strange misfortune to lose one holy father while the other two are abroad."

"Did the brothers shed any light on who might have killed Father Edmund de Grey?"

"It was the outlaw, of course. He's a known troublemaker. An agent of the devil himself, sent to sow discord among God's people."

"Did your men catch him?" She knew the answer to this already, since she'd certainly have heard if they did. Her own men had been patrolling the forest day and night, along with the king's foresters and the men of Hampshire on their side of the border.

"He's elusive as a bad spirit. As soon as someone catches the scent of him, he's gone."

A very young monk entered with a carafe of wine and two cups, then put them on a small table and poured some wine into each cup. Poore took the cups and offered one to Ela, who took it with thanks.

She took a sip. The ruby red liquid had a smooth richness that matched the beauty of its color. "What an excellent wine."

"From the vineyards of the Benedictines at Cluny," he said with a smile. "Last year's harvest was superb. Just the right amount of sun and rain for perfection."

Ela made a mental note to try to secure some casks of this particular wine for her own cellars. Then she took a silent but deep breath. "I've spoken to the villagers and what I've learned gave me reason to think that the priest's murderer is someone other than the outlaw."

Poore made a dismissive gesture with his ringed hand. "Who else would it be?"

"Almost every parishioner seems to bear some grudge against him. These simple villagers made their confessions to him and apparently he saw fit to extort fines from them in order to keep their secrets."

"Extortion is a strong word." Bishop Poore's face reddened. "If he encouraged almsgiving as a form of penance that's hardly unusual."

"It can hardly be called almsgiving when it takes bread from the mouths of their children. I heard the same story repeated until my head spun. The villagers stopped going to confession after being forced to hand over livestock and grain they needed to survive."

She studied his face, which creased into a frown. "I've heard no mention of such a thing."

"I didn't hear it from the brothers, either. Only from the parishioners. But it suggests that Father de Grey had more enemies than we suspected."

"Are you sure the villagers weren't simply griping about paying their usual tithes?"

"I'm sure of it. They'd already paid those in full and given more than they had to give. I visited the tithe barn at the abbey and the stores there were well in excess of what the abbey needs to sustain its population. Perhaps some of it could be redistributed to the people, some of whom seemed to be in quite dire need."

Poore stared at her for a moment, then laughed. His big ruby ring glittered as he waved his hand in the air. "You sound almost like the outlaw!"

"Hardly," said Ela coolly. She could tell she'd overstepped

and risked being laughed at by Bishop Poore and his cronies later, over a few cups of his very fine Burgundy wine. "I know you personally take pains to provide alms to the needy. Since the brothers of the abbey are burdened by overabundance, and the people are wanting, surely it is only sensible to direct the almoner to distribute some of the excess."

"Perhaps you're right," he motioned for the young monk, who stood over near the door, to refill their wine. "I'll look into the matter."

Ela doubted he'd do anything of the sort. More likely he'd remove the excess and sell it for profit. "Do you know what became of the contents of Father de Grey's bedroom? When I first looked at it, shortly after his murder, there were several valuable items, including a fine tapestry not unlike the one on your wall. There was also a wooden chest lined with coins and trinkets. Those items were gone when I visited this morning."

Poore's expression shifted from one of mild disinterest to keen curiosity. "A chest of coins? A tapestry? I've heard nothing of this. The brothers never showed me his room, and I never thought to ask about it. Where might the items have gone?"

"I asked Brother Ethelstan, who I believe is the oldest monk there—aside from one in his dotage—and he was as surprised as I to find the items had been removed. I was hoping you might know where they'd gone."

Poore took a swig of his wine. "I shall send men to make inquiries at once."

THE NEXT MORNING, which was the Feast of the Assumption, Ela attended early services. She itched to return to the Chute Forest, but she'd promised Richard and Stephen—and

Bill Talbot—that she'd watch a demonstration of their newly honed skill in falconry. Each boy had his own bird, caught in a trap he'd baited with a live rodent. Richard, who was older, had been taming and training his bird for nearly two years, whereas Stephen was newer to the art but had—according to Bill—already formed a close bond with the powerful raptor.

"Mine's bigger than yours anyway," bragged Stephen as they walked across the ruined remains of the old cathedral on the castle mound. His bird was a goshawk. "So it can take down larger prey, like a duck."

"Size means nothing. My sparrowhawk is faster. It can stun its prey in midair."

"There's no way yours is faster," argued Stephen. "Mine's faster."

"You haven't even been training yours for a year. Maybe it'll forget all about you and take off for the coast."

"Boys! Stop bickering. The birds themselves will show us how well they perform." Bill carried a cage filled with their intended prey. Ela refrained from looking at it. She'd learned falconry as a pastime when she was a girl in Normandy, but never developed a passion for it and had preferred stroking her bird and talking to it rather than setting it at helpless songbirds.

"I didn't feed my bird anything this morning," said Stephen. "I want him good and hungry so he'll fly fast to earn his reward."

"If he's too hungry he won't have the strength," said Richard. "I prefer to keep mine content and happy to return to me." He reached into a pouch at his waist and fished out a morsel of raw meat which he gave to his sparrowhawk. Both birds still wore the leather hoods that covered their eyes and rendered them dependent on their young masters.

"We'll start here." Bill put down the cage, reached in, and

took a small sparrow out of it, then closed the door quickly. "Richard, you remove the hood from your bird first."

Richard obliged. He got himself into position, made sure the bird was alert and focused, then Bill uttered an odd cry and released the sparrow into the air. The sparrow made a valiant bid for freedom, but as soon as Richard let go of his sparrowhawk, it shot at the smaller bird like an arrow, and grabbed it out of the air, flapping and turning before returning to Richard's arm with its prey clutched in its claws. On a cue from Richard it dropped the bird and hopped back onto his arm, where—with an ear-to-ear grin—he gave it another morsel of raw meat.

Ela shuddered and kept her eyes off the poor bird on the ground. Bill must have noticed. "It's dead. Killed on impact," he said, as if that were reassuring.

"Mama doesn't have the stomach for killing," said Stephen.

"She killed a man once," retorted Richard.

"Only because she had to," said Bill.

"In self-defense," said Ela quietly. "And I've never had a taste for hunting birds or animals."

"Just for eating the rewards. Preferably in a good sauce." said Stephen cheerfully. "Now it's my turn."

Once again Bill released the small bird. Stephen's goshawk watched it with keen concentration as it flapped in Bill's grasp, trying to take off for freedom. As it flew away, for a slim instant Ela couldn't help hoping that it might escape and live to return to its family in a little nest in a shrub somewhere. Then she thought of Stephen and all his hard work to tame his first bird and how proud he was of its accomplishments. She held her breath as he released his goshawk, and the big gray-and-white bird climbed into the sky, pulsing its powerful wings.

The goshawk struck its prey hard and fast and dropped

from the sky with the smaller bird clutched tight in its talons. Stephen also cued him to drop his quarry and sit back on his wrist for his reward of raw meat. Bill gathered up the unfortunate target and whispered reassurance to Ela that it was also dead, which was at least some relief.

"Wonderful work, both of you. You should be very proud of your accomplishments. You've gained the trust of two of the fastest, most powerful creatures on earth."

"It's good training for when we'll lead an army," said Stephen. "That's what Bill said."

Ela glanced at Bill. "I'm sure he's right." The prospect of her beloved boys leading an army into battle did not make for restful nights, but her husband had survived many a brutal encounter and returned home safely.

"Can we go again?" asked Stephen. He was almost jumping up and down with excitement. Ela noticed with some chagrin that Bill had several more small birds in his cage.

"Why not?" Bill was undoing the latch on the cage again when the sound of hooves clattering across the remains of the old cobbled roadway to the ruins made them all look up.

Two guards trotted across the worn stones and pulled their steaming horses to a halt right in front of her.

"What's amiss?" asked Ela, as one dismounted, sweating and breathless.

"There's been another murder, my lady."

"Where?"

"At the Abbey of St. Benedict."

# CHAPTER 9

"Who has been killed?" asked Ela.

"A brother at the monastery, my lady. His name is Wilfred Bedulf."

The red-haired monk with the stutter, who'd been distracted or evasive on her last visit. "What happened?"

"It appears that he's been pushed from the top of the bell tower, my lady. His body was found much broken on the ground below."

Ela crossed herself and murmured a quick prayer for the passage of his soul. "A jury must be summoned at once. Send a message to the coroner to meet me at the East Gate and we shall ride there together at once. The body must not be disturbed until Giles Haughton has examined it."

"Can I come, Mama?" asked Richard, looking up from feeding a scrap of raw meat to his bird. "So I can learn the business of being sheriff?"

"Not today, my love. There will be a great crowd of people there with the jurors and all the monastic brothers, and I don't wish to add to it.

Richard pouted slightly. Stephen looked cheered that his

brother wouldn't get to have a more exciting afternoon than his own. "I thought you wanted to be a bishop, anyway."

"Bishop Poore is both Bishop of Salisbury and Sheriff of Hampshire, so I may have need of both sets of skills," said Richard with some hauteur.

"That is not a common circumstance," said Ela. "Most bishops are content to confine their interests to the ecclesiastical realm." She wondered if Bishop Poore had yet been informed of this new murder. "I shall do you the favor of leaving Sir William here to continue your excellent education in falconry. Congratulations to you all on your fine accomplishments."

GILES HAUGHTON WAS at the East Gate, mounted on his bay palfrey, when Ela arrived there with fresh guards in attendance.

"Good morrow, my lady." He looked surprisingly cheerful for one just informed of a murder. But perhaps such was an occupational hazard for a coroner. "A fine day for a ride, at least."

"I'm grateful for the clouds to keep the sun off our backs." A stiff breeze tugged at her veil as they rode out the gate and off the castle mound. She paused to tuck it into the neck of her robe so it would flap around too much. "Do you remember the red-haired monk who did much of the talking on the day Father Edmund de Grey was killed?"

"Indeed I do."

"He's the new victim."

Haughton looked intrigued rather than horrified. "Perhaps the details of this murder will shed some light on the earlier killing."

～

By the time they arrived at the abbey, the sun had come out from behind the clouds and beamed down on them from above. Brothers stood here and there, staring or distracted rather than attending to their various duties. The gate to the abbey stood open, and Ela and Haughton dismounted outside it, left their horses with the guards, and walked in past the assembled groups of monks.

"Where is the body?" asked Haughton, since it wasn't immediately apparent. Normally Wilfred himself would have hurried forward to lead them, except for the last time when he'd been evasive. Ela looked around for Brother Ethelstan, who'd shown her the tithe barn, but he was nowhere to be seen.

A short, round monk with a freshly shorn tonsure hurried over and silently beckoned to them to follow him. He led them along the cloister, where monks parted to allow their passage. At the far end he took them around the outside of the church, across the close-grazed grass that grew up to the walls. They'd almost reached the far end of the nave when Ela saw a rumpled length of cloth spread on the grass.

Haughton approached and lifted the cloth. Ela crossed herself and murmured a quick prayer. The coroner rolled up the cloth and put it to one side, then knelt over the body. "Has he been moved since he was found?"

The short monk shook his head.

"Do you not have the power of speech?" asked Haughton rather impatiently.

"He may have taken a vow of silence," said Ela, with a glance at the monk, who nodded in assent. "Could you please find us someone who can speak about how the body was found?"

"A headless body," muttered Haughton as the monk scurried away.

"What?" Ela could clearly see Brother Wilfred's head, complete with its distinctive red hair, still attached to his body.

"This accursed abbey. No one in charge and the monks standing around like stray geese."

"Bishop Poore has taken command in the absence of the traveling fathers," she said. "I'm sure he'll send someone to manage the daily affairs." It was hardly Haughton's business either way. Though she also wasn't sure why she was defending any of them.

The body of Brother Wilfred lay sprawled on his back in a very awkward and broken way, as if his limbs had been deliberately twisted out of place.

"He's fallen from the bell tower," said Haughton without glancing up from his examination of the corpse.

Ela looked up at the tower, which loomed above them, stone shining in the midday sun.

"He'd have died on impact. Several of his bones are broken, and I'd lay odds that his broken ribs punctured his lungs and maybe his heart as well."

Ela instinctively crossed herself again. Haughton pulled his knife from his belt and cut a notch in the monk's habit, then tore it from neck to ankle in a few swift movements.

She averted her eyes for a moment as the dead man's body was first exposed to the cruel sunlight. Then, reminding herself she was sheriff and not a fainting chambermaid, she steeled herself to gaze on the monk's broken corpse.

His skin was the color of curdled milk, not a freckle or hair on it.

The short, silent brother returned with a very tall, lanky

one, with a wispy brown tonsure and a long, beaky nose. "My lady," said the tall monk. "How may I be of service?"

"Please tell the coroner the circumstances under which the body was found."

"Brother Wilfred rang the bell for Matins, as he should have, but then didn't come down to join the service. He was discovered like this just before first light," said the monk nervously. "The boy who minds the geese cried out when he almost fell over him."

"Where is this boy?"

"He ran away back to his mother once it was discovered that Brother Wilfred had gone to meet his Heavenly Father."

"Is his home nearby?"

"It's in Biddesden, some miles hence. He lives here and isn't supposed to go home but I daresay the fright of it…." He ran out of words and stared down at the hem of his robe.

Ela glanced at Haughton, who was now examining the dead monk's hands. "No signs of a struggle," he murmured. "Nails are intact." He looked up at the tall monk. "Could you help me turn him over?"

The monk's look of horror screamed a silent *no*, but he bent down and together they slowly and carefully hefted the body of Brother Wilfred until he lay facedown.

"Oh!" The exclamation rose unbidden from Ela's mouth and she wished she could take it back. The site of Brother Wilfred's back, striped with fresh red welts, had shocked her badly.

"A punishment?" asked Haughton of the tall brother.

"Mortification," said the brother, averting his eyes from the sight. "I suppose most of us bear such marks at one time or another."

"How would he manage to inflict such damage on himself? I struggle to imagine how a man can apply enough force to his own back to scar the skin like that." Now that she dared to peer at his skin, she could see the white shadows of earlier lashings.

"We have an instrument we use, my lady, with long tails on a woven handle, that allows a lashing forceful enough to sting our conscience as well as our backs." He didn't look her in the eye.

Ela wanted to cross herself again, but resisted the urge. "Have Brother Wilfred's family been informed of his death?"

"I'm not sure, my lady."

"Please make sure that they are." She said a silent prayer for his soon-to-be-grieving mother.

Giles Haughton examined the body carefully, feeling for broken bones and examining the skin for abrasions.

"Is there a sign of foul play?"

"I'd say a man falling from a bell tower implies foul play," he replied. "It's hardly something that can happen by accident. Look at the size of the window."

Ela peered up at it. The arched window near the top of the tower—on the level with the bells—was unglazed but very small. It was a wonder that Brother Wilfred even fit through it.

"Is there any indication that he was dead when he fell?" They'd recently dealt with a murder where a man had been strangled before falling to his death.

"I've found no stab wounds or marks of strangulation. If he was clubbed over the head I'd have a hard time distinguishing those marks from the contusions he suffered in the fall."

"Perhaps we can learn more by climbing the tower."

"It's a very steep climb, my lady," said the tall monk. "And the stairs are barely toeholds."

"I'm sure the coroner and I will manage."

Giles Haughton insisted on walking behind Ela as they climbed the tower, so he could catch her if she fell. The stone steps were indeed narrow, rising in a spiral along the square walls of the tower. The walls of the tower took up most of the building's thickness, leaving little interior space. By the time they reached the top, Ela felt dizzy and disoriented and in much need of a deep breath.

The view from the window, down to the bright green grass below and the crumpled form of Brother Wilfred—now hidden again by the cloth—did nothing to cure her unease. "It's a very high tower."

"It is indeed," said Haughton. "No doubt so the bells can be heard to summon the people to Mass."

"And to confession," mused Ela.

"I beg your pardon?" Haughton.

"It appears that Father de Grey, who was stabbed to death in the cloister, had been confessor to many of the villagers, then made them pay him to keep their secrets. He made many enemies among the people who were already close enough to destitution that they couldn't afford to part with what he took.

"That does lengthen the list of suspects. Are there any who seem particularly likely?"

"One big man called John Thistle was very bitter about the loss of his bull that earned him his living, but he doesn't seem like a killer. Another man, named Alfred Fletcher, gave his last bag of grain and his child starved and died."

"What were these people thinking? Why didn't they just say no and report him to the bishop?" Haughton glanced down into the yawning dark hole they'd just climbed up.

"They were terrified that their sins would be revealed. And the mind of a serf is not the same as that of a freeman. They have no experience with self-determination."

"Apparently they have enough self-determination to

commit a sin bad enough to hide from. How serious were these sins?"

"Bad enough— theft, adultery and the like—from what I could gather. Father de Grey had a chest full of trinkets and coins wrung from his parishioners, and the tithe barn is piled high with goods obtained through legitimate tithes as well as his acts of extortion. The abbey groans with riches while the people in the nearby village suffer privations."

"If the outlaw known as the Fox took it upon himself to right these wrongs—which is what people say of him—it lends credence to the idea that he killed de Grey. But that brings us no closer to learning who killed Brother Wilfred."

"Brother Wilfred took charge on my first visits here. He approached me and guided me about the monastery. Despite his stutter he seemed to offer himself as a natural leader. On my last visit he wouldn't even look at me. Something had changed."

"Who took charge instead?"

"Brother Ethelstan, one of the older monks. I wonder where he is today? I haven't seen him."

Ela peered out the narrow arched window. There were two of them, one on each side of the bell tower. "Do you see any signs of a struggle?" The wooden platform was clearly not cleaned regularly and had an array of footprints in the dust, some of them from birds who must fly in here. There were no dramatic scuff marks or signs of a body being dragged.

"I don't see anything beyond the footfalls you'd expect from normal use. You can see where the bell ringer climbs onto the platform where it meets the stairs, then walks to the bell, and pulls the rope."

"There are two sets of footprints, one on either side of the bell," observed Ela.

"Possibly one of the bell ringers is left handed and prefers to approach from the right hand side."

"We need to find out who was up here with Brother Wilfred this morning."

They descended the tower. Back on the ground they discovered that the tall monk had disappeared. Brother Wilfred's body lay unattended on the ground, and all the monks had made themselves scarce.

Haughton, growing increasingly exasperated, went striding off to find the missing Brother Ethelstan. He returned a moment later with a young fresh-faced monk with curly golden hair. "Brother Ethelstan is in silent prayer, apparently," growled Haughton. "I managed to goad Brother Philip here into answering our inquiries."

"Did anyone climb the bell tower with Brother Wilfred early this morning?"

"I don't know, my lady. It's full dark at Matins."

"Was anyone else missing from the service?"

"I don't know, my lady. There are so many of us it's hard to say."

Ela glanced at Haughton, who looked like he wanted to roll his eyes.

"I need Brother Ethelstan brought here at once," said Ela.

"He's in silent prayer," said the boy.

"He will have to be roused from it," snapped Haughton. "Obey your countess."

The boy's eyes widened, but he still hesitated. He looked at Ela, then at Haughton, then at Ela, then he turned and hurried away.

Haughton stared after him. "Do you think he'll be back with Brother Ethelstan or do you think he's just run for the hills like the goose-boy who found the body?"

Ela shook her head. "Their behavior is very strange. You'd

think they would rush forward to offer information to help determine who killed their brother."

Eventually the young monk returned with Brother Ethelstan, who looked pinched and even red-eyed. He returned her greeting with some hesitation.

Ela didn't feel like beating about the bush. "Who was the last person to see Brother Wilfred alive?"

She could swear she saw a look of panic in Brother Ethelstan's pale eyes. "I wish I knew, my lady. It's a terrible tragedy."

"The tragedy is that he's been murdered on the grounds of God's holy abbey and all of the brothers are scurrying away like startled mice. Do they not want us to determine his killer?"

"I'm sure they do, my lady," he prevaricated, with an odd hand gesture. His hands, with long pale fingers, were trembling. "But sadly his death happened in the dark and, since we were all in the chapel, no one saw it."

"Did you notice anyone missing from Matins service?"

"I'm afraid not, my lady, but I confess that sometimes I struggle with alertness at that hour of the night."

Ela suppressed her annoyance. "Is there any one of the brothers who has a keen enough mind and sharp enough eyes to notice who was missing?"

Again, he made the odd gesture. "I'm not sure, my lady. Do you need to take him away to the castle mortuary like you did with Brother de Grey, or may we prepare his body for burial here?"

Ela looked at Haughton, who spoke up. "I can't see any reason for further examination. The impact of his fall broke several bones and ruptured his organs. I have no reason to believe he was dead before the fall, so I see no further knowledge to be gained from it."

"Then you may bury him without further ado," said Ela.

A look of relief passed over Brother Ethelstan's pale, strained face. Unease gripped Ela. Did he hope to hide something by burying the body? "Perhaps Giles Haughton should take one more close look at the body before you remove it." She glanced at Haughton. "Just to make sure nothing was missed."

Giles shot her an odd look, but moved to the body and pulled back the sheet.

Ela looked at the tall monk. "Please see if you can find a witness who can tell us whether anyone else was absent from Matins service." The monk hurried away.

Giles looked up at Ela. "My initial examination was quite thorough, my lady. I'm not sure there's anything to be gained from another."

"His seeming delight that I'd agreed to a speedy burial gave me cause for concern."

"I see what you mean, but these monks are concerned mainly for the progress of his soul and would probably rather focus on that rather than having his body carted unceremoniously all over Wiltshire before he enjoys his final rest."

"I suppose you're right." Still… "Does anything strike you as odd?"

Haughton looked up at her. He had continued to examine the body, looking again at the fingers and toes, despite his protest. "You mean besides two members of a small, quiet religious community being found dead by unnatural causes within a week?"

"And that none of them seems to know anything about either one. Since these monks live so close together I would have thought they'd know every detail about each other. And where is the hoard that de Grey collected? Bishop Poore claims no knowledge of it."

"Perhaps the notorious outlaw took it. It would certainly fit his modus operandi."

Ela stared at him. "You're right, of course. And if he was here last night—"

"Then he could have killed Brother Wilfred as well as Father de Grey."

She frowned. Her surprise meeting with the outlaw had unsettled her greatly. Had he charmed her into accepting his lies as truth?

"I have a confession to make," she said softly.

Haughton looked up, then re-covered the body and stood. "Then I am your confessor."

"I trust you won't extract as keen a bribe as Father de Grey."

Haughton's mouth tilted in a half smile. "Let's hope not."

"The outlaw surprised me in the Chute Forest and held me and my men captive for a few moments. Long enough to convince me that Father de Grey was the true villain and not himself."

Haughton looked positively poleaxed by the news. His mouth fell open slightly.

"Then he escaped and hasn't been seen since. There must be fifty men—from both Wiltshire and Hampshire—hunting him in that forest and they can't even catch his scent."

"Why didn't you say anything about this before?"

Ela frowned and inhaled a slow breath. "I'm not sure. Perhaps I was embarrassed at being caught unawares. Or mortified that I had him within reach and he escaped. He lured Sir William Talbot and Richard away from me, then overpowered my men, so they're all too humiliated to breathe a word of the incident. The whole situation was just so bizarre. What did he hope to accomplish by it?"

"To put you off his scent, I'd imagine. Perhaps to make

you focus your attentions on those inside the abbey rather than on him. It seems to have worked."

"But what would he have to gain by killing Father de Grey and Brother Wilfred?"

"Revenge." Haughton wiped his hands on a cloth he'd pulled from the bag at his waist. "Hatred will make a man take foolish risks to seek satisfaction."

"I've sent to York to ask what he was originally convicted of and how he became outlawed. I've yet to hear back."

"Perhaps that's where your answer will lie, but in the meantime I'd treat him as a very dangerous man."

"I just don't understand how he could have given our men the slip and left the forest, walked into the abbey and climbed up the tower without being seen."

"Easy. In some ways the brothers are sitting targets. Everyone knows they attended service at all of the regular hours. All he has to do is sneak in while they're all busy inside the church."

"I suppose you're right. I must tell the brothers to leave some men on watch. In fact, I suspect the abbey should be under guard. I'll arrange to have some garrison soldiers sent here to keep watch." She looked off toward the cloister, the direction the tall monk had hurried away in. "What's taking so long? Why do I feel like they're all avoiding us?"

"Perhaps they're just unnerved. They're not used to dealing with worldly matters, and now they've had two fatal blows to their peace and the sanctity of their holy sanctuary."

"I can't help wondering if they have some reason to be wary of our investigation. Let's go talk to some more of them."

They abandoned the lifeless, broken form of Brother Wilfred alone in the grass, and walked back to the cloister. Oddly, all the men who were standing around before had vanished, and the entire cloister and the garden beyond it were now devoid of human life.

If nothing else, this behavior was rude. She was their countess and sheriff and they should attend her out of respect, even if they didn't give two figs about who killed their fellow monk.

She approached several of the brothers, who all acted like deaf-mutes until pressed. None of them could say if anyone other than Brother Wilfred was missing from Matins that morning, and none of them had any idea who might have killed him except for some nonspecific mutterings about "the outlaw."

"An outlaw is a convenient scapegoat for any and all crimes, it appears," said Ela, quietly annoyed at how unhelpful they were. "Every parish should have one."

They headed back along the cloister, in preparation to head out through the gates. The guards stood on the far side of the road, still holding their horses, which they started to bring to readiness at the sight of them.

"I'd almost suspect a conspiracy," said Haughton under his breath. "They're so evasive, it's as if they discussed the matter and agreed to keep mum."

Ela stopped in her tracks and stared at him. "Do you think that's a real possibility?"

He looked surprised, which told her that he'd been jesting. Still, it wasn't the most outrageous suggestion she'd ever heard. "Then what about Father de Grey's murder? Could he have been stabbed by multiple people all wanting him dead and wanting to share in the responsibility?"

"You mean the angry townspeople?" asked Haughton. His voice was polite, but his expression now suggested that he thought her touched in the head.

"Or the brothers, angry with him for extorting goods from people who'd entrusted him with their confessions."

She shook her head as if she could shake this train of thought from her mind. "It's a ridiculous idea. But no more ridiculous than the fact that we have two people dead in one cloistered community and we have no real suspects."

The sound of thudding hooves jerked their attention to the road. A rider appeared over the hill, clad in the dress of the garrison soldiers. "My lady!" he called. He slowed his horse, whose chest was lathered. "A man named John Thistle has been found trespassing in the abbey's woods. Should we arrest him?"

# CHAPTER 10

"*A*rrest him and bring him to Salisbury Castle." Ela felt a rush of relief that someone had finally stepped forward to present himself as the killer, even if inadvertently. Now she could return to the castle and take some food with at least a tiny bit of satisfaction as the reward for their morning's work.

She and Haughton mounted their horses and rode back to the castle. "I wouldn't have expected it to be John Thistle, but he was angry enough to kill, I suppose. I just wonder what he would have held against Brother Wilfred?"

"I expect you're about to find out."

BACK AT THE castle Ela ate roast chicken dressed with herbs from the garden and a fruit tart made with sweet, fat raspberries and cloaked in thick cream.

"I've been praying all morning for his soul, Mama," said Petronella, as she finished the bread and cheese in front of her. "Who would kill a holy brother?"

"That is the question I've been asking myself all morning. And why are you eating bread and cheese when Cook has prepared this tender chicken stuffed with breadcrumbs and fragrant tarragon?"

"Chicken is an indulgence I can do without, Mama. I prefer to mortify my flesh with simpler fare."

Ela peered at her daughter. "I think that making Cook prepare a special meal for you is an indulgence. And choosing to mortify your flesh is a further indulgence and an insult to the generosity of our Lord who has seen fit to provide us with this fine meal."

Petronella's face grew mottled, and her lip quivered slightly. Ela suspected that her words had mortified Petronella's very sheltered flesh rather more than she'd intended. "I'm sorry, my dear. I didn't mean to snap at you. It's been a very trying morning. I'm as shaken as you are that murder has twice touched upon a sanctuary created in the name of our Lord. But it appears that we may have the murderer in custody, so hopefully the brothers can sleep well tonight."

THAT AFTERNOON, a jury was summoned and John Thistle brought up from the dungeon. The big man lumbered across the hall, flanked by guards, with his hands tied behind his back. He seemed to shrink in the presence of all the family members and servants and garrison soldiers and jurors that peopled the room.

Ela took her seat on her dais and summoned the guards to bring him to face her. Thistle didn't look up at her. His face was redder than ever, and his mouth set in a sullen slash. Though as she studied him she noticed that he was trembling.

"John Thistle, did you kill Brother Wilfred Bedulf?"

His gaze flew to meet hers, and she was surprised to see it filled with astonishment. "I never!"

Ela peered at him. "You were found hiding in the woods near the abbey only hours after he was murdered. I would suspect that you came to the abbey in the dark to kill him and were unable to make your way back to Biddesden after the alarm was raised."

"What? No! I've never laid eyes on any Brother Wilfred. I've never been inside the abbey this morning. Or any time since I—" He broke off, and his lip twitched.

"Since you what?" asked Ela.

"Since I took my bull there," he hissed.

"Then why were you in the abbey woods this morning?"

Thistle's eyes darted from side to side. Then he looked at her. "I've hunted in those woods my whole life. Born and raised here, I was. They used to belong to the manor we all live on, and the lord didn't care if we helped ourselves to a pigeon or rabbit to feed our family. Then when the manor was granted to the abbey suddenly we weren't allowed to hunt in the woods that we all knew like the backs of our hands." Sweat darkened his tunic.

Ela considered his lengthy answer. "So you were poaching."

"I didn't catch anything at all." He shifted, uncomfortable with his arms trussed behind his broad back. "So I suppose I was just walking."

Ela studied his face to see if this was intended to be insolent, but mostly he just looked nervous. "It hardly matters since you're not here on a charge of poaching but on a charge of murder."

His face grew pale. "What?"

"Don't pretend you know nothing of this morning's murder." She peered at him.

"I never heard of any murder," he spluttered. "Who was murdered?"

*They always deny it.* She'd be more inclined to sympathy for a murderer if he admitted guilt but provided a really good reason for it. She couldn't think of one single instance where that had happened.

"Please tell the jury why you had to bring your bull to the abbey."

He looked confused. "Father Edmund de Grey made me bring it." He hesitated.

"Why?" Ela found herself growing exasperated again.

"You know why," he blurted out.

"But I need you to explain it to the jury."

John Thistle looked down at the floor and shifted his weight again. He looked to be in pain. "He said he'd tell everyone what I'd told him in confession."

There was a silence. Ela had not pressed him about the contents of his confession, but she could no longer ignore it. "What did you confess?"

Thistle's face grew red. "I parted with my best bull to keep my silence. Ruined my life it did! I'll not tell you now. Go ahead and hang me."

Ela's heart sank. Most likely that's what would happen, but a confession would make her lie easier at night. Of course the entire case would be tried before the traveling justice at the assizes, so it wasn't her responsibility to pronounce sentence, just to extract all the information she could from him in preparation for that trial. "Did you kill Father Edmund de Grey?"

"I did not." His lips pressed together angrily after he answered.

"Jurors, do you have questions for Farmer Thistle?"

"Aye, I do," said Peter Howard the baker. "Why do you feel

we should hang you if you didn't kill anyone or poach in the forest?"

"Because it doesn't matter what I say. You need a guilty man and I'm as good as any other." His meaty face had a hard quality to it.

Ela admired his lack of fear. But it didn't help her true cause. "We are not looking to hang the first handy volunteer," she cut in. "We seek to find the guilty party and see that justice is meted out where it's due."

"Then you're looking in the wrong place." He lifted his chin.

"And where is the right place?"

"Inside the abbey would be my guess." John Thistle still looked resigned to whatever fate might be handed out to him.

"Do you have any reason to suspect someone within the abbey?" Ela couldn't resist asking.

"I don't have any reason not to." His face settled into a sullen expression. "But you can go ahead and hang me, anyway. I won't be missed."

Ela frowned. This was not going well at all. At this point she had no choice but to lock him up, but also no confidence that he was the true killer of either Father de Grey or Brother Wilfred.

And no one had told the jury about today's murder. "This morning, in the dark hours during or immediately after Matins, a Brother Wilfred Bedulf was pushed to his death from the window of the bell tower at the Abbey of Saint Benedict. The window itself is high and small and pushing a man out of it would require a degree of physical strength." Something the strapping John Thistle was clearly capable of. "We've determined that Brother Wilfred was up in the bell tower to ring the bells, as he did for each Matins service, but no one at the abbey could tell us who else might have been with him. In fact, they were all suspiciously reticent when the coroner and I questioned them."

Stephen Hale, the village cordwainer and a regular member of the jury, interjected. "This man has stated reason to be angry with Father de Grey, possibly even enough to kill him, but what reason would he have for killing Brother Wilfred?" He asked the question of Ela.

Ela looked at Thistle. "Did you know Brother Wildfred Bedulf?"

"Never even heard of him." His eyes looked strangely life-less. "All those monks look alike to me. Faceless hooded eunuchs. My bull had a better life than they did, until they took him from me."

Ela really wished she had never heard of the existence of John Thistle's bull. The animal had taken on a life of its own in her mind, not unlike the minotaur in a lurid ancient tale a minstrel had sung to them over several long winter evenings before the fire.

She needed to think. "Does anyone have any more questions for the prisoner?" No one did. "Send him back to the dungeon."

THE NEXT MORNING, Ela was grateful for the reassuring routine of her morning rounds. The site of the boys feeding healthy piglets, the early bees buzzing around the bee skeps in the herb garden, even the tired soldiers attempting to stand up straight as she approached, all soothed her with their predictability. One boy swept the paths and a girl threw grain to the hens that pecked among the herbs for grubs and small insects.

Was the killer someone inside the abbey? And if so, why did none of the brothers speak up to accuse the guilty party?

She walked across the courtyard just as the great gate opened to admit people from outside onto the castle mound. Carts lumbered in, piled high with vegetables and cheeses and urns of milk, and people shuffled forward, who'd already made a long journey from a nearby village to sell their wares.

One woman pushed through them and shouted, "I need to see the sheriff!"

Taken aback, Ela hesitated until she saw the two guards accompanying her put their hands on their swords. She motioned to them to wait. "Then you must come into the great hall. I'm the sheriff, and I take petitions there."

The woman stared at her for a moment, with an intense expression on her face. "I'm here about John Thistle—"

Ela recognized Minnie Frost, the adulterous woman from Biddesden. "In the hall, she said." One of the guards roughly grabbed her arm. "And not out here."

Ela's keen interest urged her to ask the woman for details, but she didn't want to breach the protocol that she herself had instituted. "Please bring her to the hall. She may attend me at once."

She turned and strode back there herself, confident that the guards wouldn't let the woman slip away in case she lost her nerve.

Once inside the hall, Ela greeted her children, who'd come down for breakfast, and asked a serving girl to remove a small but potentially hazardous puddle recently created by a dog. Then she took up her seat on the dais.

The guards almost shoved the woman forward. She wore a plain blue gown and her hair was wrapped up in a white scarf. Now in front of her countess, she looked terrified.

"They said he killed the monk, but he didn't. John Thistle would never kill a man, never! He's a man of honor. He gave his bull to protect my reputation. And now that's made him a suspect and it's not right! He's the best man in Biddesden."

"You were the secret he confessed to Father de Grey."

"I told him he should never have confessed it. But he was such a good-hearted man and he didn't want to burn in hell."

Ela silently reflected that perhaps he should have thought of that before bedding another man's wife.

"He told you that Father de Grey seized the bull in exchange for his silence?"

"He didn't tell me until it was too late. He knows I wouldn't have let him give up his bull that made him his living. My husband's tight-fisted and dull as a bog, but he wouldn't kill me if he found out. He might not even beat me, since I'm stronger than him."

Ela blinked. Minnie Frost's protests didn't really do anything to protect John Thistle. All she'd done was incriminate herself as an adulteress, something he'd made a terrible sacrifice to prevent. Ela could imagine that John Thistle would not be at all happy to know that his mistress was here pleading for his life.

On the plus side she now knew with certainty what sin he'd given up his bull to keep secret. Ela didn't know quite what to do with this woman and her pointless confession. She could hardly be trusted as an alibi, even if she'd been with him at the time of the murder, since she'd clearly risk anything to protect him.

But since she was here... "Who do you suspect of committing the murder of Father de Grey and Brother Wilfred?"

The woman looked stunned by her question. "I don't know of anyone who could have done it."

Ela stared at her. Her protest seemed excessive. "I'm aware that several of the villagers had reason to be angry with Father de Grey for taking from them when they had so little. But who might be likely to act on their anger?"

She blinked rapidly. "None of the villagers would have dared. We've all lived our whole lives here in Biddesden."

"Your lord hasn't lived here long, though, has he?" Ela's mind wandered back to the younger Geoffrey de Wakefield. Was it a coincidence that the murders had happened shortly after he'd taken up residence in the district?

"Nay." She looked doubtful, like she might have said the wrong thing. "He sent a bailiff to collect his due but we didn't have it because Father de Grey had taken so much."

"Some of the villagers were unable to pay their share to the lord because of Father de Grey?"

The woman's face seemed to close off. "I suppose so." Her lips pressed together. "But I don't have anything bad to say about the lord. I haven't even laid eyes on him."

She was afraid to make trouble for herself. "What did he do when he found out you couldn't pay?"

"His bailiff threatened to throw us off the land but no one took it that seriously, as who would work the land for him then?"

"What do you know of the outlaw they call the Fox?"

"I don't know nothing about him," she said quickly, in a flat tone.

"You've heard of him, though?"

"Everyone's heard of him. No one's seen him."

"They say he steals from the abbeys and gives money and goods back to the poor. Someone must have seen him."

"I daresay they must."

Why was she so reticent? If she was so keen to save her lover from the noose she could have blamed the outlaw for the killings.

"It would certainly be easier to find John Thistle innocent of murder if we could find the guilty party." She let that sink in. Not that she wanted the woman to blame an innocent man, but people seemed so unwilling to help her find the murderer—or murderers.

"John Thistle would never kill anyone. You must let him go."

"It was brave of you to come plead for him at the cost of your reputation, but I'm afraid he's all but admitted to poaching so he'll be tried for that at the very least. And at least for now he's the only suspect in the murder of Brother Wilfred, since he was found hiding in the woods close to the abbey on the day the monk was killed."

"How did the monk die?" Her eyes squinted as she scrutinized Ela.

"What are people saying about it?" Ela was curious to see what rumors had reached Biddesden.

"That he fell from the bell tower. How do you even know he was murdered?"

"I've been in the bell tower and it would be very difficult to fall from the windows as they are above waist level. It would take a deliberate effort."

"Then it wouldn't be easy for someone to push him out, either." The woman was oddly self-possessed. "So perhaps he climbed up and jumped out by himself."

This possibility had flitted through Ela's mind, but it seemed so unlikely that a man of God would condemn himself to alienation from Heaven by taking his own life that she'd dismissed it out of hand. None of the brothers had suggested it either, but they had been oddly unwilling to talk. Perhaps she should return to ask them specifically about this possibility.

"He might sicken and die down there," said Minnie Frost. "And someone needs to milk his cow."

Ela hadn't realized he had a cow. She usually made arrangements for the livestock of prisoners to be tended. There was no reason for an animal to suffer or its abundance to be wasted because of the misdeeds of its' owner. "Is there someone in the village who can milk the cow in exchange for the milk."

"Oh yes. I'd do it myself if my husband would let me."

"Does he know you're here?"

"No. I told him I was going to gather dandelions for a salad."

"Then I hope you find some on your way home."

"When will he be tried?" She sounded resigned.

"Unless another suspect exonerates him, he'll be tried at the next assizes. I don't yet know when that will be."

The woman's face twitched. "It's wrong to lock up a man for something he didn't do."

"I don't ever lock up a man without good cause. But murder cannot go unpunished. If you hear any news about either murder, please come to me at once."

ELA WATCHED Minnie Frost walk away, then was soon distracted by the morning's next petitioners, with their squabbles and grievances. A sheep found mauled by a dog ignited an old feud between two neighboring farmers, and Ela spent much of the morning trying to prevent a murder rather than solve the ones already committed.

Bill tried to convince her to come watch the boys practice their sword fighting, another art he was training them in.

She demurred. "The last two times I've come to watch my sons train, we've been interrupted by the news of a murder. I'm afraid I don't have the stomach for that this afternoon." They sat eating a quiet meal of vegetable soup and a small salad from the herb garden. "I would like to visit the abbey tomorrow morning and ask them directly whether Brother Wilfred might have intentionally jumped to his death."

"That's one way to solve a murder, I suppose."

"Suicide is uncommon but not unheard of, even among holy brothers."

Bill frowned. "But if he was up in the bell tower alone, how would they know?"

"Perhaps they could speak more to his state of mind in the days and hours leading up to his death. He certainly did act odd when we came there the day before to look at the tithe barns and inquire after Father de Grey's ill-gotten wealth."

"At the very least we may gain more insight into Brother Wilfred's role in the community and why someone might want him dead."

A guard came rushing toward the table. "My lady, news from Hampshire. The outlaw has been captured!"

# CHAPTER 11

"Where is the outlaw being held?" Ela rose to her feet. "Please take a message to Bishop Poore that I'd like him brought to the castle at Salisbury."

The guard, red faced and breathless, nodded, and she sent him away to pass on the message.

"That is an interesting development," she said to Bill, as the messenger forged out of the hall.

"You don't seem entirely happy about it." He lifted a brow slightly.

"What do you mean?" she said indignantly. "Of course I'm happy. Why wouldn't I be happy?"

"Because you don't think he's the killer."

"Even if he's not the killer he's admitted to stealing from the church and that is a sin against God as well as man. He must be tried for his crimes and his reign of outlawry will finally end." She tried to sound cheerful about this.

Why wasn't she cheerful about it?

ELA AND BILL set out for the abbey in the morning, again arriving just in time for Terce. The monks parted to make way for them as they walked through the cloister and into the chapel.

Wanting to observe the brothers, Ela led Bill into a dark alcove on one side of the nave. Eyes darted toward them, and she could feel a sense of shock in the air at their sudden arrival and their intrusion on the sacred service.

Why did she feel like an interloper? Surely they should welcome strangers to hear the words of the psalms? Yet she could feel their discomfort—even enmity—in their stiff stances and averted eyes.

*I was in trouble, and cried to the Lord;*
*and he answered me.*
*Lord, free me from the lips of liars,*
*from deceitful tongues.*
*What will be given you, what will you receive,*
*deceitful tongue?*

Ela felt the words keenly in her heart. Surely the monks wanted to find and prosecute the killer or killers who'd crept into their midst? Why did she feel like no one wanted her to find out the truth?

She grabbed Bill's arm and held him in position when the service ended and the monks started to file out. Again, glances darted in her direction. As the last brothers filed out through the door, one stayed behind, holding a candle, as if waiting to escort them out.

Ela walked past the young man, who had a blackish tonsure and a pinched expression. She and Bill walked out slowly, with the monk trailing them like a shadow, as if he wanted to be sure to rid the chapel of their presence.

Once they were out into the cloister, Ela spun around to face him. "I am Ela, Countess of Salisbury."

He bowed his head slightly. "Brother James, my lady." At odds with his polite gesture, his voice was oddly dismissive.

This piqued Ela's interest. "Brother James, I find my sleep troubled by words from deceitful tongues. Can I count on you to tell me the absolute truth?"

His eyes widened and she saw—with some satisfaction—a look of panic in them. "Yes, my lady." His tone was entirely non-committal, almost a question.

"Did Brother Wilfred jump to his death?"

His jaw tightened and his eyes blinked rapidly. "I didn't see anything, my lady."

"Nobody saw anything, because you were all inside the church at the time for Matins. Was anyone—except Brother Wilfred—absent from the service?"

"I can't say I noticed, my lady." His tone was steady, but she heard a tremor of nerves under it.

"I grow weary of hearing the same platitudes uttered as if I were a fool," she said, louder than she'd intended. "I don't wish to waste a journey here again if none of you has a care for how your fellow men of God met their deaths."

She felt Bill stiffen at her newly hostile attitude.

Someone cleared his throat nearby. Ela turned to see a young lay brother with curly blonde hair and a pimply face. She saw the dark-haired monk shoot him a meaningful look. The young lay brother swallowed. "My lady…"

"Yes?"

"Brother Wilfred took his own life for shame."

"Patrick!" hissed the dark-haired man. "Mind your tongue."

"Are you commanding him to be deceitful?" asked Ela loudly, "after what we just heard about deceitful tongues?"

The dark-haired monk's lips pressed into a tight line. "Begging your pardon, my lady, but matters within the abbey—"

"Are still the business of the sheriff when they concern murder," she finished for him. "And I am the Sheriff of Wiltshire." She turned to the blond monk. "What do you know of Brother Wilfred's death?"

"He was so ashamed to be accused of stealing that he couldn't bear it, my lady."

"Accused of stealing what?"

"The money and goods that Father Edmund had collected from the parishioners." The younger man grew bolder as he spoke. "Brother Wilfred never wanted to be a monk. He was a fourth son of a nobleman, and his family paid for him to come here. His faith was weak, and he didn't feel called to devote his life to God like most of the men here."

"He admitted this?"

The blond boy hesitated. "Well, not exactly, but that's what everyone said."

Brother Ethelstan now walked slowly toward her. "My lady," he murmured, as he emerged from the shadows of the cloister to where she could see him. "May the Lord rest his soul, poor Brother Wilfred was tempted by greed. While he didn't admit the deed, his subsequent actions speak for themselves. He rang the bell for the service, as usual, but never came down to join us. When his body was found outside we all knew that he'd taken his own life rather than face the shame of his misdeeds."

"Why didn't you tell me this immediately when I arrived? His body was barely cold on the ground and—by omission as much as anything—I was led to believe he'd been killed."

Brother Ethelstan looked at the ground again. "The taking of one's own life is a mortal sin, my lady."

"I'm aware of that."

"And as such he'd be denied burial on consecrated ground here in the abbey close. For all his weak faith we were very fond of Brother Wilfred, who tried hard to be a member of the community and has been here since our abbey was founded. I admit to my own frailty in wanting his body laid to rest here where we could pray for the passage of his poor accursed soul."

Ela looked around at the assembled men. All avoided her gaze, as well they might. "Did you discuss this with each other before my arrival?"

Silence.

"Lord, free me from the lips of liars, from deceitful tongues. What will be given you, what will you receive, deceitful tongue?" she said slowly, repeating the words of the psalm they'd all just heard together. "What else are you hiding from me with the deceit of silence as the response to an honest question?"

More silence. She looked around the assembled monks. "Where are the coins and trinkets that Brother Wilfred supposedly stole?"

"We don't know, my lady," said Ethelstan. "He took that secret to the grave."

Ela wondered if in fact the money and goods had been quietly removed by Bishop Poore. "Will you insist on moving the body of Brother Wilfred?" said one monk, very softly. He knew she could insist on removing the body to unhallowed ground outside the abbey walls, since a man taking his own life was akin to murder.

"I shall leave that up to Bishop Poore." She didn't intend to meddle in ecclesiastical matters that had no bearing on the law. Her own inclination would be to leave the unfortunate monk where he lay, resting in the consecrated ground of the abbey, but she wasn't going to walk out on a limb to fight for it.

Especially when she had more important matters to discuss with Bishop Poore.

～

ELA RETURNED to Salisbury Castle to find a message from Bishop Poore. He apparently insisted on keeping the outlaw in his own custody so that he'd be tried in Hampshire. On learning that Poore was at home in his palace, she rode there at once. The monk who answered the door grew flustered and said that he was "in prayer," but Ela thought it more likely that he enjoyed an afternoon nap.

She paced impatiently in his well-appointed sitting room until he finally appeared.

"Ela, my dear." He didn't plaster on his usual delighted smile. "The outlaw has committed crimes against the Church and thus I feel it most appropriate that a representative of the Church should oversee the trial."

"Your grace, I'm sure you're aware that the murder of Edmund de Grey took place in Wiltshire, and thus the trial for his murder must take place in Wiltshire. Where exactly did you find the outlaw?"

"He offered himself right up to my men!" The Bishop's eyes glinted. "Wandered up the road to the forest and told them he was ready to be punished for his crimes."

Ela frowned. "Why would he do that?"

"I suspect his own shameful guilt led him to repentance."

Ela had a hard time believing that the man who'd leaped out of the trees on top of her would turn himself over to the authorities. More likely there was a trick or a trap involved. "Where is he now?"

"He's in custody in the jail in Winchester."

"I shall visit him at once."

"Today? It's far too late, my lady. It's a good long ride." He smiled and waved for a boy to bring over some wine he'd just carried in.

"No wine for me, thank you, your grace. I find it tires me

in the summer heat." And she wanted to keep a clear head to deal with Poore. "Have you interviewed him in front of a jury?"

"Not yet." He watched as the boy poured his wine into an engraved cup, then he took a sip. "He'll be tried at the assizes so there's no rush."

"He admitted to the murder of Father de Grey?"

"Not as such. At least not that I've heard. I haven't seen him myself. I ordered the guards to lock him up and keep him under constant watch."

Ela watched him take a deep swallow of his wine. "When did you last go to Hampshire?"

Poore's eyebrows shot up. "Why, not long ago at all, I'm sure. Though I have excellent administrators there to manage matters in my absence. Perhaps you know my very able co-sheriff, Gilbert de Staplebrigg?"

"He's worked with my co-sheriff, John Dacus. I'm curious as to why you wished to be Sheriff of Hampshire, my lord, when your responsibilities are already so many and varied?"

Ela already knew the answer to her question: A sheriffdom could be an easy route to riches. Not that Poore needed more of those. But, like his longtime associate Hubert de Burgh, he was a man for whom too much was never enough.

"I naturally concern myself with keeping the peace in the environs, my lady. If you weren't such an able and capable sheriff of Wiltshire, perhaps I'd have put myself forward as sheriff here."

"I'm glad to have saved you the trouble," she said drily. "Though perhaps it would have made more sense since you've created your own peaceable kingdom here in Wiltshire." She gestured at the extravagant palace around them and toward the window, from which could be glimpsed the great cathedral he'd built from nothing on the graveled soil of the water meadows.

"Indeed we are truly blessed here in Salisbury." The look of confusion in his eyes gave her considerable satisfaction. He probably wondered where she was going with this line of inquiry.

"Bishop Poore, where is the money that Father Edmund de Grey extorted from the people of Biddesden?"

He blinked rapidly. "The money?"

"That was found in his chambers. The evidence of his wrongdoing."

"I'm sure it's being kept at the abbey under lock and key."

"They don't know where it is. They thought Brother Wilfred stole it, but it was not found in his possession. I wondered if perhaps your men removed it."

"My men?" His face was expressionless. "I suppose perhaps it could have been relocated to somewhere safe."

*Like in your personal vaults.* "I'm afraid the money and other associated goods are at the heart of two crimes, and I must take command of them in order to properly prosecute the crime."

"Two crimes?" Bishop Poore gazed at her blankly.

"The murder of Father de Grey is the first one, as you know. The second is the theft of the money and goods by Brother Wilfred."

"Brother Wilfred is dead and I'm reliably informed that he was not murdered."

"That does not undo his crime of stealing the goods." Ela didn't actually believe that Brother Wilfred ever did steal the goods. But her accusations were part of a larger strategy.

"You can hardly prosecute a man who's no longer with us."

"No, but since the money should never have been

collected in the first place, I must look into the matter of returning it to its rightful owners."

Bishop Poore blinked at her, confusion in his pale eyes.

"Though perhaps I could overlook the matter of the... stolen goods... if the outlaw is brought to Salisbury for trial. The theft of objects from ecclesiastical building is a crime of property rather than a true ecclesiastical crime."

Bishop Poore's lips slowly flattened into a line. "I hesitate to burden you with the exigencies of trying the outlaw, especially when you already bear the great responsibilities of being castellan of Salisbury and managing a large family without the guidance and support of your late husband."

"I'm grateful that the Lord grants me the strength to meet my obligations. And of course I have the support of Sir William Talbot as well as my co-sheriff."

"I shall arrange for the outlaw to be brought to Salisbury tomorrow morning."

"I thank you."

*And the money?*

She stood waiting, expectantly. Bishop Poore shifted, and his robes brushed against the floor. "And naturally I shall inquire into the whereabouts of the money...raised by Father de Grey. Would you perhaps consider it appropriate that the money be donated to my fund that provides alms to the needy of Salisbury?"

"I think it more appropriate that the money, and the goods where possible, be used to compensate the very poor villagers who have suffered greatly from their loss."

"No doubt the outlaw would agree with you," said Poore with a syrupy smile.

Ela was now fairly confident that Bishop Poore had the money and goods and would never admit it. At least she would have the outlaw.

～

THE NEXT MORNING, Ela found herself strangely energized by the prospect of meeting the notorious Fox again. This time she'd have the advantage. She intended to find out how he became an outlaw in the first place, since there was still no news from Yorkshire on that score.

She also wanted to find out why he'd taken it upon himself to redistribute the wealth held by the ecclesiastical authorities—if that was indeed what he did. Perhaps he kept most of the stolen goods for himself.

On being notified that the outlaw had arrived and was now secured in the dungeon at Salisbury Castle, she'd summoned a jury and asked for Giles Haughton to attend. The outlaw would necessarily be tried for the murder of Father de Grey—he was still a more likely suspect than John Thistle—and they could begin building the case in preparation for the assizes.

Once the jurors had assembled, she climbed onto her dais and sent for the outlaw to be brought before them.

Her gut clenched slightly at the prospect that he might reveal that he'd met her before. She'd kept very quiet about it, as had Bill, Richard, and the guards, who were all mortified by exposing her to his attack.

The outlaw attracted a buzz of curious conversation. His outlandish exploits had caused a stir throughout the countryside—a frisson of fear mingled with silent admiration. He'd remained free for so long despite men from two counties hunting him day and night. No doubt everyone in the hall wanted to get a good look at the mysterious Fox who'd led the sheriff's men on such a merry dance.

As the side door that led from the courtyard near the dungeons opened, the din in the hall stilled to a hush. Two guards marched in, as if to clear the way through the throng of people, followed by two guards flanking the prisoner, one holding each arm as if at any moment he might break free of his chains and vanish in their midst.

Ela strained to get a glimpse of him. She wanted to see his expression. Was he here against his will or of his own volition? She couldn't imagine he'd let himself be captured unless it was on purpose. Anticipation mounted inside her until her heart beat like a drum marching into battle.

At last the two guards in front parted to give her a view of the prisoner—and her heart sank to the bottom of her chest. Ela felt the breath rush out of her lungs.

"On your knees, prisoner!" called one of the guards. "Bow to your countess."

The man fell to his knees and prostrated himself before her.

"My lady," said one of the guards. "I bring you the outlaw known as the Fox."

Ela sat up in her chair and schooled her face into a disciplined mask. "That's not the outlaw."

CHAPTER 12

$\mathcal{T}$he silence in the hall throbbed in Ela's ears until
Giles Haughton spoke up.

"What do you mean, my lady?"

"That's not him." For a moment she thought she'd have to
reveal before every man and woman in the hall that she'd had
such a close brush with the outlaw that she knew the smell of
his body. Then she came to her senses. "I know this man. His
name is Alfred Fletcher and he's a villager at Biddesden. His
child recently died of starvation after he was forced to give
his last bag of grain as penance to Father de Grey of the
Abbey of St. Benedict."

One of the jurors took a step forward. "This suggests that
Alfred Fletcher is also the outlaw."

Ela swallowed. "He isn't." She looked at Alfred Fletcher.

The man was skin and bone dressed in rags. Hunched and
bowed, on his knees on the stone castle floor, he looked inca-
pable of stealing a crumb from a mouse let alone a pair of
tooled silver candlesticks from a well-guarded abbey.

He lifted his head and his watery eyes met hers for a tiny
instant before his gaze fell to the floor. "I am the outlaw."

His voice sounded disembodied, like that of a ghost. Why would he say he was the outlaw when he wasn't? And—without mentioning her unfortunate encounter, which would raise many awkward questions—how could she prove that she knew he wasn't?

"On your feet." He didn't rise, but the guards hauled him onto his shoeless feet. Ela hoped she could tease the truth from his thin, pale lips. "Why would you pretend to be the outlaw known as the Fox when you are not?"

"I am him. You should hang me for my crimes." He looked at the floor while he spoke.

Ela frowned. "You want to die?"

"I deserve to die."

If he was, in fact, the Fox, no doubt many assembled here would agree with him. But since he wasn't... "Why do you feel that you deserve to die?"

"Because I couldn't protect my only daughter. Her mother sickened and died when she was born and I promised my wife on her deathbed that I'd take good care of little Maisie and make sure she was well settled in life. And now I've broken my promise to her and deserve no place in Heaven or here on earth." His cheek twitched as he spoke the words in a lifeless tone.

Ela's heart ached for him. His pain was so great that he'd prefer to die at the hands of the sheriff's men than to endure another day of suffering. Still, his plan made a mockery of the law and murderers of those who'd convict him for a crime he didn't commit.

She straightened her shoulders. "May God forgive, you Master Fletcher. I suspect you wanted my men to stain their hands with your blood in order to ease your burden of grief. You preferred your death to be at the hand of the judge at the assizes rather than your own hand. But don't you see that by committing this sin you'd endure yet more suffering in the ceaseless fires of hell? It's not our lot to decide when we live or die."

"Is it God's will that I suffer unbearable torment here on earth?" His voice rose and cracked.

Ela didn't know how to answer. Was it God's will that she endure the agonizing death of her beloved husband and her children suffer the loss of their father? "It is not our place to understand the will of God. You must seek solace in prayer, not in efforts to extinguish the life God gave you, no matter how hard it sometimes seems."

He swayed and for a moment she thought he might fall to his knees. She wondered when he'd last eaten. He already looked like his days were numbered here on earth.

One of the jurors raised an arm to attract her attention. She said his name. "Mathew Hart." He'd been a sturdy and reliable member of the jury for many years.

"How can you be so sure that he's not the Fox, my lady?"

"Because there are eyewitness accounts of the Fox and he does not fit the description." Was this even true? She was the only eyewitness she'd encountered. Still, she could trust her own eyes.

"The Fox is described as wearing a deep hood," said Matthew Hart. "It hides his face and keeps his identity a secret."

True. Ela hadn't seen his face. She couldn't describe his eye or hair color. "The outlaw who's terrorized religious houses in this area is a man of robust health and unusual speed and cunning. That he's evaded capture this long beggars belief. I wish with all my heart that this was the Fox here before us. It would give me great satisfaction to see him punished for his crimes."

"This man has committed a crime of deception," said Will Dyer, the cooper. "At the very least he's guilty of wasting the sheriff's time. He should be fined and given hard labor."

A look of surprise flickered across Alfred Fletcher's pinched face.

"Since he doesn't have even a penny to feed himself or an ounce of energy to lift a spoon to his mouth, I hardly think that punishment would be appropriate, Master Dyer," replied Ela. "I sentence Master Fletcher to the punishment of eating a nourishing meal in this hall while I think of how best to address his misdeeds."

Ela summoned her maid Elsie to fetch him a meal from the kitchens. She then ordered the guards to release him from his chains but to watch him closely and make sure he ate the food and didn't leave the hall.

"I'm sorry that you were all summoned here on a false pretext," she said to the jurors and to Giles Haughton. "God willing, we will soon gaze on the guilty face of the true outlaw, but in the meantime please spare a prayer for a man desperate enough to impersonate a criminal in the hope of ending his own life."

ELA FELT DRAINED by her encounter with this man who craved the smell of brimstone as sweet relief. And so soon after hearing that Brother Wilfred had ended his own life! Even John Thistle had offered his neck for hanging. To crave death so was a sickness indeed and due to Father de Grey's greed this plague of desperation had spread to infect both the abbey and the nearby village.

And the outlaw was still at large. She'd wasted valuable bargaining chips bringing this impostor here from Bishop Poore's command and had nothing to show for her efforts.

She retired to the chapel and knelt there, praying for guidance. How could she punish a man who'd deliberately sought punishment? She suspected this was a situation in which she was called upon to turn the other cheek, but how could she do that without losing face?

After some time spent reflecting, she returned to the hall and found that her maid Elsie was sitting at the table with Alfred Fletcher, whose color and demeanor had improved considerably. Elsie herself, often anxious and distracted, was talking animatedly as if telling him something very important. Ela could overhear their conversation as she approached from behind Elsie.

"Your daughter wouldn't want you to be sad." Elsie leaned forward earnestly. She was twelve now, or maybe thirteen, but her face had the serious demeanor of a woman twice that age. And with good reason. "My mama stabbed my papa and they hanged her for killing him, so I could be sad all the time but I know they wouldn't want me to cry. They'd want me to make the best of my life."

Ela looked at Alfred's shocked face.

"That's a great burden to bear," he said softly. "And you're so young and bear it so bravely."

"I'm not that young," said Elsie primly. "I have wisdom. The lady Ela has taught me a lot about being a woman."

Ela paused and blinked as emotion welled in her chest. She was endlessly lecturing poor Elsie to attend to the needs of others before her own and to pray in moments when she felt lost, but at this moment she felt she might as well have left the poor girl hanging by her heels from the castle turrets.

Alfred Fletcher noticed Ela behind her and looked up, before perhaps remembering why he was there and jerking his gaze hard down to the table.

Elsie sprang to her feet. "Oh, my lady, I'm sorry. I shouldn't have sat down, should I?"

"You most certainly should, dear Elsie. I overheard you giving a most inspiring talk to Master Fletcher."

"He's just so sad. Sometimes I'm still sad, but mostly I'm

too busy." She started to sweep some crumbs into her palm with her other hand. "It's best to keep busy."

"Can I leave now?" Alfred Fletcher rose shakily to his feet, scraping the bench behind him on the floor.

"No, you can't," said Ela firmly. "Sit down. And you sit down again, too, Elsie."

Fletcher sank back onto the bench, a look of considerable trepidation on his pinched features. "I apologize for wasting everyone's time."

"You certainly led us on a fool's errand," said Ela. "And I'm most disappointed that you aren't the real outlaw. But I believe there's a reason that you're here today."

"What is it?" asked Elsie.

"I'm not sure yet, but I suspect the Lord will reveal it to me in his own good time. Master Fletcher, do you have crops or animals at home that you need to attend to?"

He shook his head. "I should have at this time of year, but I didn't tend my seeds and they died and now I'll have nothing for the winter."

"That's why you're skin and bone," said Elsie, in a scolding tone. "It's late but you can still plant carrots and parsnips and cabbage for the winter. You need some sheep. They're fine animals as you can eat them and wear their wool and it sells for a good price."

Fletcher stared at Elsie as if she was a curiosity at the fair.

Ela had almost forgotten that Elsie grew up on a farm. After her parents died, she and her siblings had been sent to live with an aunt and uncle—who had sold the poor girl for a few coins.

Once she'd rescued Elsie from the child slaver, Ela had removed the rest of her siblings from their aunt's house for fear of the same thing happening again. She'd found an apprenticeship for the oldest boy with the brewer, but the rest of them still worked around the castle in one capacity or another. Now an idea occurred to her.

She looked at Alfred Fletcher. "The house you were living in, is that yours?"

"It belongs to the lord of the manor. I have the use of it in exchange for a portion of what I grow. So I suspect I've lost the right to it or will soon." He slumped. "I grew up in that house. And my father and grandfather too."

"It's fallen into disrepair and is hardly habitable," reflected Ela.

"I've lost the will in the time since my wife died. And now, without my daughter to care for…"

"Elsie has brothers and sisters that need a home. Elsie, which two of your siblings would you recommend to help Master Fletcher fix up his house and get his garden and vegetable plots in order?"

Elsie looked at her curiously. "Billy and Merry. Billy's young but very handy with tools so he could fix the walls and the thatch. Merry's got a green thumb and can make anything grow, even a boiled seed! She works in the castle laundry and her poor green thumb's getting scalded in the hot water all day."

"Oh, dear. We can't have that." Ela racked her mind trying to remember where Billy worked.

"Billy scrubs the pots in the back kitchen," said Elsie, as if she could read Ela's mind. "You won't send me away, though, will you?" A look of sudden panic crossed her round face.

"Absolutely not. What would I do without you?"

A smile of satisfaction crossed Elsie's lips.

Alfred Fletcher stared at them both in silence for a moment, then spoke quietly. "How am I supposed to feed two children when I can't feed myself?"

"They're not really children, more like strapping youths." Ela couldn't remember how old Billy and Merry were, but none of the Brice children had been younger than ten last year when their parents had died. "They'll help you get back on your feet if you can summon the strength to guide them. They've suffered a terrible double loss, like yourself, so hopefully you can all support each other."

Fletcher looked like he wanted to argue but couldn't find the words.

Elsie's face shone. "Shall I tell them, my lady?"

"Why don't you find them and bring them here, so we can all discuss the matter together."

It didn't take long to bring the children from their tasks. Merry was a tall, pale girl of about sixteen with mournful looking eyes. Her hands were indeed chapped almost to the point of bleeding by her washing duties as Ela saw in the few moments when Merry wasn't hiding them behind her back. Billy was younger, perhaps twelve, with bright eyes and a shock of mouse-colored hair. Ela wasn't sure who looked more alarmed and appalled, the children or Alfred Fletcher, as she outlined her plan for them to live in his house and replant his plot of land.

"Um…" Fletcher looked ready to faint from terror. "My lady, have you forgotten that my own dear child died from want in my care?"

"Don't blame yourself. You were preyed upon by Edmund de Grey, as were others in the village, and I intend to see matters restored to rights. We can spare four chickens and a rooster from my flock, and that shall start you out with a business of eggs and chicks and later meat to sell or barter with."

Fletcher looked astonished. He looked at the children, almost shy in his reticence. "I don't wish to remove you from the castle against your will."

Merry glanced at Ela, then looked at Fletcher. "I'd be

grateful for a chance to grow things and cook instead of just washing all day. I'd be a good housekeeper. You'll see."

He blinked in surprise.

"And if I never see a pot again it'll be too soon," said Billy quickly. Then he realized what he'd said. "Begging your pardon, my lady! I am grateful for the chance to earn my bread." He turned back to Fletcher. "Though I don't eat much at all."

Ela was almost offended at how quickly the children jumped at the chance of a life outside the castle. Were the boys and girls employed under her roof worked too hard and for too-long hours? She'd have to look into the matter. She knew they were well fed and had a dry place to sleep and—without much examination—she'd taken that as adequate provision for their welfare.

"It's settled then. I shall have my steward prepare a cart with supplies and you shall set out this afternoon."

ELA HAD the steward stack the cart with grain, seeds, linens, firewood, and even well-worn pots and pans. This was an effort to save a life, perhaps three lives, and she wanted to give them every chance of success. It was also a sort of test to see what might be required to lift the spirits—and hopefully the fortunes—of the more downtrodden and dejected among the villagers.

She and Bill Talbot rode ahead of them, since she wanted to guide their settling in. On arrival, Ela sent the lad to fetch water at the well and set his sister to sweeping out months of accumulated debris. She charged Alfred Fletcher with hammering some wood into simple beds for the children to unroll their mattresses on. Once they were all busy at their tasks, she beckoned Bill outside into the lane.

"Someone in this village killed Father Edmund de Grey," she said, as they walked along the dusty lane. They'd left their horses with the guards. "And I wish I was sure it was John Thistle, who's locked up in the castle dungeon, but I'm not. Today I want to question the boy that found Brother Wilfred's body on the ground outside the bell tower. "

Bill spotted a boy of about thirteen, sitting outside a small, mean cottage, mending a plough. He walked up to the lad, who looked alarmed at his approach. "Are you the boy who found Brother Wilfred fallen to his death?"

"Nay, sir." The boy stared at them.

The door to the cottage opened and a harried-looking woman about Ela's age with straggling blonde hair looked out. "What's going on?" She wiped her hands on her apron. "The boy doesn't know anything. He's just trying to mend our plough."

"What's your name?" asked Ela.

"Mildred Rucker."

"And your boy?"

"This is Harry. He's the man of the house since his father died. We don't know nothing about any Brother Wilfred."

"Do you have any other children?" Ela asked. She tried to peer around the woman into the house. She didn't hear any noise from within.

"Not anymore," said the woman sadly. She didn't expand, and Ela didn't have the heart to probe further.

"Do you know of a lad in the village who lived and worked at the abbey?"

The woman frowned. "I think young Phil Prescott did some work for the brothers. Has a mop of red hair. You can't miss him." Then she all but slammed the door in Ela's face.

Ela stepped back. The boy stared at her for a moment, then went back to making some kind of wood patch for his broken plough handle.

Bill ushered Ela away and they continued down the lane in search of a redheaded lad. As before, the villagers had disappeared inside their houses and they were forced to knock on the doors. They weren't quick to answer, either, which gave Ela and Bill more time to notice the lack of repairs to any of their dilapidated dwellings.

"It's been almost a week since I hectored young Geoffrey de Wakefield about improving this village. It doesn't look like he's so much as lifted a finger to do it. I shall have to visit him again."

Finally they found the red-haired boy hiding behind his mother in a small cottage crowded with small children. "Is this Phil Prescott?" asked Ela.

"Aye," said his mother. "Are you here about the murder?"

"Murder?" asked Ela, almost without thinking. "What makes you say it was a murder?" Even the brothers had said he jumped to his death.

"Who ever heard of a man falling from a bell tower?" said his mother. "And Phil said he saw someone up there with him."

Ela glanced at Bill, her heart suddenly pounding. "May I speak to Phil?" The boy had disappeared right out of sight behind his mother.

A scraping sound in the dark interior of the hut heralded the arrival of the boy's father. "What do you want with our lad?" asked a gruff man of short stature, with unkempt dark hair. "He's been scared out of his wits since he saw that body fall from the tower. Says he wouldn't go back to the abbey if his very life depended on it."

Ela stared at the boy. "You saw brother Wilfred fall?"

Phil Prescott, who was very young, maybe only eight, peered out from around his mother. "I did. And I saw someone up there who pushed him."

# CHAPTER 13

"*Y*ou saw Brother Wilfred pushed from the tower?" Ela could hardly believe her ears. This directly contradicted what the brothers had told her about Wilfred taking his own life.

"I didn't see him pushed, but I heard him cry out. A strangled cry like an animal in a trap. I turned as he hit the ground, then I looked up at the tower and saw someone leaning out the window looking down at him."

"This happened in the early hours of the morning before dawn. How did you see him in the dark?"

"The moon was bright that night," said the boy, still hiding behind his mother. "And I'd been outside all night so my eyes were used to it."

His mother yanked him out from behind her skirts. "What were you doing outside in the middle of the night? Didn't the brothers give you a bed to sleep in?"

"It was in the dormitory with the lay brothers, and some of them snore something awful. It was warm and quiet outside so I lay down under an apple tree. The bells had just woken me up, and I was sitting watching a badger in the grass when I heard his cry and an awful thud. I jumped to my feet and that's when I noticed the movement in the tower."

"Did you see who it was?" Ela held her breath.

"Oh, no. It was too dark and too far up and away from where I stood. But it was a man as he had short hair."

"A tonsure?" Ela tried to imagine which of the brothers might have shoved Wilfred from the tower.

"It looked more like normal hair but I couldn't see the color."

"So he didn't have a hood on?"

"No. I saw his head as he stuck it out the window but I could only see the shape of it."

"What did you do then?"

"I went over to where I heard the thud to see what fell. When I got there I found Brother Wilfred broken on the ground. I was about to scream, but then I remembered the man in the tower. I heard someone coming down the stairs and I started to run. I didn't stop running until I was all the way home."

"He was running like he'd been chased by the devil himself," said his mother, ruffling his hair.

"I can't blame him. If the murderer knew he'd been seen, he might well have tried to catch him."

His mother's eyes widened. "Do you think he's still in danger?"

"We do have a man in custody at the castle. He was found in the woods near the abbey not long after Brother Wilfred's body was discovered."

"One of the monks?"

"No, John Thistle of this village."

The woman eyes widened. "It's hard to imagine John Thistle killing a man, but he was that angry about his bull being sold away before he had a chance to buy it back."

Ela turned to Bill. "That would give him a motive to kill

Father Edmund de Grey, but why would John Thistle kill Brother Wilfred?"

"Perhaps he killed the priest and Brother Wilfred witnessed it?" replied Bill.

"Wilfred never said anything about seeing who murdered the priest. I don't believe he was a witness," said Ela.

"Unless he didn't want you to know for some reason."

Ela frowned. Then she turned to the boy. "The lay brothers, do they get up to attend Matins in the middle of the night?"

"No, they're lazy and sleep like logs right through it."

"Did any of them get up and leave that night?"

"I don't know 'cos I went and slept outside. I didn't see any of them."

Ela had largely ignored the lay brothers until now. She didn't really understand why someone would live and work in a monastery but not take the vows to become a monk. She supposed they were mostly men who'd fallen through the cracks of life somewhere and found themselves without a family to care for or lean on. "I shall have to interview them."

If the lay brothers didn't attend services, then one of them could have easily been skulking around the cloisters lying in wait for Father Edmund on the day he was killed. The monks had told her that all the brothers were in the service at the time, but she hadn't thought to ask about the lay brothers and whether that number included them.

"Keep your boy safe at home for the time being," said Ela.

"Can you tell everyone that our Phil saw nothing?" asked his mother, her expression worried.

"Until I came here today that's exactly what I thought. No one told me until now that he saw a figure in the tower. I shall keep the news secret except where necessary."

Ela drew in a breath. She wasn't sure what she'd hoped to

learn by talking to the boy, but today's information changed everything.

～

ELA SPENT some more time talking to the villagers, then stopped in at Alfred Fletcher house to see how their cleanup efforts were getting along. The cottage had two squarish rooms, and Merry had now swept them both clean. Alfred had finished constructing the two low beds for the children and set them up in the main living room, while his own bed was in the back room.

Billy had cleaned out a mountain of ash from the fireplace—which can't have been emptied all last winter—and given it to a neighbor who wanted it to make soap. They removed any broken or useless items and stacked them on the cart for removal, as Ela was worried they'd create an atmosphere of squalor if simply left outside waiting to be burned or buried.

Billy scrubbed the doorframe and the door and also the old grayish wooden table and chairs, which brightened considerably as he attacked them. Then Merry spread the fresh linens they'd brought on the beds. The colorful quilted bedding Ela had found in her stores brightened the dingy rooms.

"The walls could use a coat of whitewash," observed Ela. "That makes everything look better. We must find some lime, but that can wait for another day."

Alfred Fletcher looked rather stunned by the transformation of his humble home. "It looks as if my wife were still alive."

"How long ago did you lose her?"

"Two years last April," he said. "I'm afraid I didn't keep up with the housekeeping after she passed."

"I shall keep the place neat as a pin," said Merry with a smile. "I like cleaning."

"Lucky you," said Ela. She couldn't imagine anything more boring, though she knew that was a spiritual failing on her part. "And Billy did a marvelous job of scrubbing. This furniture looks like fresh-planed wood."

"I made those when we first moved in here," said Alfred. "Cut and trimmed them myself. It's like a new beginning."

Ela tried not to get too excited about this promising start. Still, they all seemed quite content with the modest space now that the dust and gloom had been cleared away. "What will you have for supper tonight?"

There was a silence. Then Merry chimed in. "I could make a pease pottage and add a little of the dried smoked bacon. Then tomorrow we must scratch out a garden and plant the seeds so we'll have greens."

Ela glanced at Alfred, who looked relieved that someone else had taken charge. She had a feeling the malaise that had settled over him with the loss of his wife and child would not be so quick to lift, but hopefully he'd gain strength as time went on.

"That sounds like an excellent plan, my dear." She'd taken the precautions to even bring wood for a fire, as she suspected the desperate villagers would have picked the nearest woods clean of kindling. "I'll look in on you in a few days to see how you're getting on."

IT WAS WELL into the long summer evening when Ela arrived back at the castle, exhausted by the day's events. She was surprised to find Bishop Poore in her hall, enjoying a platter of sweetmeats. He rose as she approached. "My dear Lady Ela."

"To what do I owe the pleasure of this visit?" she asked, without a hint of joy in her voice.

"I was astonished to hear that you released the outlaw from custody. I am having trouble believing that you simply released him to go about his business and I would like an explanation."

"The explanation is simple. It was a case of mistaken identity. The man in custody was not the outlaw at all."

"He announced to my men—in his own words—that he was the outlaw and that they must arrest him."

"Do those sound like words that a notorious outlaw, who's engaged in crime up and down the country, would utter to the sheriff's men?"

Bishop Poore's mouth twitched for a moment before he spoke. "Well, it was highly unusual, but I presume the Lord put it in his heart to see the error of his ways."

"Quite the opposite, I'm afraid. This man was a villager who—anxious to be quit of the cares of this world—tried to engage the sheriff's men in his plot to end his own life."

Poore stared at her, confusion in his pale eyes. "Why wouldn't he just drown himself in a pond or…or—?"

"Or jump from a bell tower?"

"Exactly." He looked delighted to recall that someone had, at least theoretically, enacted his proposed plan.

"Cowardice, I suspect. Taking one's own life is no easy feat, I'd imagine, especially when you confront the grave mistake of breaking the Lord's commandment. No doubt he wanted the matter out of his own hands."

Poore seemed to contemplate this for a moment. "Where is he now?"

"Back in his house in the village. And I sent two orphans to live with him. Losing his wife and child destroyed the poor man's joy in life, and I'm hoping they can put it back."

He stared at her as if she'd just barked like a dog. "I think it more likely that managing two unrelated children under his roof will drive him to drink."

"I admit there is some risk, but I intend to keep an eye on them. The children seem sensible enough, and I believe he's a kind man, just devastated by the loss of his family. Which solves one problem, but apparently we have two others."

"The outlaw is still at large, then."

"It appears so. Also Brother Wilfred did not take his own life. I spoke to a witness who saw another man up in the bell tower, who looked down after Wilfred when he fell."

Bishop Poore crossed himself. "The brothers all seemed sure that he'd taken his life. What reason have you to trust the witness?"

"The witness had no reason to lie. I believe him." For a moment she contemplated going into detail about the boy and his job at the abbey, but something told her not to. Bishop Poore had ecclesiastical ties to the abbey that went far beyond his role as Sheriff of Hampshire. His loyalty might lie with protecting the brothers and their interests rather than with the pursuit of justice. "What does mystify me is why the brothers would all insist that he killed himself when they didn't see it happen."

Bishop Poore swayed slightly.

"Are you unsteady on your feet, Bishop Poore? Do sit down."

He gestured for her to sit first, which she did. Sometimes she found it tiresome that no one could sit until she did.

Bishop Poore crashed back into his chair and plucked another sweetmeat from the plate in front of him.

"What do you know of the lay brothers?" continued Ela.

"The lay brothers are simple men from the village."

"Are simple men any more or less evil than complex men?" As she asked the question, she decided that they were probably less evil than the more complicated and powerful men of her acquaintance, among whom Bishop Poore was numbered. Not that she thought him evil, exactly, but she didn't trust him, either. "At this point both the holy brothers and the lay brothers must be considered suspects in the murders of Edmund de Grey and Wilfred Bedulf."

Bishop Poore popped a whole nut-tart into his mouth and chewed it, then dabbed his lips with a napkin. "What of the man in the dungeon? Do you not have a villager who felt he was robbed of his bull?"

"Yes, John Thistle." Ela had to admit she'd almost forgotten about him. Once a man was imprisoned it was hard to release him without a good reason. One of the reasons she wasn't quick to arrest people in the first place. "I suspect he was simply poaching, as he says, but he and possibly other villagers cannot be eliminated as suspects. Until we have a confession of murder we must keep an open mind. I shall return to the abbey tomorrow to interview the lay brothers and inform them that their brother did not take his own life. I suspect they'll feel some relief at the latter circumstance."

Poore looked flustered. "As their spiritual leader I must take on this responsibility for myself."

"I'd greatly appreciate it if you let me speak to them first. Then you could provide spiritual succor afterward. I suspect that catching people unawares with unexpected news is one of the best ways to flush a murderer from the undergrowth."

He looked like he wanted to argue, but instead he balled up his napkin and set it down on the table. "If you insist, my lady."

THE FOLLOWING morning Ela and Bill Talbot traveled back to the Abbey of St. Benedict. She timed their arrival to coincide with the Terce service. One of the lay brothers, a middle-aged man with tousled dark hair, greeted her at the gate.

"What's your name, brother?"

"Adam Foster, uh, my lady." He almost stammered the words, obviously not expecting her to talk to him. "You've only missed the beginning of services." He started to lead her toward the chapel, but she explained that she was there to talk to him and his fellow lay brothers.

His attitude changed to one of alarm. "They're all at work, my lady." He gestured at a nearby brother weeding the herb garden contained in the cloister.

"That's fine. I can speak to you one at a time." She tried to set him at ease with a pleasant expression. "First, do you know if the lay brothers were all in the service at the time of Father Edmund's death?"

He nodded. "I believe they were, my lady. They don't attend all the services but as I recall they were all at that one. That's why no one saw who killed him."

That ruled out yet more suspects. "What do you know of Brother Wilfred's death?"

His eyes widened. "I heard he jumped because he was so ashamed of stealing the money."

"Do you believe that?"

He hesitated for a moment, and the tip of his tongue ran nervously over his upper lip. "I don't rightly know, my lady."

"Does Brother Wilfred seem like someone who would kill himself?"

His mouth worked for a moment. "Who's to say what a man will do in a desperate situation?"

Ela wondered just how desperate his situation was. "What punishment was Wilfred going to suffer for stealing the money?"

The monk blinked. "Why…uh…a harsh penance, I suppose."

"You mean a penance of prayer, or flogging, or…?"

"I suppose you'd have to ask the bishop, since he's the one who would have pronounced it."

"Was it the bishop who accused Brother Wilfred of the theft?"

"Oh no." He looked at her, confused. "It was Brother Timothy."

"And how did he know about the theft?"

"Someone told him."

"Who?"

"I don't rightly know since he wouldn't say, but he's cutting wood in the copse behind the tithe barn."

"He's another lay brother?"

"Indeed he is, my lady."

"I'd be grateful if you could take me to him."

While they walked Ela asked him how long he'd been in the area.

"I've lived my whole life within the sound of the abbey's bells. Not that the abbey was here back then, of course. But there was a small church here before it was built."

"How did the villagers feel about the abbey being built?"

He looked non-plussed. "I can't speak for others, but I was glad of the work of building it."

"You helped in the construction of the abbey?"

"Oh, yes, we brought stones from the quarry and stacked them. We mixed up lime and even laid the foundations."

"Were most of the lay brothers involved in building the abbey?"

"I think we all were. You've seen the state of the village. It's hard for a man to scrape out a living there and the lord was absent and the steward neglectful. I suppose any man without a family to support leaped at the chance to work and live at the abbey."

"Are you all…religious men?"

He blinked at her. "I believe in God, my lady."

"Of course you do." She could see her question had shocked him. "I suppose I'm just trying to understand the difference between one of the tonsured brothers at the abbey and the lay brothers. Why do you not attend all the services?"

"I daresay we'd like to rest and sing several times a day, but we're here to work. The religious brothers are mostly the sons of rich men who donated sums of money that their offspring should have the luxury of a life of prayer."

"I see. A life of prayer is a luxury indeed." They reached the copse, and already Ela could hear the hacking sound of Brother Timothy cutting wood within it. "Do you miss life in the village or are you content here?"

"Oh, I don't miss not eating for days on end or worrying that I might starve in a bad winter. Life in Biddesden is not for the faint of heart."

Brother Timothy was wet with perspiration from his labors and pushed damp hair off his brow when they approached. He seemed every bit as disturbed as his fellow lay brother to learn that the sheriff had come to question him.

"I hear you accused Brother Wilfred of taking the money that Father Edmund de Grey collected from the parishioners."

"I...I...I..." He looked from her to Adam Foster to Bill Talbot and back to her. "I did."

"And what made you suspect Wilfred had taken the money?"

"Someone told me."

"Who?" The question shot from her mouth a little faster than she'd intended.

He blinked a few times and looked over her shoulder so intently she had to fight the urge to look behind her. Then his eyes fixed on hers. "Sir Geoffrey de Wakefield."

# CHAPTER 14

"Sir Geoffrey came to the monastery with the opinion that Brother Wilfred had stolen the money?" Ela found this most odd.

"Oh yes. He's always here complaining about something or other. You see the young man's father donated the land and endowed the abbey in memory of his late wife and young Sir Geoffrey is not too happy about it. He says his father gave away the most fertile lands and kept the worst of them. He also said that—" He stopped himself in midsentence, apparently realizing he was revealing a confidence.

Ela certainly wished he'd continue. "He also said what?"

Brother Timothy swallowed and continued more quietly. "He said that the abbey was bleeding his villagers dry."

"There seems to be some truth to that." So the young lord might also have reason to be angry with Edmund de Grey, who'd apparently masterminded the effort to impoverish the villagers. "When did Sir Geoffrey first come here?"

"When he first arrived in the district, I suppose. Right around the feast of St. John the Baptist two months ago. I remember the first time he came here complaining about the tithes and that his serfs had nothing left to live on, let alone to give him."

"And the prior and the other priest were still here at that time?"

"Yes, they didn't leave on their pilgrimage until after the feast of St. Mary Magdalene. He railed at all of them and the priests promised to pray for the prosperity of his manor."

Ela doubted that these prayers had been answered, at least going on the condition of the village. "Did he agitate to get goods back from the tithe barn? Fleeces or grain or the like?"

"He did try, I think. Whether he succeeded I'm not sure. That would be outside my purview."

"He'd have spoken to the priests?"

"Yes, and the almoner who sells or distributes the goods that aren't needed for use at the monastery. Some of the excess goes to the needy—or at least that's what he claims— and some to the markets at Marlborough or Winchester to raise funds for the abbey. I daresay that Sir Geoffrey tried to convince him to hand some of the goods over to him."

"How did Sir Geoffrey first come to speak with you?" she asked Brother Timothy, who now leaned on the handle of his axe.

"I'm one of his serfs, being from Biddesden. All of us lay brothers are. He became angry that the abbey was benefitting from our work, and he wanted to convince us to return to the village so he could profit from our labors. He's taken to following us around and hectoring us. Since his father endows the abbey, there's not much we can do about it."

Ela frowned. "That is an awkward situation. And I admit I can see his point. The abbey has sprung up in this unpromising valley like a fine strong plant that draws all the moisture and goodness from the soil. But how did Sir Geoffrey come to accuse Wilfred of stealing the money?"

"I don't know how he knew that Wilfred had it, but he seemed sure of it and he wanted me to spread the news in the abbey. He badgered me and berated me and told me he'd turf my elderly mother out of her cottage and he finally wore me down. I told the other lay brothers I'd heard that Wilfred took the money, and it spread from there."

"But you had no real proof that Wilfred took the money?"

"Nay, my lady, and I had nothing against Wilfred either, but the thought of my old mother thrown out on the road goaded me into it. I didn't think anything would come of it as it was nothing more than my word against his. But when Wilfred took his life for shame I knew it was true and he really did steal the money."

Ela glanced at Bill Talbot, then back at Brother Timothy. "Have you spoken to de Wakefield since?"

He hesitated, looking about as if someone might spring from behind a tree in the woods. "Yes. Young Sir Geoffrey sent a boy who summoned me to his manor. He did give me a coin for my pains and asked me to keep quiet about the matter." He looked around from Bill to Adam Foster to Ela. "So I'm breaking my word, but I shouldn't keep quiet about it, should I?"

"Indeed not," said Ela. "This is a matter involving the law. I intend to visit Geoffrey de Wakefield immediately."

THE SUN SAT high in the sky by the time they rode on to Geoffrey de Wakefield's manor. Ela found her nerves jangling when they left the main road and headed along the weedy track to the rustic manor house. It seemed odd for a father to pluck the plum from the pie of his son's inheritance, donate it to found an abbey, then send the son to live in the bare pastry left behind.

The sound of their horses' hooves brought Sir Geoffrey to the door of the low-slung house with its heavy thatched eaves. The midday sun lit up his light brown curls and thrust his squinting eyes into shadow.

Ela rode up to the main door and—on an odd instinct—waited for him to speak first.

He clearly had the same impulse, so there was an awkward silence while they both surveyed each other.

"To what do I owe the pleasure?" he said at last, in a voice with no hint of pleasure.

"God be with you, Sir Geoffrey," said Ela brightly. "We come directly from the Abbey of St. Benedict."

His disinterested expression didn't change. Most people would comment that it was a warm day for a ride, or some such nonsense, but he didn't. He stood, unmoving, in his doorway, waiting for her to declare her purpose.

Ela dismounted, removed her riding gloves, and handed the horse and gloves to one of the guards. She heard Bill dismount behind her. "May I come in?"

His mouth tightened and he shifted. As she'd anticipated, her request upset him. "My house isn't kept to the standards of a lady."

"Think of me simply as your sheriff. And I suspect your home is finer than most of the cottages on your manor that I've visited lately."

Now his cheek twitched. She was already walking up the short path, through a ragged herb garden that crowded the front door. He didn't bow and for a moment she thought he might stand there and block her way into the house, but at the last moment he stepped aside and ushered her in.

Ela didn't have to look behind her to know that Bill Talbot was hot on her heels. She felt a wave of…something… roll off de Wakefield as she walked past him. Irritation maybe? Possibly even fury. Almost no one welcomed the unannounced arrival of the sheriff on their doorstep.

Ela's curiosity about the inside of the manor was quickly satisfied. The door opened directly into the main room typical of such older country houses—not unlike her own great hall on a smaller scale. The room had a low, beamed ceiling, a great stone fireplace at one end and some random sticks of unfashionable but good-quality furniture scattered in small groupings.

The flagstone floor, as promised, was unswept and a great pile of ash sat in the fireplace. The remains of a meal—a chicken bone and some dry crusts of bread—sat on one of the tables, and the air was redolent with a familiar sweet scent that was probably mouse urine seeping into the smoke-blackened ceiling beams from the thatch above.

Her skin crawled with the desire to leave. "What a charming, rustic residence. Has it been in your family for many years?"

"The land was granted to our family by the conqueror himself. As the family acquired other, better manors, they let this one go to rack and ruin, and here you find me in it."

Ela wondered exactly how that had come to pass. "I learned that your family founded the Abbey of St. Benedict. Did you come here to oversee the family's gift?"

He stared at her for a moment like she might be touched, then a harsh laugh rattled his chest. "Nothing so pious, my lady. My father and I had a disagreement over some debts I accrued, and he banished me here as punishment for my sins."

His bluntness surprised her. "He wishes you to prove yourself by restoring the fortunes of this manor?"

"Or to die in the attempt," he said. His eyes glittered oddly, as if he found the situation amusing. He certainly didn't seem nervous or circumspect, like someone worried they might be accused of a crime. "Which he might prefer."

"Have you made progress in improving the lot of your villagers since we first spoke?" Having just come from Biddesden, she knew the answer to this question but was curious to hear his response.

"Any man with spirit has upped sticks and left to claim his freedom. Most of the able-bodied men under seventy are living at the abbey as lay brothers. All that's left are the elderly, the infirm, the suckling babes, and the women nursing them."

Ela couldn't argue with that, especially with John Thistle, the most able man she'd met there, locked up in her dungeon. "In some ways, having fewer mouths to feed from the same plot of land is an advantage."

"Except that there are fewer strong backs to work the land. Some of the men ran off to Marlborough or Devizes, and they've been there more than a year and a day so they've gained their liberty and are lost to me for good."

"If you can tempt them back as freemen you may find they'll work harder and longer because they have the choice."

"Or they can up sticks at any time and leave me with a crop unharvested."

Ela sighed. Clearly de Wakefield was a man who preferred his villagers oppressed by the weight of ancient laws and the ravages of want rather than enticed by a desire to improve their lot.

But that was not the reason she'd come here. "You accused Brother Wilfred of stealing the money that Father Edmund bled from your villagers."

He frowned. "Well, he did."

"How do you know?"

"He's the only one of those monks with enough wits to spark a single thought."

"I myself found him one of the most helpful brothers, but I hardly think that a reason to accuse him of theft." She paused and studied him. "Where were you when Brother Wilfred fell to his death?"

"Asleep in my bed, of course." His face revealed no emotion. "Since it happened in the wee hours of the morning."

"How did you hear the news?"

"One of the lay brothers told me the next morning when I went there to talk to them about moving back to Biddesden. They told me he was so ashamed at being accused of stealing that he jumped to his death."

A tiny prickle of doubt crept up her spine. That is not the story she'd been told when she first went to the monastery after the death. The brothers had linked arms to insist on a story of a murder so that Brother Wilfred would be buried in hallowed ground, not cast out for taking his own life. She saw no reason to believe that they'd share this weighty confidence with Geoffrey de Wakefield.

"That's not true. He was murdered." She watched for his reaction.

Sure enough he flinched slightly. She saw his hand twitch. "Murdered? Who would murder him?"

"That's what I'm trying to find out." She took a step toward him and he shrank back slightly from her. "Who would have motive to kill Brother Wilfred?"

"I can't imagine," he said quickly. "I suppose it must be one of the other monks. Who else would have any business with him?"

Ela paused to let his question linger in the air. "I find it more than strange that you saw fit to accuse him of theft on no evidence whatsoever."

"I was right, wasn't I?"

"If he'd actually killed himself for shame, you might be, but he didn't take his own life."

"How do you know?"

"Because his murderer was glimpsed up in the tower after he fell to the ground." She pinned him with a stern gaze, hoping he'd wriggle like a fish on the end of a hook.

But he didn't. His lip lifted in a slight sneer. "Impossible. It was dark at the time."

"The light of a full moon serves as well as a lantern for one whose eyes have had time to adjust to its glow."

"Who was out there?" He did seem more interested than he should have if these events meant nothing to him.

"A witness. Whose identity will be kept secret for his safety." She paused again to let that sink in. "Do *you* have a witness who can verify that you were at home when the murder happened?"

"Are you accusing me of murder?" The words burst from his mouth in a volley of rage. "Why would I bother with killing a poxy monk? I couldn't care less about any of them except I'd rather they be guiding a plough on my lands than singing psalms under a roof my inheritance paid for."

Ela felt Bill shift beside her. Probably tightening his fingers around the hilt of his sword.

"I'm not accusing you of anything, Sir Geoffrey." She said his name slowly. She wondered if he really was a knight. Most men of his class would be by his age, but the achievement demanded a level of chivalry and skill that she doubted he'd attained. Though perhaps his father bought it for him. That happened more than she cared to admit. Her own sons, however, would earn the honor for themselves. "I'm merely seeking to confirm your whereabouts with certainty since we've already established that your word alone is not to be trusted."

"What?" His face grew red. "My word is—"

"You already told us that you accused Brother Wilfred of theft on no evidence whatsoever. Surely you have a servant or kinsman who can state your whereabouts on the eve of the Assumption?"

"I suppose my housekeeper was here, though I daresay she was asleep."

"May I speak to her?" Ela could hardly wait to meet the housekeeper responsible for the disarray and dirt in this room.

"She up and left," he growled. "Lazy as a dog, she was."

"But she was here on that night?"

"I don't know."

Ela decided to take that as a no. "I hardly think you're cooking your own meals." She glanced at the plate on the nearby table, which now had a fly circling over it. "Who prepares them for you?"

"A girl from the village."

"Does she sleep here at night?"

"Nay, she insists on going back to her mama and papa at night." He wheedled the last part in a mocking voice.

Ela couldn't blame her. She wouldn't trust this man alone with a young girl. "It appears that you have a problem keeping your manor staffed," she said, running a finger in the dust on the nearby table.

"I can't help it if the folk here are lazy and shiftless."

*No one wants to work for him.* The villagers were impoverished to the point of desperation. Why were they so anxious to avoid him?

"So you have no alibi for the night of Brother Wilfred's murder?"

"Not unless you can get a testimony from the fleas in my mattress."

"And where were you on the morning that Father Edmund de Grey was murdered?" She fully expected him to say he was here at home with no humans in evidence.

A tiny smile crept across his thin mouth. "I was at your castle, my lady."

# CHAPTER 15

"What were you doing at my castle?" Ela didn't believe him. There was no way he could have visited any square inch of Salisbury castle without a witness seeing him, so if this was a lie he'd surely be caught out in it.

"I came to consult the records concerning the endowment of the abbey, and those relating to my manor, in the clerk's chambers."

Ela still didn't believe him. "What was the name of the clerk you met with?"

"Harold Pitts. And his assistant Charles dug up the scrolls from wherever they were stashed."

"Well, Harold Pitts can recall the slightest detail from a scrawled note slipped into a will from twenty-five years ago, so if you were there he'll surely remember you."

He lifted his chin defiantly. "I'm grateful for that, since it's clear that you don't believe a single word that comes out of my mouth."

"What were you hoping to find in these records? Surely you weren't planning to attempt to seize the land back from the abbey?"

"Nothing so bold, my lady," he said coolly. "I simply wanted to see the deeds and make sure everything was in order."

"And were the documents as you expected?" She couldn't wait to ask Harold Pitts about them.

"More or less. They raised a question about the right of way between the abbey and the Winchester road." His eyes narrowed slightly. "I could ask the brothers to pay a toll to use it if I wanted."

"I very much doubt that's what your father intended when he granted the land to the abbey." Ela itched to be quit of the dank and dingy room, but she wasn't quite finished with Geoffrey de Wakefield. So far, he'd raised more questions than he'd answered. "I'd like to see your manor."

"What?" His eyebrows lifted. "All of it?"

"The demesne around your house. I'd like to see what you've done with it since you've arrived back and taken control of the estate from your father's steward."

His cheeks grew mottled. "I don't see what right you have to march around my private manor."

"I am the High Sheriff of Wiltshire and your liege, and you are currently a person of interest in at least one murder."

"This is preposterous."

"You protest like a man with something to hide."

"I have nothing to hide! I have work to do."

"Then the sooner you take me on a tour of your grounds, the sooner you can get to it."

Ela was interested to see him flustered, but he led her back to the front door and he stomped through the ragged herb garden.

"Who planted these herbs?" she called after him.

"The housekeeper. Said she wanted them by the door, where they'd be easy to pick."

"That makes sense, but of course they do need weeding."

"Tell that to her."

"What's her name?"

He wheeled around, "I told you she up and left already. So if any weeding's to be done she won't be the one doing it."

"Answer your countess," growled Bill, who'd been admirably silent up until now. "And tell her your former housekeeper's name."

"Sissy's her name. Foolish name for an old woman if you ask me."

"And she lives in Biddesden?"

"Aye, I'm sure you'll find her there, bone idle like the rest of them."

Ela turned and walked to the right, she wanted to explore the perimeter of the house to see what this man was and wasn't doing on his own property before she presented him with a program of works for the village.

The remains of a path had grown slippery with moss, and Ela picked her way carefully over it. The forlorn herb garden was the only sign of industry. What fencing there was, mostly woven wattle, looked to be in poor repair. "Do you have no chickens or bees or pigs?"

"Easier to buy them. Foxes snatched the chickens, and the pigs ran off. The bees do as they please, don't they?"

Ela resisted the urge to sigh and shake her head. No wonder this man's father had despaired of him. She thought of her former maid Hilda and her young husband, Dunstan, who had inherited a dilapidated manor a good deal smaller than this one and were already creating a productive paradise spun out of hard work and the cleverness of the young man's mind.

"Your orchards will give you an abundance of apples from the look of it. And are those quince trees over there?"

"How would I know?"

"Don't speak to your countess like that," said Bill sharply.

"Begging your pardon," he said sullenly. "What does anyone do with this many apples?"

"You could take them straight to market, press them into cider, or store them in a cold, dry place that's safe from vermin. An apple will last right through the winter and still be good eating during Lent." It occurred to Ela that this lad might have had no useful education at all in the running of a manor. "If you can keep them from rotting you can sell them in the markets during the winter when they'll fetch a good price."

To his credit he looked somewhat interested.

"Of course you'd want to hire a steward to manage that for you."

Ela heard something crunch under her foot. She looked down and saw sharp pieces of glass on the path under the soft leather sole of her shoe. "Oh, dear, I seem to have stepped on glass."

Always her champion, Bill rushed into action and pulled the small shards from her shoe. Luckily none of them had pierced the leather. He gathered them into his hand. "We don't want to leave them here, where man or beast will step on them."

"What is it?" The shards were quite delicate, with no bubbles in the glass. The largest remaining piece, glittering in Bill's hand, was almost a perfect semicircle about the size of a plum, with a rim of tooled silver.

"I have no idea," said Bill.

Ela plucked the largest piece from his hand. "It's beveled so finely. And the outer edge is wrapped in silver. It looks like a magnifying glass made for reading."

"I believe you're right," said Bill, picking the last tiny shards off the mossy path. "And a finely made one."

"This way's the old kitchen garden," said Geoffrey de

J. G. LEWIS

Wakefield brusquely. "There are some carrots and parsnips growing there I suppose."

"I'm sorry about the magnifying glass," said Ela. "But how did it come to be out here on this path?"

"I have no idea. Probably been there for donkey's years."

"I don't think so." Ela ran her thumb over the smooth, beveled surface of the largest piece. "It has no moss or grime caked onto it. It's clean as if someone dropped it yesterday."

"Likely washed by the rain," said Wakefield, now striding past them and around the house. "Either way, I don't know anything about it so I won't charge you for breaking it."

Ela glanced at Bill, then handed him the largest piece and asked him to hold on to it until they could safely dispose of the shards.

The kitchen garden was even weedier and more disheveled than the herb garden. Apart from a more recently tilled plot that had just a few shoots of seedling growth, it was a waist-high riot of green. Ela could barely discern the carrot tops among the burgeoning crop of thistles and ragwort. "You need a gardener," she muttered. "Even a very young lad could keep this weeded if you showed him which ones are the weeds and which the desirable plants."

"If I knew which was which myself I suppose I could." He looked at her with slightly narrowed eyes. "I'm not cut out for country life. If I could find a way to sell this refuse heap of a manor and move into town with the money I would certainly do it."

"Has your father not deeded the property to you?" she asked.

"No. He's letting me occupy it without a single penny toward its running."

"I suspect he intends the experience to be educational," said Ela.

"So far it's educated me with the knowledge that the

172

people in this part of Wiltshire are shiftless and idle morons, and the abbey my father founded is a den of thieves sucking the lifeblood from his own manor. How were the villagers so gullible as to hand over their livelihoods to Father Edmund? They should have ganged up on him and put him six feet under when he first started."

Ela was picking her way along the overgrown track, careful not to trip over the trailing growth, and his words stopped her feet in their tracks—and not because his murderous suggestion shocked her. If anything it made too much sense. *Father Edmund was stabbed in a most haphazard and unskilled manner, almost as if a group of people—people who had no business or experience in killing a man—had taken turns wielding the knife.*

She looked up at Geoffrey de Wakefield and found him watching her. "Are you suggesting that's what happened?"

He shrugged. "How would I know?"

They made their way around the entire low-slung manor house back to the front where the guards waited with their horses snoozing in the afternoon sun.

ON THE RIDE back to the castle, Ela's brain buzzed with possibilities involving the villagers and Father de Grey. "Almost every man and woman in the village had cause to despise the priest," she said to Bill. "Is it so outlandish an idea?"

"It's hard enough to convince a phalanx of trained soldiers to act in unison. I can't imagine a rag-tag group of half-starved villagers plotting together to kill a priest in broad daylight in the cloister of his own abbey."

"True." Now that he painted the picture of the event for her, it did seem unlikely if not downright impossible. "It's hard to imagine any of them having the daring to kill a man. Even John Thistle, though he's the sturdiest of them, doesn't seem a likely suspect." She suffered another pang of guilt for keeping him in the dungeon without a sincere conviction that he was guilty.

"Far be it from me to agree with Sir Geoffrey on anything, but the villagers seem more like sheep than men," said Bill.

"It's their condition," said Ela. "They've been knocked down and kicked and need a firm hand to help them up. Unfortunately I can see that firm hand is not going to be extended to them by Geoffrey de Wakefield. Do you think he's really a knight of the realm?"

"I doubt it sincerely. I've heard nothing of him. He doesn't display the character of man who's earned his knighthood, but I'll make some inquiries and try to find out more about him."

"It is disturbing to see a man waste the advantages offered to him by noble birth and property." Ela sighed. "I wanted to goad him into repairing the water courses to the village and giving the villagers guidance and support in restoring their fields and homes, but he can't even keep his own home in order. If he fired the steward and doesn't intend to replace him, the manor will surely fall to rack and ruin."

"No wonder his father wanted him at arm's length," said Bill.

"I shall have to think of a way to turn the situation around at his manor, for the sake of the villagers, if not for him. But first we must determine if he's a real suspect in Father Edmund's murder."

~

ELA HEADED STRAIGHT to the clerk's chambers when she returned to the castle, but he was nowhere to be found. Harold Pitts was a man of great age and Ela strongly suspected he was catching a late afternoon nap. She told his young assistant that the matter could wait until tomorrow, and she retired to her solar to change into fresh clothes.

Elsie unpinned Ela's fillet and barbette and brushed out her hair. "I wonder how my brother and sister are getting on with the old man."

"He's not old at all! He's younger than me." Ela found herself offended on his behalf. "He's just worn by care and sadness."

"I'm worn by care and sadness too, I suppose." Elsie's serious voice made Ela turn to face her. The girl's round face bore its characteristically placid expression.

"Your resilience in the face of suffering is a great credit to you. Your siblings as well. They settled in very well and had the place looking like a home before Sir William and I left them there."

"I'm glad for them, then."

Ela remembered Elsie's comment about her sister's green fingers getting scorched in the castle laundry. "Are you happy in your work, dear Elsie?"

"Oh, yes, my lady, very happy," she said flatly. Elsie never showed much emotion of any kind so it was hard to know if she was just saying what Ela wanted to hear, or if this was the true expression of her limited capacity for joy.

Ela sensed that her direct gaze was intimidating the girl, so she turned around and let Elsie continue brushing her hair. "What would you like for your life, Elsie, if you could choose your future?"

"I'm sure I don't know, my lady." Elsie brushed vigorously, and Ela could tell there was more that she wasn't saying. Elsie had seemed rather jealous of her predecessor, Hilda, who—despite her willful misdeeds—had stumbled into a sort of dream life as mistress of her own manor with a handsome and intelligent husband and a baby to love.

"I'm sure you'll be married one day, when you're old enough."

"Oh, no." Elsie's startled response coincided with her tugging on Ela's hair with the brush almost hard enough to make her yelp. "Never. I'll never be married to a man."

"Because of what happened to your parents?" Ela hesitated before speaking, but sometimes it was better to unwrap a festering wound and expose it to the air.

"Yes, and my uncle was horrid to my aunt. He's the one that sold me. She tried to stop him."

Ela hadn't done anything to pursue punishment for his foul deed other than removing Elsie and her brothers and sisters from their care. Reprehensible and ungodly as their act had been, it wasn't actually against the laws of the land to trade children for money—which in itself was appalling.

"Do you think you'd like your own business, like Una Thornhill, the alewife?" Ela knew that most female sole proprietors were widows, but she'd come across a few that had forged their own destiny from a young age, usually with the help of a father or mother in the same trade.

"I don't think I'm clever enough for that. Maybe I could be like Cook and still work in the castle when I'm older."

Ela wanted to laugh. "Don't take Cook's skills and talents for granted! She shows the courage and fortitude of a general in commanding her helpers as well as creating meals to feed our household and all the staff and a good many of the soldiers as well. She's a rare creature and more valuable than half the garrison soldiers put together."

"I suppose I wouldn't be clever enough for that, then, either," said Elsie glumly.

Ela reflected that she probably wouldn't. Elsie was steady

and faithful but not exactly the kind of firebrand who could run a huge kitchen with flocks of pheasants and rivers of almond sauce flowing across its boards. "You're still young yet. We must wait and see what the Lord calls you to do."

"I think the Lord has called me to pin on your clean fillet and barbette," said Elsie crisply. "As Albert the porter said that your mother is expected here tonight."

"What?" Ela hadn't heard this. She'd been tempted to leave her head bare, as the day's travels and travails had left her with a slight headache. But the sight of her unadorned forehead might send her fastidious mother into a fit of apoplexy.

"Oh, dear. I think I was supposed to tell you."

"And you just have. I shall stand as still as a statue while you make me fit to greet her, my dear Elsie."

# CHAPTER 16

*A*lianore swept into the hall, her two poodles at her heels, just as the bells rang for Compline. Ela hurried to greet her.

"Darling!" Alianore kissed her on both cheeks. "I simply had to flee. Jean's nephew from Rouen has been staying with us for nearly three weeks. He's the most awful bore and talks of nothing but hunting. Jean can't resist teasing him, and he's so stupid he doesn't even notice. If I have to hear about the running of the boar along the banks of the Seine one more time I'll lose my mind."

"You've arrived just in time for an eel roulade the cook has prepared," said Ela.

"As long as I don't have to eat any more game birds, I shall be quite satisfied." Ellie rushed forward and hugged one of her grandmother's fluffy dogs. "Ah, my poppet. Have you been keeping your brothers in check?"

"I try, Grandma, but all they want to do is fight," exclaimed Ellie, flinging her curls with a toss of her head.

"Bill Talbot is training them in the art of swordplay," explained Ela.

"Aren't they a bit young for that?" asked Alianore, handing her cloak to an attendant. "Oh, I'm so hot. If it wasn't for the dust of travel I'd have ridden in my shift!"

Ellie laughed. Alianore probably wore a trimmed velvet gown even in bed. "They're eleven and thirteen, Grandma. Bill says they're almost grown men and must be able to fight for the king. I don't like to hear their swords clashing."

Alianore feigned a shudder. "Not one of my favorite sounds, either, but better in practice than when your castle is being besieged."

"Were you ever in a siege, Grandma?" asked Stephen excitedly.

Alianore clutched him to her and planted a kiss on his cheek. "Oh, many times." She winked at Ellie, who giggled. "It makes me quite tired to think about it. Would you fetch me a cup of wine, my dearest?"

Stephen turned to find Elsie and another girl hurrying over with a jug of wine and several cups. *Well done, Elsie*, thought Ela. The girl was learning to anticipate her needs and those of her guests.

Soon they were all seated at the high table, enjoying delicate summer fruits and pastries as light as air along with the cook's rich eel roulade.

"I was half afraid to travel here today," said Alianore, after dabbing her lips with a napkin. "As I hear there's an outlaw on the loose, killing priests and monks and robbing innocent travelers."

Ela's bite of roulade caught in her throat. This outlaw and her inability to catch him was a continued embarrassment to her as sheriff. "The sheriff of Hampshire's men thought they had him in custody but it was a case of mistaken identity. I've not heard of him robbing travelers. His specialty is stealing from churches and monasteries."

Alianore shook her head in disgust. "Why can't you

179

J. G. LEWIS

apprehend him with all of these brawny idle men at your
disposal?"

"He's slipperier than this eel, unfortunately." She hoped
Richard wouldn't say anything about her meeting him face-
to-face in the woods. Her mother would have a fit about
her exposing herself to danger. Luckily he was as embarrassed as Bill and the guards about their failure to keep Ela
safe.

"I'd run him through with my sword," said Stephen,
making the gesture with his hands. "A man who steals from
God's holy church doesn't deserve a fair trial."

"Quite so," said Alianore. "Fear not, for he'll get his just
deserts on Judgement Day!"

"In the meantime, a fair trial is as much about deter-
mining whether the accused is actually guilty of the crime, as
much as deciding what punishment they deserve. We have
no proof that the outlaw was involved in the two murders at
the Abbey of St. Benedict."

"Of course it was him," said Alianore, waving a pastry in
the air. "Who else would commit such brazen acts in a
cloister of all places?"

"That's a very good question," said Ela. "And one I've
spent the last few days trying to answer. It seems that almost
everyone within hearing distance of the abbey's bells has
motive of one kind or another."

"To kill a priest?" Alianore exclaimed. "I've never heard
such nonsense. Why would villagers want to kill their own
priest?"

"He was apparently taking money and goods from them
in return for not spreading rumors of their sins."

"Who gives half a moldy fig about the sins of villagers,
anyway?" asked Richard.

"They do, of course. Every man's petty cares are important to him, just as yours are to you."

"I'm quite sure Richard doesn't have any cares worth murdering anyone over," said Alianore. "Do you, my dear?"

"Not yet, Grandmamma."

Ela inwardly crossed herself and praised God for giving her the strength not to share with her children the conviction that their father had been murdered—by the second most powerful man in the land. Such knowledge would warp his young life and set it on a course that could end in disaster.

"The villagers have good reason to despise the priest, from all the information I've gathered," said Ela, "But they're quiet and unassuming people disinclined to take action even in their own interests."

"Which, I suppose, is how he got away with robbing them," said Alianore archly, plucking a fresh berry from the platter.

"Exactly," said Ela. "The outlaw seems to consider himself a man charged with stealing from the wealthy abbeys and returning their riches to the poor, but he's not shown any murderous intent."

"That you know of!" said Alianore. "Perhaps he came to steal the silver and Father Edmund caught him at it?"

"How do you know the dead man's name?" Ela had certainly never mentioned it to her.

"It's the talk of all Wiltshire, my dear." Her mother leaned in. "And people are whispering that this outlaw is running circles around the lady sheriff."

*Unfortunately, they're right.* Ela felt a fresh fire under her to make this outlaw pay for the damage he was doing to her reputation, quite apart from his crimes against God's holy church.

"Sir William has applied to Yorkshire to determine the exact crimes that the outlaw was charged with up there and the cause of his outlawry." She looked at Bill, who was far enough down the table not to overhear her. "Bill, any word from Yorkshire?"

"Not yet, my lady."

"He's probably left a trail of bodies across the moors and dales, my dear!"

"I doubt it. Most outlaws are simply unfortunates who find themselves unable to pay a fine or similar. Once they become outlaws they have no legal means to support themselves and they compound their crimes with new ones in the struggle for survival."

"But this one is wilier than most, it seems, if he can have the men of two counties chasing him for days or weeks or months with no results."

"He seems a most unusual character."

"I'd wager my best gold chain that he's your killer."

"You may well be right." Ela—for reasons she couldn't explain—felt fairly sure that the outlaw hadn't killed either Father Edmund or Brother Wilfred. Since she couldn't justify her conviction with facts of any sort, she kept it to herself. "God willing, we shall soon have him in custody here at the castle."

THE NEXT MORNING Ela visited the clerk's chambers immediately after the Prime service. She found Harold Pitts already bent over his books. He sprang immediately to his feet, which took some effort due to his advanced age. "Good morrow, my lady." He bowed his hoary head. "How may I be of service?"

"God be with you, Master Pitts. I'm here to tax your formidable memory. Did a man name Sir Geoffrey de Wakefield come to your rooms on the day Father Edmund was murdered at the Abbey of St. Benedict?" She could have gone into some description of the young man, but decided to see what sprang to the old clerk's mind.

"Indeed he did. He wished to consult the records concerning the land transfer to the Abbey of St. Benedict."

*So he was telling the truth.*

"What time did he arrive, and when did he leave?"

"He arrived before the bells for Terce and stayed until well after Nones in the afternoon, going over the ancient records concerning the boundaries of the manor owned by his family near the Chute Forest."

"Was he hoping to find anything in particular?"

"If he was, he didn't say. He asked to see every deed and document dating back to before the Domesday book was written. It took most of the day to find the scrolls he needed, for some were buried very deep in our archives."

"And he stayed here the whole time?"

"Indeed he did, my lady. He sat right there in that chair while he was waiting." He indicated a sturdy wood chair with a leather seat tucked into a corner of the room. "It surprised me that he didn't want to go away, then come back after we'd had a chance to dig through the archives, but he insisted on sitting right there."

*Almost as if he were trying to establish his presence here, in case he might be called upon to prove it in court.*

"Was he satisfied with what you found?"

"He seemed to be. I dug up the original parchment granting the manor to his ancestor during the time of William the Great. Quite an impressive document it is, written in a hand we don't often see today and with a colorful drawing of the manor and its boundaries. Of course, it looked quite different then—far more densely wooded than it is today."

"Did he say what he hoped to accomplish by finding these documents?"

"He muttered something about wanting to know the full extent of his family holdings. I told him his family should also have a copy of these documents in their possession, but he said he thought they were lost, so he wanted to see our copies. I did tell him that our scribe can make a fresh copy and stamp it with the official seal for a very fair price, but he didn't seem interested."

"And he didn't leave at any point during the day?"

"No, my lady. He was sat here reading them for a long time. He complained about how difficult the ancient hand was to read."

Ela found herself disappointed that his alibi held water so well. She'd half resolved to set John Thistle free if there was a solid chance that de Wakefield might have killed the priest. In terms of monetary loss, de Wakefield's grievances against de Grey were far greater. The priest had all but ruined his estate and crushed the morale of his tenants—though this couldn't have happened if the estate was under proper management.

"Does young Sir Geoffrey have any ownership rights to the manor?"

"No. The manor is held by his father these forty years. He inherited the manor on the death of his father and there's been no transfer of ownership since."

"Did the son inquire about ownership or express any desire to alter it?"

"No, my lady."

It seemed that the younger Sir Geoffrey was living here on sufferance from his father, who might require him to quit it at any moment. Perhaps that's why he showed so little interest in improving the manor. He'd moved down here hoping to enjoy the cash flow of the estate and found that the spring had dried up completely and that it could only be restarted by hard work which he had no inclination toward.

Still, he hadn't killed Father Edmund de Grey and unfortunately she was no closer to learning who had.

∾

BACK IN THE HALL, Ela had her usual crowd of petitioners waiting to see the sheriff to address their grievances. She kept the procession moving, mediating disputes, levying fines, and even issuing a warrant for the arrest of a man accused of theft by another.

One of the last petitioners of the day, an older woman in a faded blue cloak with a ragged hem, begged for a private audience with her. Ela was loath to make such an exception, but the woman was very stooped and aged and whispered that she was there on a very personal matter, so Ela finally acquiesced. She summoned her guards to follow her and led the woman to the nearby armory, where she could hear her away from curious ears.

Weapons lined the walls, arranged in patterns, their sharp steel gleaming in the reflected shaft of light from a single high window.

"All this shining steel speaks of many deaths," rasped the woman, staring up at it. The skin of her hands was brown like tanned leather from decades of hard work.

"Think of it as the sharp edge of freedom," said Ela. "These weapons keep us safe from usurpers and invaders."

The woman didn't reply. Instead she turned to Ela and peered at her with a soot-smudged face containing surprisingly sharp dark brown eyes. "John Thistle didn't kill anyone."

"Are you his mother?" asked Ela. Under her hood, the woman wore a dull green cloth loosely wrapped around her head that covered her hair and forehead completely and obscured her features with its folds.

"Nay. I've never met John Thistle."

Ela felt a wave of irritation. Sometimes people came to the castle just to waste her time and feel important. "Then how would you know he's not the killer?"

The old woman held her gaze.

A frisson of unease crept up Ela's spine. "What's your name?"

"They call me the Fox."

# CHAPTER 17

*E*la found herself struck speechless for a moment. "You're a woman?"

Then she remembered someone saying that the Fox was a master of disguise.

"Does that really matter?" The outlaw's voice was deep for a woman, but not unusually so.

*I must have him arrested.* The thought flashed through her mind. But if she called for a guard the outlaw might snatch a weapon off the wall and kill her before they could even open the door. She'd never have brought a stranger in here if she hadn't thought she was just an infirm old woman. Petitioners were checked for weapons before being granted entry to the hall, so she knew the visitor was unarmed, but now she also knew he was swift and cunning as his—or her—namesake.

"Did you kill Father Edmund de Grey?" she asked, as calmly as she could manage.

"I did not. Nor do I know who did, before you ask me that."

"Then why have you come?" Ela's mind scrolled through increasingly wild scenarios—could she pull the knife from her belt and hold him captive with it at his throat? Could she grab a halberd off the wall and—

"A good man is locked up for a crime he didn't commit. You have a reputation for fairness and I know you wouldn't want that."

*This outlaw is not the killer.* She couldn't explain why, but she was as sure of that as she'd ever been of anything in her life. "Why are you an outlaw?"

"A sad story involving a corrupt sheriff. What matters is that John Thistle, probably the most able man in Biddesden, is at risk of losing his life when he's already been wrongly deprived of his property."

Ela now found herself strangely relaxed in the outlaw's presence. "I heard you're from Yorkshire. Why are you now in Wiltshire?"

"I've traveled here and there over the years. This area has many wealthy monastic houses and a great forest to hide in. Once here, I heard of the injustices being perpetrated on the people of Biddesden by the abbey and resolved to take back what was theirs and return it to them."

"And have you managed to do so?"

"There has been some small redress." The beady brown eyes simply looked at her for a moment. "But if I had succeeded, would the townspeople still be ground by the millstone of poverty?"

"Where is the money that Father Edmund took?"

"If I knew that, I would seize it and return it to its rightful owners."

"You're not very helpful," said Ela, fully cognizant that this was an untenable situation.

"The truth is often unhelpful, dull, and trite. But a miscarriage of justice is a mote in the eye of God."

"I agree entirely about that." *The Fox is a woman.* Ela found herself growing increasingly convinced of it. The outlaw's sun-weathered skin and coarse features could belong to a man as easily as a woman, though there was no shadow of mustache or beard to be seen on the lip, chin, or neck. The gnarled fingers and scarred hands could belong to either gender. The graveled voice was low but not too low.

"How old are you?"

"A few years older than you." The outlaw spoke the last two words with a sort of mock deference that raised Ela's hackles. "But this land has weathered me like one of its ancient trees or stones."

"For how long have you been stealing goods and money from the Church?"

"About five years. Before that I was a more typical outlaw, scraping a living from the land."

"Poaching."

"If you consider that every wild bird and beast is the property of some great lord or bishop, then yes."

"What made you decide to take on God's holy church as your adversary?"

"A sense of injustice. Jesus told us that the meek shall inherit the earth, not be bled dry by those above them. A rich man is less likely to find entrance to the kingdom of heaven than a camel to pass through the eye of a needle, so why are bishops arrayed in gold rings and purple cloth?"

Ela's gold rings—gifts from her mother that she'd worn today to please her—suddenly seared her fingers like fire-brands. Her own elaborate plans for the monasteries to honor her husband and herself seemed like expensive indulgences.

"You're one of the wealthiest people in England," continued the outlaw. "You could do great works to lift up the downtrodden instead of throwing them in your dungeon."

Ela tried to speak but found that her words had dried up.

She cleared her throat. "I sought the role of sheriff precisely because I want to seek justice for rich and poor alike. I do indeed concern myself with the poor of each parish and frequently offer alms. It's a lord's responsibility to ensure that his villagers are supported and I already had words with Sir Geoffrey de Wakefield about the deplorable conditions in his—"

The outlaw made a dismissive sound. "That man is a carbuncle on the backside of humanity. He'll do nothing for his villagers but bleed them white. If anyone's your killer, it's him."

"He has a cast iron alibi for the murder of Father Edmund de Grey. My trusted clerk said he was in his chambers the entire morning and afternoon—and de Wakefield had no reason to kill Brother Wilfred."

*I can't believe I'm trying to reason with an outlaw inside my own armory.*

"I realize that blaming me for the deaths is the easy way out. I'm not the killer."

"I would be fully convinced of that if you stood trial and were declared innocent by the traveling justice," said Ela grimly.

The Fox snorted. "They'd hang me as soon as look at me. Probably burn me as a witch as well. I'm everyone's worst nightmare, an outsider who shines a light on the inequities at the heart of this godless society."

Ela blinked, certain in the knowledge that Salisbury was far from godless. Bishop Poore was perhaps not the ideal representative of God among the people of Wiltshire, but still…. "You do realize that I can't let you leave?"

The outlaw leaned toward her slightly, dark eyes unwary. "You will, though. You know I'm not the killer and you have no desire to see me punished for crimes that benefit the downtrodden and punish only the exploiter."

"Two days ago a man got himself arrested claiming to be you because he wished to die and saw an easy path to it. Unless you also wish to die your presence here makes no sense."

"Ah, well, I am tired." A slight smile creased the outlaw's weathered face. "Eternal rest does sometimes seem like a soft feather bed. But I have work to do."

"Stealing from the Church and flouting the laws of the shire?" Ela found herself growing equally angry and frustrated. In truth she didn't want to arrest this outlaw. Especially if it was a woman. There would be an inevitable gossip about the clash of two unusual women—one of them herself —who dared to step outside the domestic sphere and command the affairs of men.

The outlaw met her question with a cool gaze and a studied silence.

Ela's curiosity overwhelmed her. "How did you overpower and truss my two guards in the forest?"

"Most people aren't paying attention to what's under their nose. If you're quick and quiet you don't need strength."

Ela lifted her chin. "What can you do for me? Can you find out which of the villagers killed Father Edmund? I think it has to be one of them, but I have no way to find out which."

"Does it matter which one of them it was?"

"Of course." Ela became indignant. "Once a man has killed, he's far more likely to kill again. I don't want a murderer running amok in this shire."

"Not when you already have an outlaw running circles around you."

"That has been a source of considerable embarrassment. As you can imagine I always have detractors at the ready."

"And they must, of course, never know that I was here, surrounded by your gleaming weapons, or that would be awkward for you." A crooked smile tugged at the outlaw's wrinkle-lined mouth. "I'll never tell."

Frustration, mingled with fury, surged through Ela. "I could kill you myself, right here."

"You could, but you won't." The outlaw didn't flinch. "What would they think of you killing an old woman too frail to harm a fly? And I've done nothing to you and yours."

"Not true! The abbeys you've robbed are under my protection as sheriff. You've defiled these holy sanctuaries."

"Would that they followed the teachings of Christ, providing loaves and fishes to the poor and needy instead of piling up wealth in their grand buildings and offering empty prayers for the shriveled souls of the wealthy patrons who fund them."

Ela swallowed. This accusation came a little too close to the bone, and she didn't have the humility to accept such a slap to her own face. She spun and walked away, before turning back to hiss. "Do you have no faith in the Lord our God and his commandments?"

"I'm not sure what I have faith in anymore, my lady." She said it without mockery or deference. "I have no certainty of a place in Heaven, for I've done things that break both the laws of man and God's commandments. But today and tomorrow and the next day I shall try to do good in this world before I depart it."

Ela wondered how much good she could do from inside the castle dungeon. Her confidence that she wasn't headed there seemed delusional. Even if the outlaw was to snatch a weapon off the wall and strike Ela down with it, the guards outside would stop her at the door. She'd never even make it back to the hall. "How do you intend to escape my castle and the laws of Wiltshire?"

"With your blessing, my lady." The graveled voice spoke softly now.

"I begin to wonder if you are touched in the head," said Ela drily. "I have a reputation to protect and having an outlaw on the loose is bad for it."

"Then you should have hanged the man who pretended to be me. That would have saved your reputation and done the poor man the favor of delivering him from his misery."

"I have instead lifted him from his misery with the company and assistance of two lively youngsters to brush the cobwebs from his hearth and his heart."

"One of many selfless acts you've done. I do believe that your own heart is filled with Christian charity. I admire you immensely, my lady. Your determination to govern Wiltshire confounds the men of the shire and impresses them so they hardly know how to look at you or talk to you."

"The men of Wiltshire are not witless fools. And I am not easily swayed by flattery."

"What is more important to you: imprisoning the outlaw who makes fools of your men, or finding out who murdered a priest and a monk?"

"Finding the killer."

"I can help you do that."

"You already said that you don't know who killed them."

"I can find out. I'm in a better position than you to gain the confidence of the villagers."

"Hardly. You're an outlaw who inspires fear among them."

The Fox looked at her quietly, brown eyes thoughtful in her weathered face. "I've won the trust of several villagers already."

"Who?"

"I wouldn't betray their trust by telling you. But I do know that John Thistle is innocent." She straightened her shoulders beneath her ragged cloak and grew a full inch taller. She was the same height as Ela. "If you let me leave

193

here unmolested today, I shall find you the killer and I promise to leave Wiltshire forever."

Ela frowned. "Why would you do this?"

"Why would I do anything at all? I have a sense of self-preservation often at odds with my own desire for justice. You of all people may understand that."

Ela wasn't going to say it out loud, but she did understand. Her own children often berated her for putting her life and reputation at risk by pursuing criminals when she could be embroidering fine linen handkerchiefs to pass the time. "What if you can't discover the killer?"

"Then I shall offer myself up to you. To preserve your reputation as an effective sheriff, you can hang me for the crimes." The woman's eyes did reveal a flicker of emotion.

Her promise struck Ela in the chest—because she believed her.

*Am I about to let this notorious outlaw make a fool of me? Or would I be a fool to turn down her solemn pledge and risk letting a murderer walk free?*

The outlaw now frowned, which made her look older than her years. "I had suspected young Sir Geoffrey of killing Father Edmund de Grey, but since he has witnesses placing him elsewhere at the time of the murder, I shall redouble my efforts to find the true killer."

*Am I really going to let the Fox walk free?* Misgivings jangled in Ela's fingers and toes. But in her heart she knew that she wanted to take the chance. "How will you give me the information you find about the killer?"

"Don't worry about that. I'll bring it to you myself."

*That alone is a worry!* "Why did you risk coming here today?"

"Because I don't want an innocent man to hang for a crime he didn't commit. And I had faith that you'd want the same."

Ela drew in a slow breath. "Follow me back into the hall in your shuffling gait, and I'll conclude our meeting, then you must leave the castle at once."

"Yes, my lady." She seemed to shrink in stature as her shoulders hunched over once more, and she pulled her cloak around narrowed shoulders.

Ela led her to the door. Just before she pulled it open, the outlaw whispered, "We're more alike than you think."

ELA FOUND herself deeply shaken by yet another unplanned and uncontrolled encounter with the Fox. She dismissed the few remaining petitioners and retreated swiftly to the chapel, where she could count on being undisturbed for a few moments of reflection.

Had she just made a deal with the devil?

THAT EVENING as the family gathered for supper, John Dacus arrived back from his journey to the coastal ports.

"Did you even go to France?" asked little Nicky. "It seems like you just left."

"I never left the shores of England, my lad," said Dacus indulgently. He was sweet with Ela's children, which she greatly appreciated. "For I was not able to find the port they left from. There's no record of a prior and a priest from the Abbey of St. Benedict, or even two monastics from anywhere at all, getting on a ship within a week of the feast of St. Mary Magdalene."

"How odd. I thought priests traveled constantly," said Ela. "Not just pilgrimages but petitions to the pope and for their studies."

"I daresay they do, but none left either Southampton, Brighton, Poole, or Topsham in the last few weeks."

"Do you suppose they could have left from London?" asked Ela.

"I made inquiries and found no record of them at all or any nearby harbor, so it made no sense to cross the sea on a wild goose chase after them."

"That is perplexing," said Ela. "But speaking of goose, you must join us for supper. "Richard, please fetch a chair next to me for Sir John."

Richard leapt up to fetch a chair from another table, while one servant removed Dacus's cloak and another brought him a bowl of fresh water and a linen cloth to clean his hands.

John settled down into the chair Richard has set on her left hand side. Bill Talbot sat on her right. Flanked by two brave, good men she trusted with her life, she found herself cut by deep unease.

*Neither of them can know that the Fox came here, and that I let the outlaw go.*

"Where can the priest and prior be after all this time?" asked Bill.

"I've been asking myself that question all the way home from Exmouth. It's been nearly three weeks since they left, by all accounts."

"Do you suppose they abandoned their calling and have run off to live a life of sin?" asked Bill.

Servants set a platter before John Dacus, and he helped himself to roasted goose and candied baby carrots and a summer salad of dandelion and watercress.

"From everything I heard, they were highly respected pillars of the order," said Dacus. "Both of them were mature men, over sixty and possibly closer to seventy. I hardly think they'd have run off to live in the woods like outlaws."

Ela's knife clanged noisily against her plate as the word *outlaw* brought her secret encounter to the forefront of her mind. Why did she feel like everyone around her could read her guilty thoughts?

"If the priests from the abbey stole enough money from the villagers, they could sneak away to live independently," suggested Bill. "Are they accused of the same?"

"Not by the villagers. They made themselves somewhat unpopular with local landowners by aggressively pursuing the tithes they were owed in what was a difficult year for some, but nothing out of the ordinary. From all accounts they were good churchmen, one from Canterbury and the other from Lincoln, both with decades of experience shepherding a rather larger flock. This was almost a retirement position for both of them."

"Perhaps they both thought they'd been forced to take a step down in the world, coming from great cathedral towns to a tiny backwater monastery," suggested Bill. A servant refilled his cup with wine, and he took a swig of it. "How did they end up on the outskirts of the Chute Forest?"

"I imagine Bishop Poore had something to do with it," said Ela. "I shall ask him about it tomorrow."

ELA RODE out early in the morning to New Salisbury. Such visits had sometimes caught Bishop Poore still in bed and bleary-eyed, but this morning he was already up and dining on a large plate of poached eggs and sardines that quite turned Ela's stomach, which had been in knots since she let the outlaw leave her castle.

"May God grant you health and strength, Bishop Poore," she said.

"Indeed he has been generous enough, my dear lady," he

replied, rising only a little from his chair. "Won't you take a seat and join me to break your fast?"

She sat, only so he could reseat himself without undue rudeness. "Thank you, but I've eaten already. I'm here to find out more about the pilgrimage that Prior Hode and Father Billow left for at the time of the feast of St. Mary Magdalene almost three weeks ago. Do you know where they were headed?"

"I'm afraid I don't know, my dear Ela. John Dacus asked me the same some days ago, and I told him I was quite taken by surprise to learn of their departure."

"They didn't ask your permission to go?"

"Nay, apparently they obtained the funding from Sir Geoffrey de Wakefield and took off forthwith, with the promise to light a candle to the saints at each stop along the pilgrimage route, in honor of their benefactor."

*Sir Geoffrey de Wakefield? He hated the abbey and all it stood for.* "Who told you this?"

"One of the brothers at the abbey. When I went to take charge of the place after the priest was killed, they told me it was all very sudden." Poore mopped egg yolk off his lips with a napkin. "This was the old Sir Geoffrey that funded the pilgrimage, of course. Not the young one, who apparently railed against the waste of money."

"Ah, that does make more sense. I couldn't imagine the young Sir Geoffrey giving them a clipped half-penny."

"A most unpleasant young gentleman." Poore wrinkled his nose as if one of his poached eggs had turned rotten.

"You've met him?"

"I paid him a visit to introduce myself and to thank his family for endowing the Abbey of St. Benedict. I was surprised by the...modesty of the manor. Sir Geoffrey de Wakefield, his father, is a man of wealth and influence."

"It seems he sent his son here to rid himself of the burden

of his company, rather than to bless Wiltshire with his presence."

"As I discovered. And his father does not appear to have provided him with the funds necessary to live the life of a gentleman, let alone to make generous donations to the church, as one would hope."

*Of course Bishop Poore had gone to de Wakefield's manor on a fundraising expedition.*

"I can't imagine the son was thrilled to have his father pay for two clerics to make a lengthy pilgrimage when he can't afford to staff his manor properly."

"He did indeed seem angry about it and wouldn't discuss the matter."

"What do you know of the priest and prior?"

"Not much. They were translated to the Abbey of St. Benedict from their respective benefices to make way for fresh younger men to lead their large flocks."

"Because they didn't go on a pilgrimage at all. Sir John Dacus has inquired at the major ports and they didn't board a ship to France or anywhere else. Nearly all pilgrims from this region embark from Southampton so they can land at Cherbourg and start their pilgrimage by visiting the shrine at Mont St. Michel. So I find myself wondering if they can have flown their holy coop."

Bishop Poore stared at her, pale eyes rather watery. "Goodness. I can't imagine…. They were both older men ready for a quiet cloister to spend their twilight years, as I recall."

"I had the same thought."

"In fact, now that I think on it, their superiors had recommended each of them for a less demanding position due to some slight loss of faculties due to their advanced age."

"So they are very unlikely to have suddenly decided to abandon their calling and seek a secular life?"

"Without actually having met either of them—I handled their appointments by letter—I would say that it's impossible."

"Which begs the question—where are the two missing men?"

## CHAPTER 18

*E*la summoned Giles Haughton to the castle.

"I heard that the outlaw is still at large, my lady," he said, as soon as preliminary greetings were over. "How is this possible?"

Ela felt her weight shift from foot to foot. "The outlaw is a nuisance akin to a fly, but I don't think he's the murderer. Don't get distracted by his presence." She made a very deliberate effort to refer to the Fox with the male gender. "I've called you here about a very concerning and not unrelated matter. The two other men from the Abbey of St. Benedict have disappeared. The prior and a priest. The monks say they went on a pilgrimage, but there are no records of their embarkation."

"How very odd."

"The trip was sudden, unplanned even, according to the monks at the abbey. Apparently one day Father Edmund de Grey arrived back from Geoffrey de Wakefield's manor with the news that his father had privately funded a pilgrimage for them to visit the holy shrines along the way of St. James in his honor, and that they'd left at once, with mounts and baggage bearers provided by their benefactor."

Haughton stared at her. "And they believed this?"

"Apparently so. Or at least they didn't trouble themselves to question it."

"Those missing clerics are dead as sure as I'm standing here."

"I believe the same, which is why I summoned you as soon as I pieced together the story." She'd visited the monastery after her discussion with Bishop Poore, and found that no one had more than a half-baked account of their departure, which was described to them by Edmund de Grey—now dead himself and unavailable for questioning.

Haughton pondered in silence for a moment. "It must be the outlaw. Who else would wage a war of revenge on a holy sanctuary tucked away on the outskirts of the forest? They speak of him in hushed tones at the Bull and Bear. They say he's traveled the country for years, robbing churches and monasteries from Scotland to the south coast."

*I know.* Ela kept the thought to herself.

"He's left a trail of mischief crisscrossing the land going on five years or more."

Ela inhaled. "Has he been known to kill anyone?"

"Not that I've heard, but one who'll break the laws of God and man to steal so willfully and for such a long period of time is surely not above taking a life."

Ela felt the floor unsteady beneath her feet. Constant movement enabled the outlaw to conceal her true identity. As soon as she came close to capture and detection in one jurisdiction she started anew in a different shire. It was probably only now, with the outrage surrounding the murders, that people were starting to stitch together the stories of outlaws in different counties and realize they were the same person.

Was the outlaw the killer? Ela truly didn't believe she was. She'd staked her reputation on it.

"Have you encountered Sir Geoffrey de Wakefield?" she asked, hoping to deflect his attention. "He despises the abbey because his father donated a vast sum to found it while keeping him on a short leash, then sent him here to inhabit the rather unpromising manor next to it."

"I've had no cause to meet with him thus far, but if he funded this imaginary trip then he's certainly a suspect."

"Unfortunately he has an iron-clad alibi for the date Father Edmund was killed. He was my chief suspect for that killing until I discovered he'd been in my clerk's chambers all that day."

"We now have three other bodies to inquire into. I intend to visit de Wakefield at once."

ELA SPENT some quiet time listening to her youngest children sing her songs they'd learned from their tutor. She looked forward to enjoying the peace of the Vespers service, and was just about to excuse herself from the hall to go change her veil before the service, when her mother hurried toward her. "Get dressed, my dear." Alianore's face was wreathed in smiles. "We're going to visit the king."

"What?" Ela didn't relish the prospect of making small talk with young King Henry III when she had four unsolved murders—in addition to a rogue outlaw—gnawing at her conscience. "Why?"

"Do I believe my ears?" Alianore looked around at Bill and the children, who clustered around her in the great hall. She went to sit in Ela's favorite chair, ready to hold court as if she were still Countess of Salisbury. "Most noblewomen would be overjoyed by a royal invitation."

"Most noblewomen aren't sheriff of a county as large and populous as Wiltshire," said Ela.

Her mother took a cup of something from Elsie's offering hand. She had a sip and smiled at the girl. "Very refreshing. Thank you, dear Elsie." The girl smiled shyly. "Dear Henry is spending a few days at Clarendon, and we've been invited to sup with him."

"How did this invitation come about?" Ela felt suddenly wary.

"My dear friend Sir Nicholas Fitz Ralph is visiting from Suffolk, and I do look forward to spending time with him."

"So you thought a royal invitation was the best way to do that?"

"It was either that or invite him to your home, my dear, and I worried that might be too much of an imposition." Her mother's lips pressed together in a wry smile that suggested she'd considered and rejected the latter idea. Her lips were slightly reddened with pigment, and she wore a dark blue gown trimmed in silver. "I'm ready to depart as soon as you've had time to change your veil. And perhaps a more festive gown would suit."

*She has an ulterior motive.* "How old is Sir Nicholas?"

"Not old at all! And quite youthful for his age. Recently widowed, poor man, and with seven young lads to manage."

*I knew it.* "Let me guess, he's seeking a new wife, preferably one with vast estates and perhaps a grand title he could assume?"

"Ela! I'm shocked at you. What will your dear children think?" She looked around. The children were now caught up in a game—chasing one of her mother's dogs—and weren't even listening. "He has a fine title of his own and a castle with a delightful view over the sea. And he's the most charming conversationalist. You can hardly condemn the man before you've even met him."

A weight settled in Ela's chest. "I'd prefer to spend the evening in prayer," she said quietly.

"If that were truly the case you'd be treading the cloisters of Bradenstoke like your dear departed grandmother. The truth is that you enjoy the hum and bustle of life in the secular world more than you'd like to admit. And now your king is expecting your company."

"I visited him not two months ago, Mama. And asked him a great favor, which he was kind enough to grant. I don't wish to presume on his kindness."

"I'm sure he'd be most put out if you don't come with us. I told the messenger to let them know that you would be joining us."

"And Sir William, of course," said Ela.

"Uh, no, I'm afraid I didn't include dear Bill. I'm sure he has important duties here that he can't neglect."

"Quite so," said Bill gallantly. Ela wondered if he felt slighted, or if he realized that her mother wouldn't want Ela's right-hand man present when she introduced her to a hopeful new prospective husband. "I'm planning to teach them a new chess move I learned from a visiting soldier."

Ela racked her mind for a decent excuse to beg off an evening of wearisome festivities, but, failing to come up with one, she headed for her solar to change.

"You might have chosen a more radiant gown, my dear." Alianore peered down her long nose at Ela, who had chosen a demure gray-blue trimmed in white embroidery. "Perhaps a jeweled belt?"

"We should leave at once or we'll miss supper altogether," said Ela, anxious to get the visit over with so she could return home for a good night's sleep.

Alianore had arranged for a carriage, and the moon lit their way admirably over the relatively short distance to the king's newly renovated palace.

The king welcomed them warmly and was gracious enough not to mention the circumstances of Ela's last visit. She would rather not have her mother know that she'd now plied him with a total of seven hundred pounds in gold and silver just to keep her title of sheriff and role as castellan of Salisbury. Her mother would likely have died of shock at what she would have considered a gross extravagance.

Alianore introduced her to Sir Nicholas Fitz Ralph, a surprisingly handsome man of impressive height. With clear brown eyes and a head of wavy black hair he appeared to be a good ten years younger than Ela.

"His poor dear wife died more than four years ago," Alianore exclaimed. "And he swore that he would never marry again."

"Indeed I did," he said, in a voice deep enough to draw attention. "Her loss was a grave shock to me. I lost all joy in amusements for quite some time."

Ela liked him more already. "My condolences on your terrible loss. I know just how hard it is to lose your partner in life."

King Henry led them into his dining chamber and drew their attention to the walls, which had been recently painted with hunting scenes in gorgeous colors.

"The hunting in Wiltshire is quite unrivaled," exclaimed Henry. "Which is the main reason I've been fitting out this palace to spend more time here. Your family enjoys great good fortune to live surrounded by such lush and abundant country."

"Nor do we take it for granted, your grace," said Ela. "My sons enjoy hunting as much as their dear father did." This led to a discussion about her sons and Sir Nicholas's sons and her eldest—William—recently married and man of his own household. The king encouraged the subject, asking indulgent questions about his young cousins.

Unease rose in Ela's gut as the first course of oysters was cleared and the second of fat goose and suckling pig arrived. Had Henry himself arranged this meeting between her and Sir Nicholas Fitz Ralph out of a desire to see her safely married off to someone?

"We hear there's a great stag in the Chute Forest," said Henry, after their food was served. "And I'm keen to give chase to it, but even keener to give chase to this outlaw we've heard much of lately."

Ela stiffened. She hated that the outlaw was now cause for gossip—since it meant that her failure to catch and try the Fox was also a subject of discussion.

"The outlaw is a wily character, to be sure." She managed to sound calm and even lifted her engraved silver goblet of wine to her lips without shaking. "And is proving to be something of a distraction as we seek the murderer of a priest at the Abbey of St. Benedict." She hadn't mentioned to anyone other than her closest confidantes that the other two clerics were likely dead as well.

"But surely the outlaw is the killer? We heard that he robbed the abbey only a week or two before the priest was stabbed."

"Our inquiries suggest the events are unrelated. I believe that the priest was murdered by a local villager he had wronged."

"Do you have the man in custody?" asked King Henry, with keen interest.

"We do." Ela hoped her color didn't change. "He's in my dungeon awaiting trial." This was not entirely a lie but certainly not the truth. Poor John Thistle was a convenient scapegoat so she could save face at the king's table, even if she didn't think he was the murderer. At the very least the fib bought her time to keep searching for the true killer without alarming the monarch that chaos loomed as large as the great stag in his royal forests.

"I'm glad to hear that, my lady," said Sir Nicholas. "It must be quite a weight on your shoulders to maintain order among the common people in the absence of your husband."

"I'm glad to take a firm hold on the reins handled by my husband and by my father and his father before him," she said primly. "With our good king's blessing."

Henry raised his cup. Ela dearly wished to change the subject, but that was the king's prerogative.

"Ela shows uncommon spirit," said Henry warmly. "I trust her entirely with the management of the shire."

"Your confidence is much appreciated." She said a silent prayer of thanks, and a further prayer that he wouldn't have cause to lose faith in her. If any of these people knew that she'd entertained the notorious Fox in the glittering light reflected from the sharp blades in her armory—and that she'd then let the outlaw walk freely from her castle—she'd probably be brought before the next assizes in chains or committed to a nunnery as a simpleton.

Henry mercifully steered the conversation to a topic dear to his heart, the attempted reconquest of his father's lands in Normandy. Ela found the subject both expensive and boring but was glad of the chance to wax on about her childhood in Normandy and her memories of the Continent in happier days.

Anything to avoid discussion of the unholy tangle of misdeeds unfurling around the borders of the Chute Forest.

# CHAPTER 19

*I*n the carriage on the way home Alianore positively glowed. "What a charming man Sir Nicholas is! And he has great estates in Suffolk. Vast tracts in Ireland as well, though I'm not sure if that's a benefit or a burden to a man already blessed with great wealth."

Ela wondered if she could simply say nothing.

"Isn't he handsome?" continued her mother. "Those eyes!"

"He's quite tall," said Ela, when she realized her mother would insist on a reply.

"As tall as William, I think," said Alianore, with a faraway look in her eyes.

"William was the only husband I shall ever want or need," Ela said firmly. "Another man may be his equal in height or looks, but he could never be equal in my affections."

"Now, now, my dear. You can see that King Henry himself approves the alliance. He may well see fit to grant you both a fine gift of property on your marriage."

Ela couldn't conceal her exasperation. "He can give the gift to Sir Nicholas Fitz Ralph and another lady, because I'm not marrying again. I'd shut myself up in Bradenstoke first, and I don't intend to do that either. Not yet, anyway. When my new monastery at Lacock is built and I am truly ready, I shall take the veil."

Alianore shuddered. "The life of the cloister is not for everyone."

Ela wanted to laugh at the idea of her luxury-loving mother having to share crude and modest utensils with a gaggle of other nuns, or wear one simple homespun habit for an entire season. Even the wealthiest and best-endowed abbeys had to play at poverty or contravene the rules of their order, which invariably glorified humility and modesty in all earthly things.

"Imagine how you'd feel if I had begged and pleaded for you to become a nun when Father died? That's how I feel when people suggest I remarry."

"It's so...eccentric, though, my dear, to be unmarried and not a nun."

"Why is the sight of a woman in command of her own fortune so alarming to people? The Magna Carta protects my right to remain a widow if I so choose."

"Quite, my dear, but you're not an alewife or washer-woman. You're a person of status and people talk about you."

"Then let them talk. I've done nothing to call for their reproach." Ela wanted to cross herself and pray that her agreement with the outlaw would never become public knowledge. And perhaps a further prayer that the outlaw was indeed *not* the murderer.

"But what example are you setting your children?"

"I trust that I am showing them how to live a good Christian life where I can be of service to the community as well as to my family." Even as she said it, Ela knew it sounded pompous and overly pious. She didn't look up, but if she had she suspected she might have seen her mother roll her eyes.

"And what of your son William?" asked her mother. "He

must be keen to become earl. Your presence here in Salisbury prevents that."

"William is not yet mature enough to manage the business of the castle, let alone of Wiltshire."

"He's managing fine up north with Idonea. I suspect you just don't want to give up control to him."

"I don't." Ela didn't want to stare too hard at her reasons, and she certainly didn't want to discuss them with her mother. "William has not even attained the status of a knight yet. All in good time."

"I daresay the king himself will let you know when he's ready for William to take over from you," said her mother primly. "You can hardly ignore his royal command."

Again, Ela wondered what her mother would think if she knew about the king's ransom she'd paid to keep control of her title and castle. Ela felt fairly confident that Henry wouldn't try to wrest them away from her after the exchange of seven hundred pounds. Besides, once her son demonstrated the maturity and wisdom of an earl she'd be glad to hand him the castle and estates.

At least she thought she would. Luckily, the time for that had not yet arrived.

"The king has been my ally and supporter thus far," said Ela. "He's shown faith in my abilities and has always responded positively to my entreaties. I'm glad to consider him a friend as well as a family member."

Her mother took out an embroidered handkerchief from her sleeve and blew her nose very thoroughly into it before refolding it and tucking it back into her sleeve. "Dear Ela, your confidence is a credit to you."

"And to you, dear Mama."

～

ELA AND HAUGHTON set out early the next morning, resolved to question the monks and the villagers and determine—at the very least—if John Thistle was the right man to keep in custody.

Once again they arrived at the abbey during the Terce service and waited in the cloister until the service let out. Ela walked to the spot where Edmund de Grey was stabbed and stood exactly there. She wanted to get an idea of how easy it would be for someone to kill a man—undetected—in that spot. "There's only one sentry at the gate. The entire cloister is unguarded. You could slay me with your sword right now, and no one would be any the wiser."

"But the guard at the gate saw me come in and leave and would know it had to be either me or one of the brothers," replied Haughton, apparently unperturbed by the idea of him slaying her.

"And the guard that day said he saw no one. Which suggests that the murder was committed by someone resident at the abbey."

"Except that they were all present and accounted for in the abbey during services at that time. Even the lay brothers were there."

Ela looked toward the chapel door. "I do wonder why Father de Grey left the service and commanded them to stay and pray a few more decades before leaving. Perhaps he'd arranged to meet someone?"

The doors opened and the monks filed out, followed by the new priest Bishop Poore had found and installed. Ela and Haughton hurried forward to intercept them, and they scattered like geese spotting a predator."

"God's blessings upon you, dear brothers," she said quickly, before they could all vanish out of earshot. "I require your presence for a few moments."

"Attend your sheriff," barked Haughton, when they hung back.

"Come closer," said Ela. "I must ask you about the prior and the priest who went on a pilgrimage. We hear there was very little notice between when the journey was proposed and when they embarked on it."

"Notice?" A brother stepped forward. Ela recognized the wheaten-haired monk who'd spoken with her during her first visit to the abbey. "There wasn't any notice. They left that afternoon, shortly after Sext service, to visit the son of our benefactor, and it was Father Edmund who informed us that our benefactor had sent them on a pilgrimage. We didn't even have a chance to wish them well."

A very nasty sensation twisted Ela's gut, all but confirming her suspicions.

"And you didn't think it strange that he should simply tell you they'd be gone for several months without so much as a by-your-leave?"

"Well, they were the superiors so they didn't need our permission. I suspect Bishop Poore approved the trip."

Ela knew this wasn't true. "Did Father de Grey say which port they were leaving from?"

"Southampton, I think," replied the monk. "I'm not sure where else they would leave from."

Ela glanced at Haughton. "We've inquired at Southampton and other ports on the south coast, and they didn't board a ship at any time between then and now."

"Who told you it was Southampton?" asked Haughton.

"Father de Grey, I suppose," replied the monk. "We heard all about the journey from him."

"Unfortunately we can't confirm this with Father de Grey because he's now dead," said Haughton. "But the young Sir Geoffrey de Wakefield has said they left from Norwich, where his father has shipping concerns."

The monk looked confused. "Ah, then I daresay Father Edmund got it wrong."

"How did Father Edmund seem to feel about this sudden voyage?"

The monk blinked. "Well, he sounded cheerful enough when he told us. It is a once-in-a-lifetime opportunity to visit the relics of the saints and pray in the great cathedrals and most of us will never have that chance. I do remember that he did seem distracted and anxious afterward. I expect it was just the prospect of bearing all the responsibility of the abbey and the parish by himself."

The tall gray-haired monk nodded. "He was somewhat churlish over the next few days. I suspected him of being upset that they got the chance to travel and he didn't. I admit to experiencing the sin of envy myself."

"I daresay they'd never have left if they'd known Father Edmund was about to be murdered," said the wheaten-haired monk. "What a terrible shock."

Ela glanced at Haughton. She wasn't sure whether to reveal that there was a strong possibility that Father Billow and Prior Hode were also dead. She suspected they should wait for news from Norwich. Though she was already fairly certain what the news would be.

"Did either Prior Hode or Father Billow use a magnifying glass?"

"Oh, yes," said the gray-haired monk. "They both had weak eyes on account of their age. Why do you ask?"

A nasty cold feeling settled in the pit of Ela's stomach. "And did they carry one with them, when they went about the countryside?"

"Yes," said the wheaten-haired monk. "They both did. Prior Hode's was a flattish disk of blown glass, and Father Billow's was a half-round translucent gemstone. They needed them to read from their prayer book while giving last rites and such. And since they're among the few lettered men in these parts, sometimes they'd be called on to read a letter or will or similar."

Ela glanced at Haughton. She suspected that she'd stepped on Prior Hode's glass disk. *We need to arrest de Wakefield.*

But he didn't kill Father Edmund. So who did?

She looked back at the two monks. All their brothers stood around in silence like they were under a spell. "Do you know John Thistle from Biddesden?"

"Yes, my lady," said the older man. "One of the parishioners. Used to be a regular at Sunday services until…" He tailed off.

"Until what?" pressed Ela.

"I don't know exactly. One week he was coming here every week of a Sunday and the next he wasn't. Father Edmund said he'd call on him and make sure he wasn't ill, and he reported that he had some minor ailment of the leg but would be back in the congregation soon."

So Father Edmund had lied. There was nothing wrong with John Thistle's legs, or any other part of him.

"And he never came back after that? Outside of service hours perhaps?"

"No, my lady."

So he'd never come here ranting and angry. And why would he when he'd given his prize bull to keep his guilty secret? It wasn't until later that he started to realize how cruelly he'd been wronged and gained the courage to speak out.

"Do you think him capable of killing a man?"

The wheaten-haired monk looked startled. "Well, I don't know, my lady. I suppose any man that's capable of killing a calf is capable of killing a man, at least physically."

Ela turned to Haughton. "An experienced farmer like

John Thistle would likely make a quick job of killing a man, not stab him haphazardly almost as if he were pecked at by diving birds."

"Very true, my lady."

"Sir Giles, do you have any questions for the brothers?"

Haughton looked from one man to the next. "I'd like to know if any of you has any suspicions about who might have killed Father Edmund or Brother Wilfred?" The monks all stood around like mutes. Haughton looked around the cloister. Some of the men started to shuffle. "It's a crime to hold your tongue when you have knowledge of a murder."

"Truly, sir, it is a great mystery to us," said the one she recognized as Brother Ethelstan. "We live a retired life here, rarely leaving the abbey grounds. The priests have more interaction with the local people than we do. If you can find Prior Hode and Father Billow where they've gone on their pilgrimage, they may know more—if revealing that knowledge wouldn't violate the sanctity of the confessional."

"If I may speak, my lady." Ela looked up to see the new priest that Bishop Poore had installed, speaking from a more distant part of the cloister. He was a youngish man with a neat brown tonsure. "Although I wasn't here at the time the murders took place, I've been getting to know the brothers in this abbey and I feel confident that no one here committed the crime."

"How can you be so certain?" asked Ela, wondering how Bishop Poore chose him out of all the available clergy in this part of England.

"I can't be certain, my lady, not without the eyes of God himself, but surely the killer is someone from Biddesden, where Father de Grey unfortunately managed to make himself the enemy of half the people in the village."

Ela nodded. She would have laid odds that Geoffrey de Wakefield was the killer—except that he had a most reliable witness to prove he was elsewhere at the time of the murder. "Please send word at once if you gain more knowledge about either murder."

As she turned to leave she felt almost a sigh of relief from the brothers in the cloister. Her presence there made them tense and anxious. Why?

ELA AND HAUGHTON remounted their horses and rode away from the abbey as the sun rose in the sky. "I think we should arrest Sir Geoffrey de Wakefield for the murder of the Hode and Billow," she said, as soon as they were out of earshot. "The magnifying glass I stepped on must have belonged to one of them. It lay there, abandoned on the path, and was intact until I stepped on it. No man would leave such an expensive and hard-to-obtain item as a good reading glass lying in the weeds. If he found it missing he'd retrace his steps until he found it."

"Unless he didn't notice its absence until later that day," said Haughton. They trotted up a short hill and down past fields of grazing sheep that belonged to the abbey. "While I understand your concern, we've sent a messenger to Norwich. I think we should wait until we get confirmation from him about whether they did or didn't depart from the port."

"We may never get that if they were supposedly guests on a private vessel rather than booking passage on a commercial one. And how many days might that take?"

"The problem is that, with Sir Geoffrey de Wakefield being a knight of the realm and a man of property, the burden of proof is rather higher than if he were a simple villager. He's proven—at least with me—that he can display a degree of charm that might manage to sway the jury to see him as a man wrongly deprived of his liberty on a supposition, with no actual evidence."

"The broken glass is evidence."

"Only if we can prove its ownership." He rode along, looking ahead.

Ela found herself growing increasingly frustrated. "I suspect the bodies of Prior Hode and Father Billow lie in the disturbed soil behind his neglected manor house." She trotted right up next to him. "Would that meet the burden of proof?"

"Indeed it would, my lady."

"Then I, as sheriff, wish to have his herb garden excavated and any freshly turned soil examined in great detail."

# CHAPTER 20

*E*la instructed the soldiers that they intended to make an arrest and would need reinforcements. One rode back to the castle to fetch more guards, and they arranged to meet under a particular spreading oak tree on the public road half a mile from de Wakefield's manor house.

In the meantime, Ela decided to take Haughton with her to visit Biddesden to see what he would make of the villagers.

Their arrival clearly made the villagers nervous. Similar to the monks at the abbey, some of them disappeared into their houses and others stood around in a state of watchful distraction as they approached.

Ela rode into the middle of the single lane that made up the dismal hamlet and dismounted. Haughton followed suit. One woman stood more steadfastly than the others so she approached her, recognizing her as Agnes Crumb whom she'd spoken to on her first visit to the village.

"God be with you, Mistress Crumb. This is Giles Haughton, the coroner. We're here to further our investigation into who killed Father Edmund de Grey."

"You have John Thistle in custody." Her statement had a hint of accusation about it.

"Indeed we do. He's awaiting trial for the crime, but I'm not entirely convinced he's the killer."

"Good, because he isn't."

Ela frowned. "What makes you so sure?"

"He just isn't, that's all. He's a good man who got swindled out of his property like the rest of us. He'd never kill a priest, even one who's a thief."

"If the true killer would come forward of his own accord, that would protect John Thistle from suffering the consequences of another man's crime." Ela looked up at the few villagers hovering nearby. They all looked down at the ground.

Two children ran by, one chasing the other, oblivious to the adult business until their mother emerged from the house and yelled at them to get inside. Then she looked apologetically—or warily—at Ela, before disappearing back into the dark void of her doorway.

"Where's Phil Prescott?" asked Ela. The boy who'd worked at the abbey had been one of her most useful witnesses so far.

"I'll fetch him, my lady," said another nearby boy, who stood digging at the ground with his bare toes. He hurried off, then soon returned with Phil and behind him another slightly older boy striding to keep up.

"You come back here, Harry!" called a woman from behind him. Ela now recognized the boy as the one she'd seen mending a plough on a previous visit. The woman chasing him now, face half-hidden by a loosely tied kerchief, was not his mother, but perhaps his grandmother.

The boy turned. "I need to—"

"You need to come back in here and sweep the floor before I tan your hide!"

The woman caught up with him and tweaked his ear hard. The boy cringed under her grip but turned for home with her still holding his ear.

Phil Prescott now stood in front of her. "Good day, my lady," he mumbled, looking down at the hem of her skirt.

"Good day, Phil. This is Giles Haughton, our coroner. I'd like you to describe for him the man you saw in the tower on the night that Brother Wilfred fell from it." Now that she had a suspect in mind—Geoffrey de Wakefield—she wanted to compare the two.

The boy didn't look up. "I didn't see anything but a shadow," he mumbled.

"But you saw enough to know that it was a person and not a shadow."

"I don't know, my lady. Perhaps it was just a shadow." She could barely hear him.

"Don't be scared. I'm the sheriff. I wish to arrest the evildoer so you have no cause to fear. If a killer is allowed to roam free, he could kill again." She thought of another tactic. "Do you know John Thistle?"

"Of course, my lady." Finally his eyes met hers. "He lives right here in this village. I've known him all my life."

"Do you like him?"

He squinted at her, no doubt wondering why she'd ask such an odd question. She could tell he thought it was some kind of a trick.

"I don't know, my lady. I suppose so."

"So you wouldn't want him to hang for a crime he didn't commit?"

He hesitated for a moment. His lip quivered. "No, my lady."

"Would you say the man you saw up in the tower was John Thistle?"

He paused again, probably wondering what kind of a trap he was about to fall into. "I don't think so, my lady."

"What makes you say that?"

"John Thistle is a big man, tall and broad. He'd make a big, fat shadow. The one I saw was more ordinary sized. At least from what I saw in the moonlight." He said this long speech quite fast and looked almost breathless when he was done.

"Could you tell what color hair he had?"

"No, my lady, but it wasn't a tonsure because it was full and thick—it made his head big."

"Like curly hair?"

"I suppose so, my lady."

Ela's fingertips pricked. *It's de Wakefield. I'm sure of it.*

Still, he hadn't killed Father Edmund, so that problem still remained.

They spoke to several more villagers without gaining any useful information. Everyone had been asleep—or so they said—in the dark hour of the morning when Brother Wilfred fell to his death. And they'd all apparently been in the village at the time of Father Edmund's murder, where each had some kind of alibi to confirm the presence of another one there. One neighbor had visited another to barter for an egg, another had borrowed his neighbor's plough, and three mothers had gone together to beat their washing on the rocks by the stream, and so on.

They found Sissy Richards, de Wakefield's former house-keeper, who was a woman of fifty or so with a careworn face. She said that she'd cleaned and cooked for him for about three weeks but one day he dismissed her and she hadn't heard from him since. She said he still owed her money for her work but he'd had a temper and she was afraid to claim it.

As they interviewed the villagers, the Brice children

whom she'd deposited to live with Alfred Fletcher emerged from his cottage and stood quietly outside the door.

Ela walked over to them. "Good day to you, Billy and Merry. How are things in your household?"

"Come in and see, my lady," said Merry with a hint of pride in her voice.

Ela had to stoop a little as she stepped through the low doorway, but inside she could see that all was neat and tidy and the bed covers were spread out smooth. It was a relief not to see Alfred Fletcher sprawled on the bed like a corpse. In fact she didn't see him anywhere.

"Where's…" She paused, struggling for the words to use. Not their father. Not their master.

"Alfie's in the vegetable rows, my lady. He's planted all sorts and there's plenty of summer left for them to grow. I've been carrying water from the stream and they've started to sprout," said Billy brightly. "We'll be eating like kings."

"That's wonderful." A mix of relief and joy swelled in her chest. "I'm so proud of you both for setting this household to rights."

"It's a lot easier than scrubbing pots in the kitchen all day, my lady," said Merry with a shy smile.

"It isn't easier, Merry. If anything it's more difficult." Ela admired the dramatic transformation in the whole feel of the house. "But far more satisfying, and that makes a big difference."

"It does, my lady," the girl agreed. "And Alfie's more cheerful, too."

"Not exactly cheerful," said Billy. "But not nearly as sad, either."

Ela nodded. "That's as much an achievement as this swept floor."

～

As they walked back to their horses, Ela saw a woman striding toward them. She recognized her as the grandmother who'd seized the boy by the ear and dragged him back into the house. Ela wondered if the woman would speak to her, and if she'd scold her for her rough handling of the boy.

But as the woman drew close Ela had a chilling realization.

*It's the outlaw.*

The woman wore a plain linen kerchief, like any village woman, and a very faded green gown almost the color of lichen in some places. Her unremarkable features might go unnoticed in any marketplace or congregation. But her eyes fixed right on Ela's with unmistakable intensity that sent recognition shooting to her core.

*Is she going to accost me in front of Haughton and all the guards?* Her whole body tensed and her mind scrambled with possibilities as the outlaw, unrecognized by anyone except her, marched forward.

"God be with you, my lady," said the outlaw as she drew close. "I'm sorry about my grandson interrupting earlier. An unruly boy, he is."

Any scolding words that had hovered on Ela's tongue a few moments ago had long evaporated into a sort of stunned silence. She struggled to come up with a suitable response. "I quite understand, mistress. Raising boys is a constant challenge. Good day to you."

She sounded rather more abrupt and dismissive than she'd intended, but whatever the infamous Fox had in mind, she did not intend for it to unfold in the middle of Biddesden.

The woman bowed her head very slightly. "Thank you for understanding."

Ela swept on toward her horse, heart pounding. Every inch of her itched to leave this village with all possible speed.

~

ELA'S HEART didn't stop pounding until they were almost at the oak tree. She felt great relief that the guards had not yet arrived so she had a few moments to catch her breath and pretend that she hadn't just been startled almost out of her wits.

She wasn't even sure why she was so surprised to see the outlaw among the villagers. The Fox had promised to uncover the murderer, and how else would she do it than to get close to them and peer into their thoughts and motivations. But what story had she told about herself?

Haughton startled her out of her thoughts. "It seems that not a one of them has a solid, verifiable alibi for the morning that Father de Grey was murdered. Each of them just says he was with another, and that other with the first, and so on. If they didn't seem lamentably simple, I'd almost suspect them of a conspiracy."

"Don't be deceived by simplicity. It doesn't shield a man from sinful desires and actions. A man doesn't have to be a cunning villain to be a common criminal." The killer was almost certainly one of the villagers. It pained her that she intended to consider the word of a criminal outlaw in deciding which one had committed the crime.

"Perhaps we must consider the possibility that they are all somehow involved in the death." Haughton's brow furrowed. "The dead man was stabbed in a rather unusual and erratic pattern."

Ela stared at him. "You really suspect that half the village of Biddesden could enter the cloister of the Abbey of St.

Benedict—without being seen—and stab a priest in broad daylight?"

"Well, put like that it does seem unlikely." He heaved a sigh. "But none of them had a kind word to utter about the dead priest and they all seemed relieved to be quit of him."

Ela resisted the urge to growl with frustration. "If it weren't for their admitted sinfulness they'd never have gone broke trying to buy Father de Grey's expensive silence. Perhaps they're all lying. We could arrest the entire village and put them in the dungeon. That might bring the truth to the front of their minds."

Haughton looked like he wasn't sure if she'd lost her mind or not.

"Of course we can't do that," she admitted. "Not without making provision for what's left of their animals and crops. And I have no desire to make myself a worse villain to them than Father de Grey."

The sound of distant hooves heralded the arrival of a phalanx of guards—twenty of them—arms shining in the summer sun. Before they reached the tree, Ela headed toward them and told them to lead the way to the manor and arrest its occupant, preferably without disturbing any workers who might be there. She rather dreaded this type of arrest, as a wealthy and powerful man might push his servants and serfs out in front of him to field the blows, and those innocent of wrongdoing would end up injured, killed or in commission of a crime they would be tried and possibly hanged for.

She prayed that they could arrest Sir Geoffrey de Wakefield without incident and secure him safely in the castle dungeon.

THE MANOR WAS ODDLY quiet on their approach. No sign of the busy workers that Haughton had observed on his visit. This time, though, the manor looked maintained—its paths weeded, the walls whitewashed and new woven fencing sectioning parts of the demesne.

The guards clattered right up to the house, bridles jingling, and Ela waited for the young lord to make an appearance in his doorway as usual.

"Attend your sheriff!" cried out one of the guards in front, an older man with wind-reddened skin. "Come out at once."

Ela watched the door, then her gaze darted around the gardens. The eerie calm unsettled her. She wondered if he lay in wait somewhere, ready to rain arrows on their party. If he were indeed a knight his training would have included numerous ways to slay an adversary, should he so wish.

Movement in an upper window made her breath catch. "Someone's upstairs," she called.

"Come out now or face a forced entry!" called the same guard.

Ela's horse shifted under her, sensing her growing unease. She glanced at Haughton, who stared stolidly ahead.

The upstairs window creaked open and de Wakefield's tousled head poked out. "What's amiss? I'm abed with the fever."

"That's a new one," muttered Haughton. "I admire his ingenuity."

Ela sensed the guards' hesitation. No man wanted to catch a fever, especially in the summer when they were more likely to be dangerous. "Come down right now," she called. "And surrender to my guards or they shall come up and take you."

True to form, his expression didn't change much. "Have I offended you, my lady?" de Wakefield called down. He'd assumed a quizzical air, as if a mistake had been made and they must simply get to the bottom of it.

"You are a suspect in the disappearance of Prior Hode and Father Billow," called Ela calmly. "Unless you can produce them—alive—you must let my men arrest you so you can stand trial for their murder."

"I told the coroner—who I can see among you—that they departed from Norwich on one of my father's ships."

"We've sent to Norwich for confirmation, but in the meantime you must be taken into custody."

His face darkened. "This is preposterous. A made-up story to cover up your inability to arrest the outlaw who is the true villain." He leaned out toward the guards. "One ragged man running circles around a hundred soldiers in the Chute Forest. You should be ashamed of yourselves."

Ela could hear ire stirring among the men as evidenced by the prancing of their horses, who now tossed their heads and sent their harness jangling.

"Go take him," she said in a low, decisive voice. She fixed her eyes on the window, half expecting him to raise a bow and arrow, but instead he'd disappeared, leaving the casement open, a scrap of linen curtain blowing about it. "Don't let him escape."

# CHAPTER 21

*S*everal men dismounted and handed their reins to their fellows, then one heaved himself against the door.

"It's bolted," he called. Four men ran around the back of the house, while the first took a knife from his belt and shoved it into the crack between the door and the door frame, and pried them apart. The door quietly splintered near the hinge, and he kicked it open.

"Surrender yourself or risk death," he growled, as he set foot inside.

"He's gone out the back!" called one of the men.

"Give chase!" called Ela. She gathered up her horse and urged her forward. If de Wakefield escaped they might never find him. She cantered around the house, through his newly planted herb gardens and over the freshly swept paths, to where three men pelted toward the edge of a nearby oak copse.

She caught a glimpse of his blue tunic as he slipped between the trees. Other guards had followed her around the house and galloped toward him and into the wood.

"Got him!" came a cry.

Ela rode to the edge of the woods where two guards emerged, arms locked around de Wakefield's.

"You're hurting me," he moaned, as they tugged his arms behind his back and lashed them together with sturdy rope they'd clearly brought with them for the purpose.

"You had your chance to go quietly," growled one of the guards. "Now you'll go whichever way we see fit."

The other guard struck him a sudden blow behind the knees and he fell to them, then pitched forward, unable to catch himself with his now-trussed hands.

"Take him back to the dungeon at once," called Ela, not wishing to chastise her guards for excess roughness in front of the prisoner, but not wishing to humor his complaints, either. "Unharmed if possible."

Guards sometimes struggled to maintain their composure in the face of the insults and attacks that occurred during an arrest, especially when strong drink was involved. Still, she expected them to comport themselves like good Christians and turn the other cheek to such behavior, even if that was not their first instinct.

She rode back toward the house, then rode around it and surveyed the newly laid gardens that Haughton had seen under construction. Once the guards bearing the prisoner had left, with him trussed to a wagon brought along for the purpose, Ela summoned the rest of the guards.

"Dig up these beds. I strongly suspect that the bodies of the missing priest and prior are buried beneath these tender seedlings. And given the indolence of the property's owner, I don't expect them to be buried too deep."

"A pond is even easier burying." Haughton tilted his chin toward a nearby fishpond. Ela hadn't noticed it before, probably because it had previously been overgrown with foliage that had now been cut back.

"If he's not in the beds, we shall search the pond."

As she suspected, it didn't take long to find the remains of the two dead men, still dressed in their clerical robes, less than three feet below the tilled surface.

Ela crossed herself and said a prayer for them, hoping that their piety here on earth had secured passage for their souls, even though they'd died unshriven. She ordered for them to be brought to the castle mortuary for examination into how they'd died, and for Bishop Poore to be alerted that two more members of his ecclesiastical flock had been cruelly murdered.

~

ELA BRACED herself before entering the castle mortuary. Viewing the body of one dead priest had taken a good deal of fortitude. Two at once, and in the lamentable condition of having been buried underground for several weeks, took every bit of courage she could muster.

But it was summer and the long hours of sun allowed plenty of time to examine the bodies in daylight so she couldn't find an excuse to avoid the examination.

She took a deep breath and crossed herself before opening the door. Giles Haughton stood bent over one of the bodies. He held one eyelid propped open with a thumb and appeared to be examining the eyeball with a magnifying glass not unlike the one she'd trodden on those few fateful days ago.

"It appears that they were poisoned with belladonna."

The smell of the decaying corpses turned her stomach. "How are you able to tell?"

"Do you see this dark discoloration of the skin?"

"A little." She could see signs of what looked like mild bruising. "A reddening of the skin is typical of belladonna poisoning. Once the victim dies it fades to a dark, purplish discoloration. Extreme dilation of the victim's pupils is another sign of such toxicity." Ela tried to see the dilation he spoke of but the man's sunken eyes were hard to gaze upon.

"Do you think de Wakefield poisoned them before burying them in the garden?"

"I have little doubt of it." He lifted himself somewhat creakily to his full height. "I can find no signs of brutal beating, strangulation or any other method of injury."

Ela still couldn't bring herself to look fully at the desecrated bodies and kept her gaze focused on Haughton. "Praise be to God that de Wakefield's in the dungeon. Even as a knight of the realm and the son of a noble, he's not likely to escape punishment for the murder of the prior and the priest found poisoned and buried in his kitchen garden."

"God willing he'll hang for it at the next assizes."

Ela couldn't resist crossing herself again. "I've sent a messenger to Bishop Poore to ask for holy brothers from the cathedral to come to clean the bodies and dress them for burial in consecrated ground."

Haughton pulled a length of stained linen back over the corpse nearest him. "Would you like a jury to witness the condition of the bodies before they are prepared for burial?"

"No." She suppressed a shudder at the thought of parading the villagers in front of these poor, ruined bodies. "Your word as coroner shall suffice for their condition."

"Then I shall return to de Wakefield's manor to search for the source of the poison."

THE PROMISED report from Norwich arrived the next morning not long after the bells for Terce. The messenger that Ela had sent to the port city came straight into the hall.

Ela asked the guards to bring him straight to her dais in the hall and called for Bill Talbot to act as a witness.

The messenger, a young man dusty from the road, approached and pulled a small scroll from the scrip that hung from his shoulder.

"What is this?" Ela took the proffered scroll and broke the seal.

"It's a list of cargo and passengers on the *St. George*, a ship out of Norwich, bound for Calais, departing on the 25th of July, 1227."

"I hardly need to look at it, as I know our two passengers weren't on it." Still, she unrolled the tight piece of cheap parchment and held it stretched out. A cargo of fleeces and casks of salt fish followed by a list of about thirty names, written in a crabbed hand, slanted across the surface. Among them were the names of Prior Hode and Father Billow.

"This was presented by the steward of Sir Geoffrey de Wakefield, a nobleman of the area, who owns the ship that sailed."

Ela glanced at Bill. "A deliberate falsification, compounding a crime of murder with a crime of deception." She looked back at the messenger, who looked too tired to care if his news was important or not. "You can take a meal and rest after your long journey. If I need you to testify at the trial I'll send for you."

"Have the prisoner Geoffrey de Wakefield brought up from the dungeon," Ela commanded her guards.

Three murdered clerics made for shocking news that would no doubt spread the length and breadth of the land, so the case excited enough interest among the townspeople to draw a large jury.

Almost twenty men had assembled in the hall by the time the appointed hour arrived. They pulled up chairs to the usual U-shaped arrangement of trestle tables that Ela preferred for trials, and a hum of excitement and anticipation filled the air.

Ela took her seat at the head of the table and summoned Bill Talbot to sit on one side of her and Giles Haughton on the other. The two men always greeted each other cordially, but sometimes she sensed a tension between them, almost as if they were both her jealous lovers.

Which was ridiculous. Haughton was happily married—or married, at least—to his wife of more than twenty years and Bill Talbot had never shown the slightest sign of interest in the female sex despite her ardent efforts over the years to find him a wife.

He had been briefly married at one point, when he was barely in his majority and shortly after he'd retrieved Ela from Normandy. Talbot's wife, chosen for him by Alianore and married under some duress, if Ela recalled correctly, had been a quiet girl from some remote Normandy castle who'd died of the flux during her first summer in England. They were married less than a year, but Bill had used her death as an excuse to remain single for decades now.

Ela had long since ceased to badger Bill about his solo status and took pleasure in his company, especially in the wake of her husband's death. Their utterly different social status meant that not the slightest hint of romance could ever have evolved between them, even if he didn't prefer the male form, as she secretly suspected. Bill's quiet, supportive presence went a long way to assuaging the loneliness of widowhood.

The prisoner, Geoffrey de Wakefield, was settled into chairs in the space between the tables. Her husband had preferred for the accused to stand and suffer the blows of justice on their two unsteady feet, but Ela felt safer with the miscreants chained to a sturdy piece of wood furniture.

De Wakefield had an oddly intense expression on his face, and kept looking around the tables of jurors, as if trying to pick the ones he hoped would believe him.

Once silence had been obtained by Bill repeatedly asking for it in increasingly loud tones, she stood to address the jurors. "As you know, there are now four murders connected with the Abbey of St. Benedict. All three of the senior clerics connected with the abbey have been cruelly murdered, and one brother—who was most helpful to me during my initial inquiries—has been pushed to his death from the bell tower."

Geoffrey de Wakefield stared at her with hatred that could curdle milk. Which only stoked her determination to see him hang for his crimes. She fixed her gaze on him. "News has arrived from Norwich." She watched his expression, which quickly turned to one of keen interest. "And the ship's inventory states that Prior Hode and Father Billow were on the St. George out of Norwich."

A hum and rustle arose among the jurors, to whom this was news.

"What do you have to say about this?" she asked of de Wakefield.

"I told you they left from Norwich to go on the pilgrimage. They're probably halfway to Santiago de Compostela by now." His familiar cocky expression returned. "And as you know I was in the clerk's chambers when Father Edmund de Grey was killed. And why would I care whether Brother Wilfred lives or dies? You must let me go free at once or I shall pursue redress from this court of lies."

"Silence!" Ela had let him ramble on purpose. She wanted him to dig a hole for himself to fall into. "While the ship's inventory suggests that Billow and Hode were in Norwich, their very dead bodies found buried in the freshly dug vegetable gardens directly behind your manor prove this list to be fraudulent."

His face paled and his chains rattled. If he wasn't tied to a chair his knees might have buckled.

"How did they come to be buried in a shallow grave, piled on top of each other like refuse, under your lettuce seedlings?"

"I don't know," he stammered. "I had nothing to do with it."

"Come now, Sir Geoffrey. As a knight of the realm—if, in fact, you truly are one—you must obey a code of chivalry that includes telling the truth in all matters. The Lord your God knows the truth of the matter and will be your final judge, but I find myself placed as an intermediary between you and him and charged with making sure you commit no more crimes here on earth. There is no doubt in my mind that you killed Prior Hode and Father Billow. My only question is why?"

De Wakefield looked to have gone into a sort of trance. His eyes stared forward, but not really at her or anyone else. His lips trembled. His feet even seemed to dance on the floor beneath his chair as if he was having some kind of attack. Was he pretending to have lost his wits to avoid being questioned?

Ela sent a serving girl to fetch a cup of strong vinegar. A sip of that would soon revive him.

"Jurors, do you have any questions for the prisoner?"

Peter Hardwick, the butcher, rose to his feet. A man in his mid-twenties, with a solid build and a ruddy handsome face, he was known for his good character. Usually busy quartering hams for the people of Salisbury, he couldn't often spare the time to serve on a jury. Ela was glad when he did because he had a sharp mind and never wasted words.

"I have a question for the coroner, who I believe has

examined the bodies." Hardwick spoke politely to Ela. She nodded. He then turned to Giles Haughton. "In your opinion, how did these men meet their end before being buried?"

"The decomposition process had unfortunately begun before they were exhumed," said Haughton. "However their eyes were intact enough for me to determine that their pupils were excessively dilated. Combined with purplish discoloration of the skin, I concluded that they were both poisoned with belladonna."

"A premeditated crime," said Hardwick.

"It would appear so," said Haughton. "As belladonna is not found in the kitchen of a normal household."

"I don't know what you're talking about," burst out de Wakefield, who had apparently come to his senses.

"I found a small, green glass phial of the substance in the spoil from the burials," said Haughton. "On testing it, I found it is indeed belladonna, as the victims' symptoms suggested."

"I didn't put it there!" protested the prisoner.

"Oh?" said Haughton. "Did you force some of your unfortunate serfs to bury the bodies and throw the poison in after them?"

The prisoner apparently didn't think it wise to respond to this. Ela wondered if he actually had browbeaten his impoverished tenants into committing his crimes, but thought it unlikely.

Peter Hardwick interjected. "Why were the two clerics at your manor in the first place?"

"I don't know," spat de Wakefield.

"You're lying," said the butcher confidently. "In my business I can tell when a man is lying, either about the weight of his lambs or the speed with which he pays his debts. Did you invite them to your manor or did they come of their own accord?"

De Wakefield's cheek twitched. A not uncommon

symptom when a man was struggling to come up with a tall tale to save his neck. "They turned up by themselves. Why would I ask them?"

Hardwick regarded him suspiciously. "What was the reason for their visit?"

De Wakefield hesitated. "They wanted to collect tithes for the abbey. I told them they'd been given a great portion of my inheritance already, and they should remove themselves from my property before I chased them off it." He spoke with considerable vehemence.

Was he going to confess? Ela sat up in her chair.

"And how did they react?"

"They said that my steward cheated them of a third of last year's portion and that I owed them a full forty fleeces, eight bags of millet, and five pounds of silver. I told them to go find the steward in Wales and tell him themselves. Then they left."

"No, they didn't," said Hardwick.

Ela was surprised by the way one juror had taken command of the proceedings. She wondered if his persistence in questioning might undermine her authority before the room.

"You weren't there," snarled de Wakefield.

Ela spoke up. "No one was there. You kept the manor empty of anyone except yourself, which is a very strange way to conduct yourself as the lord of a manor. I asked you why you didn't employ your villagers to enrich both your manor and their livelihoods. You told me that they were too lazy and idle to be of use." She leaned forward. "But I can now see you kept them away because you were worried that you'd be found out if your tenants started turning earth in the garden and discovered two dead bodies."

De Wakefield shifted, rattling the chain that tied him to the chair. "When your coroner visited he saw that I had taken your advice and hired villagers to dig my gardens and build fences for me." He looked at Haughton, who looked silently back at him.

"By then you had presumably buried the bodies just deep enough to avoid discovery by unsuspecting gardeners. But by then I already had my suspicions about you."

Ela straightened her shoulders, and looked from one juror to the next. "While I was at his manor I stepped on a piece of glass abandoned on the path running around one side of the house. It broke under my heel. It can't have been there long or someone else—likely de Wakefield himself—would have stepped on it."

She now stared hard at de Wakefield. "But, to all appearances, no one had been there since the visit by Father Billow and Prior Hode."

Ela looked back at the jurors. "The magnifying glass that broke under my shoe almost certainly belonged to one of the fathers, who were both men of advanced years who needed assistance to read the fine script of their prayer books and psalters. It was the clue that goaded me to ask my men to dig up the gardens on his manor."

"You can't prove that I killed them."

"The burden of proof is not on me. It's my duty as sheriff to gather evidence to present to both the jury and ultimately the justice at the assizes. Out of curiosity, let me conduct a quick poll of our jurors assembled here today." It was a gamble, but could any of them still think de Wakefield was innocent of the murders? "Which of you think it likely that the priest and prior were killed by someone other than Geoffrey de Wakefield and were then buried in his garden, perhaps while he slept in his bed at night?"

The jurors jostled and rustled a little in their seats, but not one of them raised his hand.

"And which of our jurors assembled here today believes

that the evidence suggests that Geoffrey de Wakefield killed Prior Hode and Father Billow and buried them in his own demesne?"

Again there was some shifting and shuffling, and for a horrible moment Ela thought she'd rushed to assume their agreement and lost their confidence.

Then Peter Hardwick raised his hand, followed by Will Dyer, the barrel maker, Stephen Hale, the cordwainer, Hal Pryce, the young thatcher, Hugh Clifford the wine seller, and finally by every last man assembled around the tables, including Giles Haughton and Bill Talbot, who joined in last of all, not wanting to influence the votes of the others.

Ela looked down the length of her nose at de Wakefield. "As you can see, you are almost certain to be hanged by the neck until you are dead." She said the words with cold satisfaction which was probably sinful. She'd say a penance in the chapel at Vespers, but she couldn't help take some pleasure in condemning this ruthless murderer of two—if not three—clerics and possibly a monk as well.

"As you can see, you won't escape with your life. So perhaps you'd like to be a man of your word—as a knight of the realm—and tell the truth about what happened to Father de Grey and Brother Wilfred."

De Wakefield's once arrogant face had drained of blood, but as she spoke, some color returned to flush it and he leaned against his chains. "You may as well kill me right here and now because I'll die before I say another word to you."

He proved to be a man of his word in that, at least, as they were unable to extract further confessions. Flushed with the success of gaining the jury's confidence in convicting de Wakefield, Ela decided they'd proceeded far enough to prepare for the assizes, and de Wakefield could rot in the dungeon until the traveling justice arrived to pronounce his sentence.

Of course, John Thistle was still down in the dungeon, and she'd have to decide what to do about him. With the outlaw still at large and two unsolved murders still gnawing at her conscience and the lips of village gossips she couldn't simply let him go.

The jury was dismissed, and Ela headed back to her dais to deal with the last of the day's business. She braced herself to hear a long train of villagers squabbling over a pail of spoiled milk or a broken stool, but luckily there was just one woman waiting to speak with her.

The woman was older and stooped, wearing a long cloak so old that it was somewhere between black and brown, with a frayed hem that brushed along the floor as she shuffled forward.

"God be with you, mistress," said Ela by way of greeting.

"And with you, my lady," replied the outlaw.

# CHAPTER 22

*E*la's heart seized. She didn't want to be seen talking to the outlaw in her great hall, even in disguise. "Ah, Mistress Cratchett. I wish to hear news of your family, but let's sit somewhere quiet. Come with me."

She wasn't foolish enough to take the notorious Fox into her armory again, but instead led her into a windowless closet of a room near it that was used to store flags and banners and tents and poles and such items. She had one of the guards light the small brazier on the wall, then told them to wait outside, and she led the outlaw in and closed the door behind them.

There were no chairs, but the chests containing banners embroidered with the Longespée crest provided ample seating. Ela didn't wish to sit. "What have you discovered?" She kept her voice low so the guards wouldn't hear it through the heavy door.

"I'm here to surrender myself to the court."

Ela blinked. "As an old woman?"

"I am a woman, as you've no doubt discerned by now. And not a young one."

"You're not much older than me. Why are you dressed as a crone?"

"I didn't want to surprise you by presenting myself in person. I know that no good can come of people knowing you gave me a chance to find the killer. I wanted to give you the opportunity to decide how to take me."

"But why?" Unease chilled her. "Did you kill Father de Grey?"

The outlaw no longer stood hunched. Her full height made her an inch or more taller than Ela, tall for a woman, which had no doubt helped her lengthy deception. She pushed back her hood so Ela could see her weathered face, but not her hair, which was hidden under a knotted kerchief. "I didn't kill him but I haven't been able to find the killer, so, per our arrangement, I shall accept the blame myself."

Ela stared at her in disbelief for a moment. "A hanging is not like a jousting tournament where you can just switch horses and no one cares. Do you think I'd take satisfaction in hanging any living body that confesses, whether they are the true killer or not?" She blew out. "If that was the case, I'd have gladly hanged poor miserable Alfred Fletcher, who offered himself up as a sacrificial lamb some days ago. I wish to hang the true murderer, not a willing substitute." She realized her voice had risen while she was talking, and she turned to the door quickly as a reminder that listeners stood nearby.

The outlaw swallowed. "I had hoped to be able to determine and even produce the killer, but alas, I cannot."

Ela frowned. "But why did you offer to do that? You despise Father Edmund de Grey for how he abused the people of Biddesden. Why would you care who killed him?"

"I care nothing for him or his kind, who in the main I find to be as feckless and greedy as any man, but—"

Ela bristled at this. "I've been blessed to know many true

holy men, including Father—" She cut herself off. Her personal feelings about the clergy were irrelevant. "But what?"

"But I didn't want to see an innocent man like John Thistle hanged for the crimes of another."

"Are you sure John Thistle is innocent?"

"As sure as I'm standing here. Everyone in the village vouches for him. Though he's a big man with an impressive, even menacing, physical presence, he's as gentle as a lamb and you should let him go."

Ela thought as much but wasn't about to start agreeing with an outlaw who was trying to use her for some purpose she couldn't yet determine. "Why did you call out to that boy who tried to run up to me in the village? You pretended to be his mother."

The outlaw's expression didn't change. "Just a foolish boy about to stir up trouble putting his nose into other people's business."

"Was he about to reveal you as the outlaw in front of my men?"

"Perhaps. But I stopped him."

"Giles Haughton has a theory that all the villagers were in on it together. That they somehow came up with a plan to kill Father de Grey and possibly even set upon him as a group. Are you perhaps intending to stand in for all of them in an act of misguided heroism?"

The outlaw faltered for the tiniest sliver of a moment, but enough for Ela to see that she'd hit upon something dangerously close to the truth.

But the outlaw shook her head vehemently. "No. While they all have reason to detest the man, I don't think they have the wit and will between them to plot to take his life, even if he did deserve it."

"What is your name?"

"Why do you need to know it?"

"If I'm to hang you, I'd like to do it properly," said Ela coolly. Had this woman come here to call her bluff? Perhaps she did know the identity of the killer and hoped he'd walk free.

"Ellen Godwinson. I've gone by Allen these last few years, but Ellen is the name I was christened. I doubt there's anyone alive who'd recognize me as the pale, soft-spoken miller's wife I once was."

"Tell me the truth about how you came to be an outlaw."

"My husband died, and the sheriff set his sights on stealing the mill from under me. He accused me of cutting the flour with chalk and levied fines I couldn't pay. He got what he wanted in the end and I was forced to leave or be imprisoned. I had nowhere to go so I fled into the forest and fended for myself. I grew up with brothers, both long dead, so I knew how to hunt. A female outlaw is not something people could imagine or tolerate. Since I've always been tall and lean, I decided to wear men's clothes and hide my face under a hood."

Ela found her audacity unsettling. "I could hang you just for the trouble you've caused wasting manhours that could have been put to better use than searching the Chute Forest from top to bottom for you."

"And I'm here to offer you that chance."

Ela's heart sank. Part of her wanted to hang the outlaw who ran such merry circles around her, but the rest of her recoiled from the prospect. Truth be told she saw a lot of herself in this woman. Ellen Godwinson had been let down by the laws of men and their executors. With seven hundred pounds of gold, a grand title, great estates and a family relationship to the king, Ela had purchased the right to wield those laws herself. In the absence of those great advantages, this woman had taken her limited power into her own hands and wielded it as she saw fit—removing luxury goods stored in the great abbeys of the land and giving that wealth back to the local people.

"Would it not gall you to be hanged for another man's crime while the guilty one goes free?" asked Ela.

"As you said, I'm guilty of enough to justify a hanging." Ellen Godwinson looked bold and steady as a knight about to ride into a joust.

"I'd be remiss in my duties to let you go unpunished." Ela spoke quietly. If any of the men in the castle knew she had the notorious Fox in here, the outlaw would be clapped in irons before she could finish a sentence.

"You must let John Thistle go free," she replied. "Do you believe me when I say he has nothing to do with the crimes?"

"I do believe you, and I shall release him. Though, as you clearly know, that puts pressure on me to accuse someone else of Father de Grey's murder in his place."

"And thus I surrender myself." The look in her eyes was one of resignation, almost of relief.

"People won't take kindly to the news that the elusive Fox is a woman."

"I don't expect them to. Are you worried that my gender will reflect poorly on you?"

Ela let her silence on the matter speak for her. "I do not relish the prospect of walking back into the hall with a bent old woman and saying, "Here's your outlaw." Especially after I've just been in private conference with you. If you are truly intent on being arrested, you must present yourself as the Fox of legend and let them capture you in a conventional way."

"Dress myself in green and be their quarry in the forest, like a great hind that has eluded capture by the hunt?"

Ela watched her face. She almost looked amused by the idea. "Yes. Either that or leave Wiltshire, as you promised, and never visit this county or Hampshire again. At least not while I live and breathe."

An odd expression lit the outlaw's eyes. "You don't want me to die."

"No, I don't. However I won't hesitate to recommend you for hanging if you are indeed captured." Ela tried to reinstate her authority. "I leave your fate in your hands."

"You're breaking your part of our bargain."

"No, I'm not. I'm just offering the opportunity to disappear back into the forest, as long as it's one a very long way from here."

A smile played around the outlaw's lips, which suddenly looked more feminine than the hard almost lipless slash she normally bore. "I'm not sure if you're a very bad sheriff or a very good one."

*Sometimes I'm not sure either.* Ela would have to pray on this moment. But she certainly would never admit it to her confessor.

"Follow me back into the hall and play your part and don't do anything to reveal yourself until tomorrow at the earliest. I don't want our conversations to ever become known. What happens after tomorrow is up to you."

"I won't betray you, my lady."

Further unsettled by the outlaw's first use of her polite title, Ela exited the room with the Fox hooded and hobbling behind her like an old woman. Back in the hall she muttered some words about alms and visiting her soon. Then she watched from the corner of her eye as the outlaw shuffled back toward the main doors.

Unease crouched in her stomach. She was playing a very dangerous game with this outlaw. Her enemies would love to learn that she'd colluded with the Fox. Perhaps Bishop Poore would use the opportunity to put himself forward as sheriff of Wiltshire as well as Hampshire. His old friend Hubert de

Burgh would happily prepare the documents with his own hands.

Still, she'd followed her conscience. She must let her conscience—and her faith—guide her in all things because her deeds would one day be judged by a far greater power than the traveling justice at the assizes.

ELA TRIED to conduct the rest of the day's affairs with equanimity she didn't feel. She longed to head to the chapel and lose herself in prayer. Much of her afternoon was stolen by two farmers arguing over a dam that had burst on the land of one man and washed away a swathe of the other man's crops, leaving him too little time to replant before winter.

When she finally got rid of the pair of them, she rose to her feet, ready to finally head for the shelter of the chapel. She'd barely stepped off her dais when she noticed a boy staring at her, his gaze so intense that it caused a hitch in her step. He wore ragged clothing and bare feet, so she knew he wasn't one of her servants. He stood there, like someone waiting to meet with her but too intimidated to approach— which was not especially unusual with first time visitors to the hall.

Ela walked up to him. "Who are you?"

His lips worked for a moment while he struggled for words. Up close he looked familiar, and Ela realized he was the boy from Biddesden who'd had his ear tweaked by the outlaw in disguise.

"H-H-Harry Rucker."

"Why are you here?"

"I killed the priest."

# CHAPTER 23

*E*la bustled the boy into the antechamber where she'd met with the outlaw. He could have been armed for all she knew, but something told her he wasn't and that he'd present no danger to her.

She closed the door behind him and led him away from it. "Such an utterance could get you thrown in the dungeon. Do you have any idea what my dungeon looks like?"

He shook his head. He fell somewhere between Richard and Stephen in age. Eleven or twelve, perhaps. His greasy light-brown hair hung about his big, heavily lashed eyes. The realization sank in that he was the boy who'd run toward her in the village and been stopped by the outlaw. Had he intended to confess then, and the Fox had stopped him? She now found herself half wanting to do the same.

"My dungeon is dark and windowless with damp, dripping walls and rats the size of cats. Prisoners are chained to the walls and given barely enough food to keep them alive for their trials." She wasn't actually proud of these features, but they were difficult to improve without seeming to pamper criminals.

The boy's lip quivered, but he lifted his chin. "Don't let them hang the Fox. He didn't do it. I don't want him to die for my crime."

She'd warned the lad of the risks of incriminating himself, so now she couldn't do much but listen to his confession. "Tell me of your crime."

"I stabbed the priest. I used my dad's old knife. I even sharpened it beforehand on his whetstone. Then I walked to the abbey. I climbed the wall around the back so the monk at the gate didn't see me, then I waited in the shadows for Father de Grey. He'd told me to come, so he was expecting me after the service ended, while the others were still praying. He thought I was there to give him our last hen, but instead of a chicken I had the knife and—" He choked on his words.

Ela wanted to interrupt him, to reassure him that she didn't believe him and that he didn't need to cover for anyone. But something about his earnest manner and the tension racking his young body told her that every word he spoke was the truth.

"I had a basket with me, covered with a cloth. I put it down on the ground…." The boy's voice shook. "And I told him the chicken was in it."

He looked up at her, as if checking to see if she believed him.

"He told me that if it was dead it wouldn't fulfill the debt and that it had to be alive and I told him that it was alive and if he lifted the cloth he'd see—" Once again he seemed to choke on a lump in his throat. Ela found herself strangely rigid as she stood listening to him. "Then, when he bent over the basket, I pulled the knife from my sleeve and stabbed him in the back."

Ela held herself steady as the image flooded her mind— Father de Grey lying dead on the cloister floor, in a pool of his own rapidly congealing blood. She wanted to cross herself but didn't want to interrupt his account.

"He made a strangling sound and fell to his knees, and then I stabbed him again." The boy now looked past her, into an apparent hell of his own making. "I stabbed him over and over. Then he fell backward and I stabbed him in the belly. When I was sure he was dead, I grabbed the basket and ran."

It took Ela a moment to gather her thoughts, and that last image struck her as odd. "Why did you take the basket?"

"My mam would be cross if I lost her good basket. She uses it to take eggs to the market. She still has her chicken as I didn't give him that last one," he said with an odd note of triumph. "And that bad old priest can't take it now."

Ela blinked, her heart sinking. This young lad had tried to save his mother's last chicken and condemned himself to the gallows—or worse—which would surely break her heart. "Where is your father?"

"He's dead these five months. A cow kicked him and broke his leg, and it didn't heal right and got infected and he died." The boy spoke with little emotion, as if this were a simple historical fact. "And my mam was pregnant and while she fretted over how to feed us all, she thanked God every day that a piece of my dad was still alive inside her. Then Father de Grey made her give him nearly all her chickens and she couldn't buy food and the baby died."

Now Ela did cross herself. The thought of this boy's poor mother suffering two losses back to back and now the even worse loss she was about to face…

But some things made sense. "Did you tell the outlaw about this?"

"I did. I wanted him to take me into his band of outlaws so I could go live in the forest with him so my mam wouldn't get in trouble for what I did."

"And what did he say?" Ela thought it interesting that the

outlaw had kept the boy convinced that she was a man, even while dressing as a woman to move among the villagers.

"He said I was to never tell anyone a soul of what I did. That it was a secret between me and God and that God would understand why I did it. He said that I couldn't come live in the forest with him but I was to stay and look after my mam." His pale face showed little emotion. "And then I think he came here to say that he committed the murder so that he could be hanged instead of me."

Ela turned to look at the door, where her guards stood sentry outside. Her first instinct was to tell the boy to keep his voice down, but she realized that was fruitless. This boy would have to be tried at the assizes. Even with a mother's soft heart she could not let a confessed murderer—who described his grisly crime in intimate and accurate detail—go free, even if he was a foolish boy who'd acted in a misguided attempt to save his mother's livelihood.

"Why did your mother give her chickens to Father de Grey when it was a matter of life and death to keep them?"

The boy's face stayed oddly impassive. "I can't say."

"Why not?"

"Because it's a secret or my sister's life will be ruined." He realized at once that he'd said too much and froze, mouth slightly open.

"Why will your sister's life be ruined?"

"I can't say."

Ela's chest ached with exasperation. "Your sister's life will be ruined because her brother is a murderer. She'll have to see you hanged and comfort your grieving mother. You're not sparing her anything with your secrets. Tell me the truth so I can do what's best for your family in my role as sheriff."

The boy's eerie composure was cracking. Ela saw his shoulders subtly shake beneath his rough brown tunic.

"I won't tell anyone else unless it's absolutely necessary," she said, as softly as she could manage. "Tell me what happened."

"He raped my sister." The boy spat the words out as if they might poison him on the way out of his mouth.

"Father de Grey?" Ela felt shock cascade through her.

"No!" The boy's face scrunched. "Geoffrey de Wakefield raped her and my sister confessed to the priest and he told my mother that he'd tell everyone that my sister's virtue was sullied unless she paid him his due." The boy's eyes had a lifeless quality, like one already half dead. "Then no one would ever marry her."

Ela stood blinking. "Why did your sister not come forward and accuse de Wakefield of rape?"

The boy's jaw tightened. "Because she's just a girl and he's the lord who owns our whole manor and everyone on it!" He shouted so loud that her ears rang. "He'd say she was lying and have us thrown out of our home and then we'd all die." The rage in his voice suggested that he thought Ela was the stupidest person on earth for not understanding all this on instinct.

And for a moment she felt like she was.

"My mam was so angry with Mirabel for telling the priest what happened. She said she should have kept quiet about it. But Mirabel thought she would go to hell for her sins if she didn't confess."

"It wasn't her sin. It was de Wakefield's." Ela felt cold fury at the man. "But she confessed to Father de Grey?"

"Yes. That gave him the power to take my mother's chickens. And my sister's still afraid of the evil lord. What if he comes for her again?"

"Sir Geoffrey de Wakefield is in custody, accused of killing Prior Hode and Father Billow. He won't trouble you again."

The boy's eyes grew wide. "Truly?"

"Yes." Not that it would help him, poor lamb. It wouldn't make him any less a murderer.

"Then I can tell you that he made me stab Father de Grey." The words tumbled from his mouth. "He said he'd rape my mother if I told anyone about him raping my sister or me killing the priest. He told me how to do it—and when—and said he'd leave us alone entirely if I did it for him."

"You should never have killed anyone. It's a sin and a crime of the worst magnitude even if your reasons are good."

"No, it isn't," the boy argued. "Soldiers kill their enemies in war. Father de Grey killed my baby sister with his greed so he was my enemy." His half-dead eyes glittered slightly. "If I could have thought of a way to kill de Wakefield I'd have ended his worthless evil life as well."

Ela felt a slight frisson of fear. The cold fury and murderous rage in this boy felt dangerous, even though he was shorter than her and unarmed. "Come with me."

She hurried to the door and quickly issued an order for the guards outside to arrest him. She had no choice but to put him in the dungeon. Despite his tender age he'd proven himself to be a ruthless killer and now he had nothing to lose.

Ela found herself shaking, and she crossed herself three times as she hurried to the chapel to pray about the horrible turn of events that had just unfolded.

AFTER SOME TIME in prayer to gather her wits, Ela gathered Bill as her companion and rode back to the dismal village of Biddesden. She went at once to the house where the boy lived with his mother and broke the terrible news to them as gently as she could.

The boy's mother, Mildred Rucker, looked like a living

ghost. "He's damned his soul for all eternity and now his poor young body, too, by his confession." Her voice was barely audible. "He wanted to turn himself in after John Thistle got arrested for his crime."

"Did the outlaw try to stop him from confessing?"

She nodded. "Said that the priest deserved it for the lives he'd ruined."

"The outlaw offered himself as the murderer, to die for your son, without telling me what happened."

"Some people are too good for this world, whether they break its laws or not."

Ela wasn't sure if she referred to the Fox or to her own son, and she didn't ask. The girl, Mirabel Rucker, sat silently in the back of the room, on the low pallet that passed for a bed. Ela walked over to her and crouched down to her eye level. She was about fourteen, her youthful face marred by strain and the traces of recent tears. "You mustn't blame yourself for any of this."

"How can I not?" whispered the girl. "If I'd kept my mouth shut my brother wouldn't be a murderer."

"And you'd be suffering agonies in lonely silence."

The girl stared at her like she was simple. "I still am."

"Geoffrey de Wakefield will hang, and you don't need to come forward in court. He'll die for killing the two clerics we found buried in his garden. No one needs to know your story. I'll take it to my grave."

Ela wished she could undo the horrible violation now engraved on the girl's heart, that might sour even loving encounters with her future husband. "Prayer can heal," she said hopefully. "And if you decide that you wish to take the veil I can find a place for you at Bradenstoke or the new convent I'm building at Lacock."

A fat tear rolled down the girl's plump cheek. "I don't believe in God."

Her admission pierced Ela like a knife to the belly. "You believed in God enough to confess to a priest and seek help for your wounded soul. Give yourself time to heal, and I'm sure your faith will return. In the meantime I'll pray for you."

The girl blinked and another tear fell.

Ela stood, her knees creaking, and walked back to the mother. Today she felt twenty years older than her true age under the weight of this horrible case. "I wish I could find a way to save your son, but his crime is too great for me to pardon him. His fate will rest in the hands of the traveling justice at the assizes, and I'm afraid I can't offer much hope."

The mother nodded, tearless and gray-faced, as if all the emotion had already been wrung out of her and there were no tears left to shed.

ELA ARRIVED BACK at the castle downcast and almost weepy. Sometimes the course of justice crushed the innocent under its wheels as well as the guilty.

As she rode in through the main gates, Albert the porter rushed up to her in a frenzy of excitement. "They've got him, my lady! He's in the dungeon."

"Who?"

"The outlaw, my lady. The Fox himself!"

# CHAPTER 24

*B*ill strode toward Ela as she entered the hall. "I'm sure you've heard the good news! Shall we call a jury and bring him up from the dungeon?"

"Not today." Even summoning her voice to reply took a great effort. "This day has gone on long enough already." Sometimes these long summer days, where darkness didn't come until nine in the evening, could seem interminable. She craved the silence of her solar. The outlaw had committed enough crimes to stay in the dungeon overnight—or even forever. "Summon a jury for after Terce tomorrow morning." The delay would give her time to think.

The outlaw likely didn't know the boy had already surrendered and her sacrifice of her life in his place was futile. Now they might both hang. Was it her responsibility to save the guilty from their fate? No, it was her job as sheriff to mete out punishment where it was due.

Sometimes the burden of her duty was a heavy one to bear.

"Mama!" Little Nicky ran up to her and clutched at her dress. She half wanted to scold him. At nearly eight some might say he was too old for such displays of affection. Then again the period of youthful innocence was so short she wanted to clutch him in her arms and hold time still so the precious moment could last forever.

She stroked his hair. "What have you kept busy with today, my pet?"

"I taught Grayson how to jump onto the table!"

"Oh." Probably not the best idea.

"But then he was afraid to jump down, so Bill had to lift him."

Bill looked rather sheepish. "And he wrote out the Lord's Prayer in Latin on parchment."

"Did you really?"

"Yes. But then I spilled the ink on it and blotted it." Nicky said brightly. "Do you want to see Grayson jump?"

"Another time, my love. I must wash and change before supper."

She hurried upstairs, with Elsie trailing behind her, carrying a bowl of fresh water. Was she rushing through her children's tender years, too busy to cherish the precious moments that would never come again?

She envied the women for whom the burdens and joys of motherhood were enough to make their life whole. Sometimes her ambition and sense of duty almost felt like a curse. But surely the Lord wouldn't plant these seeds in her heart if he didn't want them to flourish?

ELA AWOKE with dread crouching on her heart like a gargoyle. Both young Harry Rucker and the Fox, or whatever she was calling herself that day, were due to face the jury that morning.

"Are you alright, my lady?" asked Elsie, looking curiously at her face.

"Of course I am. Why do you ask?"

"You just look a bit...green around the gills."

"I'll be fine."

Ela chose a blush red gown in the hope that it would impart some much-needed rosiness to her complexion. After Elsie had pinned her fillet and barbette into place, she pinched her cheeks and bit her lips to redden them.

"Do I look half alive now?"

Elsie looked doubtful. "Lovely as ever, my lady."

"False flattery is sinful," scolded Ela, but with what she hoped was an indulgent look. Elsie wisely held her tongue and primly fastened Ela's veil into place.

EXCITED MUTTERINGS ECHOED off the high ceilings of the hall as the jurors filed in and took their places. Ela's light breakfast of fruit and almond cakes sat in her stomach like lead. She took her place at the head of the table with a growing sense of unease.

Would the outlaw somehow reveal that they'd met and even made a deal of sorts? The awful possibilities were endless. She had both new prisoners brought up at the same time and resolved to question the boy first, so the outlaw would know that all attempts to protect him were futile. De Wakefield was also brought up in the hope that he'd admit his part in the death of the priest.

Young Harry Rucker comported himself bravely during his public confession and questioning. He seemed resigned to his death and keen to make sure that Geoffrey de Wakefield would hang for his crimes alongside him.

Every now and then Ela glanced at the outlaw to see what

effect the boy's words had on that weathered and inscrutable countenance. She was surprised but rather relieved to see no trace of emotion.

Ela made her speech that the boy had been driven to his crimes by the cruelty of both the priest and his liege lord, but that she knew she couldn't pardon him for murder but must present the case to the traveling justice at the assizes.

The jurors peppered the boy with questions. Ela almost wished the lad would show a quivering lip or a tear or an escaping sob like a normal boy, to elicit sympathy from the men of the jury, but he held himself steady, apparently resolved to meet his fate without cowardice.

One question still remained, though. And Ela waited until they had finished interrogating him about the bloody details of Father de Grey's demise. "Do you know who was responsible for pushing Brother Wilfred from the tower?"

The boy shook his head.

"I do," said the outlaw. The Fox's voice, low and masculine, didn't betray her gender. Nor did her now-visible hair, which was crudely chopped to chin length. All eyes turned to face the outlaw. Ela's heart started to thud. Would she attempt to claim guilt for this crime, too?

"What do you know of Brother Wilfred's death?" asked Ela, almost too roughly.

"That he was pushed to his death by Geoffrey de Wakefield." The outlaw looked at de Wakefield, who shifted slightly in his seat. "Brother Wilfred knew that the two clerics had gone to visit him. When Brother Edmund returned from his manor and told all the brothers that Father Billow and Prior Hode had left on a sudden pilgrimage, Wilfred started asking awkward questions. He didn't like or trust de Wakefield, who came to the abbey to complain and rage about the tithes that he felt should have been his property. When Father Edmund was killed, he was sure that de Wakefield had something to do with it."

"How do you know all this?" asked Ela.

"Because I was living in the abbey all this time."

A sudden hush fell over the hall and everyone, including Ela, stared at the outlaw in disbelief.

"You thought I was hiding in the Chute Forest—and I did go there when it suited me—" *Such as when I jumped out of a tree onto you.* Ela held her breath. "But your men couldn't find me because I was living in the attic above the cloister."

Ela didn't believe this was possible. "The cloister has a ceiling of stone arches. There's no attic above it."

"It's not an attic such as you could stand up in, but there's several feet of space between the vaulting of the arches and the beams of the roof above. Like most cloisters, the attic is small enough that no one would think to look there, but large enough for me to move around and overhear all the abbey's business and find opportunities to steal their valuables. I've done the same in abbeys up and down this land."

The outlaw's smug expression stunned Ela. A shocked murmur rose among the jurors. This confession would tie the noose around the Fox's neck as surely as if she'd killed a man.

One of the jurors rose to his feet, anger plain on his face. "How do we know you didn't kill the prior, the priests and brother Wilfred?" Ela recognized Will Dyer, the cooper, known for being a hard task master with his apprentices and a tough bargainer at the market.

"I don't suppose it matters if you do or not, since you'll hang me anyway. But I'd prefer to see the murderer punished for his crimes and the greed that drove them."

Ela could no longer see the outlaw as anything other than a woman. Did anyone else suspect her secret? If they did they'd probably want to burn her as a witch rather than try her as a thief, as she'd said herself. Especially once word got out that she'd overheard almost every conversation in the cloister of the Abbey of St. Benedict over the last who knows how many weeks or months.

Geoffrey de Wakefield had brightened during this last exchange. "The outlaw did kill them all," he said in his strident voice. "And sought to blame an upstanding member of the nobility out of his misguided hatred for those with any degree of wealth and power."

The jurors seemed to warm to this theory. They asked de Wakefield questions, and he replied with convincing lies. Ela watched the Fox's face tighten as de Wakefield swung public opinion in his favor.

After watching this disturbing turn of events unfold, Ela raised her hand and Bill Talbot called for silence. "I'd like to hear the opinion of the coroner. Sir Giles Haughton is our expert in matters of murder. Please tell us your thoughts on who committed these crimes."

She was confident that Haughton wouldn't be swayed by de Wakefield's nonsense.

Haughton nodded. "Prior Hode and Father Billow were buried in Geoffrey de Wakefield's garden. I hardly think the outlaw would have had the opportunity to dig their graves there under de Wakefield's gaze, thus I am confident that de Wakefield killed them and buried them there himself. Dilation of their eyes and discoloration of their skin suggest that they were poisoned with belladonna. Since de Wakefield's manor was devoid of servants—most unusual for a property of that size—I think it entirely possible that he invited them there with murder foremost in his mind. My question is why?"

De Wakefield lifted his chin. "I didn't kill them."

"I'm convinced that you did." Ela hated that de Wakefield seemed so composed. She'd previously discovered something of a talent for getting under the accused's skin and making them reveal more than they should. She needed to find the gap in de Wakefield's armor. "I know you found your own manor to be too remote and rustic for your tastes. You said your father banished you here as a result of a disagreement over some debts. I've written to him to hear his side of the story and to learn what I can of your life in Oxfordshire before you came here."

She watched him closely and saw his expression change very slightly.

"Since you bear his name I can only assume you are his firstborn son and rightful heir. I wonder if he intends for you to inherit your full titles and estates or if he exiled you here with a view to giving those to another?"

She watched his mouth tighten.

"Perhaps you already proved yourself to be a wastrel and unsuited to managing a large inheritance?"

"My father spends freely and raised me to do the same." He pinned her with a flinty gaze. "He can hardly scold me for extravagance."

"So you feel that you've been wrongly exiled here?" She tried to sound sympathetic. She wanted to draw him out.

"He raised me to be a great man and to live as one. A great man must have horses and armor and fine clothes and a luxurious residence, not live like the peasants scraping out their bread on the fields around."

"I agree completely," she said, as if with sympathy. "As Countess of Salisbury I must live according to my station. Did he not allow you access to enough money to do such a thing?"

"At first he did, thus confirming my tastes and inclinations. Then he tightened his purse strings and left me in an awkward position."

"He left you owing debts you couldn't pay?"

"Indeed he did." He spoke with some vehemence. "And I was forced to turn to gambling at dice to raise the sums needed to pay my debtors."

*Aha*, thought Ela. She nodded. "How unfortunate. Such efforts often soon lead to far greater debts."

"And to my life being threatened by scoundrels who are in the business of wringing either money or blood from men." His voice rose as he spoke. "What kind of position is that for a nobleman to find himself in?"

"A very difficult position, I'm sure." Another possibility occurred to her. "Did one of these lawless ruffians threaten to harm you over these debts?"

"Not for long!" he boasted. "I ran him through with my sword. Wiped the smirk right off his ugly face." His expression had brightened. "The sheriff agreed that I had defended my life and committed no crime."

Ela's gut tightened. "You killed a man and suffered no punishment?"

"He was at fault for threatening my life!"

Ela looked at the jury. "I'd like the jury to make note of the fact that the defendant has just confessed to a murder."

"That was last year!" protested de Wakefield. "And as I said I was proved innocent of the crime."

"Not being convicted and hanged is not at all the same thing as being proved innocent," said Ela coldly. "You've now demonstrated a willingness to resort to violence and bloodshed to solve your problems. I suspect that Prior Hode and Father Billow visited you at your manor and somehow enraged you— perhaps by demanding tithes—and you lost your temper and killed one or both of them. Then, on reflection you realized it might be hard to convince the sheriff that two elderly clerics had threatened your life and limb, and that it might be wiser to make them vanish without a trace."

De Wakefield's lips had shrunk back to a thin line.

"Father Edmund de Grey was also a problem for you. He'd extracted money from your villagers and beggared them, in turn beggaring you. For all we know, he had every intention of continuing to do the same."

"He did! And what does a priest want with coins and trinkets? He was like a magpie stealing everything that shines and hoarding it in his nest."

"Some men have such an affliction. That is no excuse for ordering them to be killed in cold blood, especially by a small boy."

De Wakefield's eyes narrowed. "You have only a boy's word against mine that I encouraged him. He had plenty of reasons of his own to kill the priest."

"The boy has confessed to stabbing Father Edmund. The dead man's wounds were consistent with his story and his stature and the weapon he claims to have used, so I see no reason not to take his full confession at face value. I now find myself satisfied that you were instrumental in committing the first three murders. Brother Wilfred's death is more difficult to parse out. We have a witness who says he was pushed to his death, but that witness did not see the killer in enough detail to accuse a particular man. On learning that you killed a man in Oxfordshire, and now two men in Wiltshire, I feel thoroughly convinced that you also took the life of Brother Wilfred to cover up the earlier crimes. Does the jury have any questions?"

The jury turned their attention again to de Wakefield, now contenting themselves with picking apart his lies. Since Ela didn't possess the power to sentence him to death, their role today—in addition to forming their own opinion of each defendant's guilt or innocence—was to gather information for the trial at the assizes.

Next they grilled the Fox, who revealed the details of many crimes, known and unknown, and said that he was

ready to meet his fate for contravening the laws of God—
who he didn't believe in—and man. Ela listened with a mix of
fury and chagrin. She hated the outlaw's crimes against the
Church and her blatant disregard for the law, but couldn't
help admiring her courage and cunning. She could also see a
twisted logic behind her project of stealing fine trinkets from
the rich abbeys, who drew their wealth from the purses of
the common people. She refused to breathe a word of how or
where she sold the goods she stole, or who had received the
profits of her efforts. She also claimed not to know what had
happened to the box of coins and trinkets from Father
Edmund's room, confirming Ela's suspicion that Bishop
Poore had quietly claimed it. Ela was also fairly sure that the
bishop would avoid payment of the ten pound bounty for
capturing the outlaw, on account of the Fox surrendering to
the authorities.

There was nothing Ela could do to save the outlaw, even
if she'd wanted to. She did want to save herself, though, from
the discovery that she'd had any kind of arrangement with
the Fox or that the outlaw was a woman.

She rose as soon as she felt was appropriate. "The confessions of this outlaw make further discussion unnecessary.
His guilt is certain and his crimes of such a nature that I'm
sure the traveling justice will deal with him most severely."
The extra effort required to use the male pronoun—even
though she knew it was a lie—exacted further payment from
her nerves. "I hereby adjourn today's trial, and you shall all
be summoned to testify at the assizes."

Before the day ended, Ela quietly released John Thistle
from the jail without pursuing the poaching charge against
him.

THE ASSIZES TOOK place at the end of September. She knew the justice, Robert de Lisle, from the last assizes. A tall, lugubrious Scottish noble with pale, glassy eyes, he'd proven to be both bold and compassionate in the sentences he'd doled out.

Ela welcomed him and his party to the great hall, and they feasted and rested before the trials, which began the next morning.

A large jury assembled and it took some time to get everyone settled around the tables in the hall. All three defendants, de Wakefield, the Fox, now known as Allan Godwinson, and young Harry Rucker were seated in chairs in the middle of the tables.

As expected, evidence was presented and de Wakefield and the outlaw quickly sentenced to hang at dawn. Additional evidence of the Fox's misdeeds in Yorkshire and elsewhere had arrived to paint the picture of a very dangerous and lawless individual, even if no murders had been committed in "his" name.

Finally, the jury presented the evidence against Harry Rucker. The justice then summoned the boy to stand. Chained to the chair, the boy was unable to move, so de Lisle had the guards release his chains so he could go stand directly in front of the judge.

The boy looked weak from his time in the dungeon, but he shuffled forward and stood, eyes downcast, in front of the judge.

De Lisle leaned forward, elbows on the table between them, big pale head hovering ominously. "Look me in the eye, boy!"

Harry lifted his head and met the judge's gaze.

"You killed Father Edmund de Grey with malice afore-thought?"

"I did." Harry spoke clear and plain. "He threatened my family."

"And in addition to having your own very good reasons for killing him, you were commanded to do so by your liege lord, Sir Geoffrey de Wakefield?"

"I was." The boy spoke less boldly now. "Though I know I shouldn't have listened to him."

"Nonsense!" barked the judge, so suddenly that Ela jumped in her chair. "An order from your liege Lord is like a command in battle. Your loyalty summons you to obey."

Ela peered at de Lisle. Where was he going with this? He'd managed to save another young boy at the last trial by installing him in an abbey to spend the rest of his youth learning to be a religious brother. That boy's crimes were not so heinous and were at least partly the result of him being a fool. They also hadn't resulted in a death—certainly not a death of the priest in the abbey in question.

"Did it cross your mind to disobey your lord?"

The boy hesitated, then said, "No. He said he'd rape my mother if I did." Ela noticed that he didn't say that de Wakefield had already committed the atrocity against his sister. She almost wished he would, since it might draw clemency. But she'd promised to protect the girl from prying eyes and whispering tongues.

De Lisle looked at the jury. "Is there any man among you who wouldn't hesitate to take a life to protect his family from violence and scorn?"

The jury shuffled awkwardly, clearly stunned by the odd question. There was some grunting and murmuring.

"Speak up!" commanded the judge.

Peter Howard, the baker, rose to his feet. "Well, my mother's been dead these twenty years, but I'd have taken any man's life who tried to tamper with her!"

The others soon joined in a chorus of agreement.

The boy swayed oddly from foot to foot, clearly confused by this strange direction the judge had embarked on.

"But then, my lord," said Stephen Hale, the cordwainer, a stalwart and thoughtful member of the jury. "Wouldn't it make more sense for the boy to kill de Wakefield, who made the threat?"

"Would you have the boy kill his liege lord who owns the very manor he lives on? Why such a thing would shake our realm to its core and bring it to its knees!" His voice boomed across the hall. "In Scotland our lords rely on the loyalty and boldness of all their serfs and vassals to defend their territory and sovereignty in the conflicts that erupt between the ancient clans."

Ela had only a vague understanding of how Scotland functioned as a society. The Norman invaders—her people—had not conquered that wild land by the sword but rather through marriage and various treaties. The old families that traced their lineage back to the ancient kings had somehow managed to keep most of their fiefdoms and—from the stories she'd heard—occupied themselves with constant internecine warfare. The Norman authorities were apparently content to have the Scots occupy themselves in this manner. Every now and then, however, conflicts broke out that threatened the status quo, and Ela suspected that de Lisle—whose name revealed his Norman ancestry—was referring to that.

The boy stared at de Lisle, hardly blinking.

"While this boy's crime is reprehensible in its unexamined nature, he has clearly rid the district of a poisonous and corrupting influence in Father Edmund de Grey, a man who bled the district dry of resources and left its people to starve, by exploiting the simple faith that led them to make confession of their trifling sins."

Ela nodded in agreement with this, and she could see the

jury was also on board for this argument. But surely he wouldn't attempt to install the boy as a lay brother in the very abbey where he'd committed a violent murder? As sheriff she'd have to protest such a move as a threat to the peace of the shire.

"His bravery and valor in killing a full-grown man with a simple knife is nothing to sneeze at." He looked directly at the boy, whose eyes now grew wide as spoons. "I propose that his courage and daring be employed where it is sorely needed. If King Henry commands our troops to fight his wars on the Continent, as I believe he soon will, this will leave us bereft of good fighting men here on our home isles. I propose installing this young man in my own household in Galloway for training as a man-at-arms to defend our people and our way of life from the marauding ruffians that surround us."

Ela looked at the boy, now blinking rapidly, then at de Lisle, who turned to look at her to gauge her reaction. She drew in a steadying breath before replying. "I'm not opposed to this course of action. I hate to see a young life wasted, and he was provoked into his crimes by both his victim and his lord."

Her heart lifted at the thought of sparing his mother and sister the sight of seeing young Harry hanged in the market-place. She scanned the crowd and found the pair of them together, hunched in the shadows of an archway at the edge of the hall, clutching each other and staring at the justice as if he were completely mad.

"I'd like to ask the jury their opinion," said Ela quietly. She certainly didn't want to ignore their thoughts when such a seemingly outrageous solution to the ugly problem of needing to hang a twelve-year-old boy presented itself.

To her surprise, they all seemed to agree with the judge. If they didn't, they kept quiet about it.

The justice then returned his gaze to the boy, who'd done an admirable job staying steady on his feet while all this went on. "Harold Rucker, would you prefer to hang by the neck until you are dead at dawn—" The boy faltered and swayed. "Or travel with my men to Scotland to be trained as a fighting man?"

"I'd like to go to Scotland and learn to fight, my lord," said the boy, calmly.

A satisfied expression settled over the justice's broad, pale face. "Then it is done. The boy will journey up north with my men and spend his minority as an apprentice soldier in my fighting forces."

A great wail rose into the air, and Ela looked at where the boy's mother had now fallen to her knees, sobbing.

"That's the boy's mother," she whispered to the justice. De Lisle summoned the woman forward, and de Lisle commiserated with her on losing her boy to the rugged wilderness of Scotland, but assured her that it was better than the alternative. She tearfully agreed.

CHAPTER 25

$\mathcal{T}$he hangings took place at dawn. Ela chose the early hour to minimize the crowd at the gruesome spectacle. Also because she half-expected the outlaw to have some final trick up her sleeve. Would she vanish into the darkness, never to be seen again? Ela both hoped and feared for it.

She didn't. Allen—or Ellen—Godwinson made no last statement condemning the church, the nobles and Ela above all. She kept her gender secret until the last, though most men would have at least something of a beard after weeks in the dungeon and—of course—she didn't. Ela suffered a pang of loss as the outlaw met her death bravely.

Geoffrey de Wakefield was hanged first, still protesting that it was a gross miscarriage of justice and that his father would have their heads. His father was nowhere to be seen and had not responded to any missives sent to him about how two dead clerics came to be on the ship's manifest of one of his boats leaving the port of Norwich.

Ela hated executions, but now felt compelled to attend—if

nothing else, to ensure that they took place properly. Her sons begged to attend and she finally relented. If they cared enough to rise at dawn, the grisly sight would perhaps prepare them for the horrors that awaited them as fighting men.

They watched, unflinching, as both hangings took place.

"Did the boy leave for Scotland yet?" asked Richard.

"He's leaving today with the traveling justice and will stay with his men as he returns north. I suppose there are some more trials to be held along the way."

"Would you have hanged him if you were the judge?"

Ela frowned. "Probably. It wouldn't have occurred to me to put his combination of loyalty and violence to good use. I'm grateful to Justice de Lisle for his creative thinking."

"I'd kill anyone who tried to hurt you, Mama," said Stephen.

"While I appreciate your loyalty, my love, there are men charged with that duty."

"Myself, for example," chimed in Bill Talbot. "So don't jump in front of me."

"Seriously, though…" continued Ela. Richard's words had rung a warning bell inside her. "Don't risk your life on an emotional whim or in a foolish quest for vengeance. Your destiny is greater than that."

She'd been so careful not to share her conviction that the king's justiciar, Hubert de Burgh, was responsible for poisoning their father. She knew they'd reshape their whole destinies in a quest for revenge, and she didn't want her enemy to steal their lives as well as her husband's.

She hoped that one day de Burgh would suffer the punishment due to him, but she didn't want her sons distinguished future careers swept away on that tidal wave when it came.

Ela arranged for both hanged bodies to be sent to the castle mortuary, where they'd be prepared for burial in unmarked graves outside the walls. She'd asked Giles Haughton to attend them himself. This was her last-ditch effort to keep the outlaw's greatest secret.

Her sons and Bill Talbot went off to practice their jousting. With a promise to come watch as soon as she could, she followed Giles Haughton and the bodies to the mortuary.

"Your interest in these corpses surprises me, my lady," he said once they were alone in the mortuary, where the two enemies in life lay side by side on his scarred wood table.

"My interest is in seeing them safely buried without fanfare. I worry that the outlaw has excited enough interest and sympathy among the local people that his grave could become a shrine of sorts if its location was known. For that reason, I propose burying them at the east end of the old orchard yard, where they can fertilize the new apricot trees we're about to plant."

"A sensible precaution, my lady. But that location is inside the castle walls. Isn't it more customary to bury criminals outside the pale, as it were?"

"It is, but in this case I'd rather keep them in my custody to avoid martyrdom."

"I hardly think anyone could make a martyr of Geoffrey de Wakefield. You were right that he was never knighted. He merely assumed the title much as a man puts on a feathered hat."

"The deaths of four members of our local clergy rest on his head. I prefer for no one to know where that head lies that he may be forgotten as soon as the earthworms make their meal of him."

"What will happen to his manor?"

"The manor still belongs to his father, who only suffered

him to use it. I have, however, applied for custody of it as payment for the gross suffering that its occupant inflicted upon the local population and the prior and priests of the nearby abbey. Bishop Poore has also put in an application to confiscate the lands for the benefit of the abbey. Should either one of us succeed, I look forward to improving the lot of the people of Biddesden."

Giles Haughton removed Wakefield's clothes, examined him briefly, then placed him in a winding sheet. As he went to do the same to the outlaw, Ela held her breath. "Is that really necessary? Can you not just put the winding sheet on over his clothes?"

"I could, but I presume you want me to examine the body."

"Not at all. You are merely part of my ruse to take custody of them." Her words came out faster than she'd intended.

He shrugged. "As you will." And he wrapped the burial cloth around the outlaw's comparatively slight form. "He's a good deal smaller in body than in reputation."

"Perhaps that explains why he was able to evade capture for so long. A heavy man couldn't live by creeping around above a cloister." Ela still wasn't breathing. The outlaw's secret wasn't safe until earth had been shoveled onto the corpse.

"There's something very odd about him. The cut of his chin is almost feminine and surprisingly hairless."

Ela's heart started to beat faster.

"And sometimes the timbre of his voice sounded almost like that of a woman."

"Oh?" She glanced casually across the bodies as if his observations were of little interest to her.

"But in death that hardly matters, does it?"

"Not at all."

Haughton sewed up the ends of the winding sheets, and they left the mortuary together. Ela then walked to the ruined cloister of the old cathedral, where her sons prepared to ride at each other again.

THE END

# AUTHOR'S NOTE

The outlaw in this tale was inspired by the mention of an outlaw called—variously—Robert Hod, Hobbehod and Robert Hood in the records of the 1226 and 1227 York assizes. In the first mention, a church called St. Peters of York claimed his goods—worth thirty-two shillings—in a debt and they were confiscated, whereupon he became an outlaw. I couldn't resist exploring the idea of a legendary Robin Hood character during this exact period, even though the real one wasn't in Salisbury.

Only a few vestiges of the ancient Chute Forest remain today, but during Ela's time it was a vast tract of woodland almost a hundred square miles in size, with its southernmost boundary running along the old Roman road from Old Sarum to Winchester. Spanning two counties, it seemed an ideal place for my imaginary outlaw to lead the authorities on a merry chase.

I thought it might be useful for my story to have a Sheriff of Hampshire who was slightly at odds with Ela. When I researched who the sheriff was at this time, I almost died laughing when I discovered that the actual sheriff was Bishop Richard Poore, who I've employed as an antagonist throughout the series. That really underscored for me how the local power structure was an old boys' club, since Bishop Poore and Ela's archenemy, Hubert de Burgh, had been largely running the country together during Henry III's minority.

Serfs still existed as a sort of permanent underclass in Ela's time. Often called villeins, the most common types of serfs were tied to the lord's land and couldn't leave it of their own accord. They paid rent for their cottages and land and would have to provide labor at planting and harvest time, but could keep and sell their surplus produce. Their lord could choose whom they married and they could typically gain their freedom only by escaping and remaining free and uncaught for a year and a day. This system persisted until the plague of 1347 decimated the population and forced changes in the social order.

During the Middle Ages the lives of rich and poor were structured around the tolling of church bells that heralded each of the Canonical Hours of the Divine Office. Each service was held at the same time every day (some varying with natural day length) and followed a particular pattern of psalms, hymns, prayers, readings, etc. While the average person wouldn't have had the luxury of taking time to attend all the services, the bells provided a handy alarm clock that all could hear.

Matins or Lauds, 3 a.m.

Prime, 6 a.m.

Terce, 9 a.m.

Sext, 12 p.m.

Nones, 3 p.m.
Vespers was typically held at sunset, so times would vary.
Compline, about 7 p.m.

If you have questions or comments, please get in touch at jglewis@stoneheartpress.com.

# AUTHOR BIOGRAPHY

J. G. Lewis grew up in a Regency-era officer's residence in London, England. She spent her childhood visiting nearby museums and riding ponies in Hyde Park. She came to the U.S. to study semiotics at Brown University and stayed for the sunshine and a career as a museum curator in New York City. Over the years she published quite a few novels, two of which hit the *USA Today* list. She didn't delve into historical fiction until she discovered genealogy and the impressive cast of potential characters in her family history. Once she realized how many fascinating historical figures are all but forgotten, she decided to breathe life into them again by creating stories for them to inhabit. J. G. Lewis currently lives in Florida with her dogs and horses.

For more information visit www.stoneheartpress.com.

96961158R00169